Sennett, Richard
An evening of Brahms

AN EVENING
OF BRAHMS

Richard Sennett

AN EVENING
OF BRAHMS

Alfred A. Knopf
New York
1984

THIS IS A BORZOI BOOK
PUBLISHED BY ALFRED A. KNOPF, INC.

Library of Congress Cataloging in Publication Data
Sennett, Richard, 1943–   An evening of Brahms.
I. Title.
PS3569.E62E9   1984   813'.54   83-49091
ISBN 0-394-51300-2

Manufactured in the United States of America
First Edition

for

PATRICK O'CONNOR

and

JON GACIOCH

For by grace are ye saved through faith;
and that not of yourselves; it is the gift of God:

Not of works, lest any man should boast.

EPHESIANS 2: 8, 9

All the more honor to you then
If, weaker than some other men,
You had the courage that survives
Soiled, shabby, egotistic lives.

W. H. AUDEN,
"NEW YEAR LETTER"

CONTENTS

ACKNOWLEDGMENTS

For information on Robert Schumann's medical history, the author wishes to acknowledge E. Slater and A. Meyer, "Contributions to a Pathography of the Musicians," *Confinia Psychiat.*, 2, 65–94, 1959, and E. Sams, "Schumann's Hand Injury," *Musical Times*, December 1971. The letters of Clara Schumann and Johannes Brahms which appear in the novel come from *Letters of Clara Schumann and Johannes Brahms*, edited by B. Litzmann (New York: Longmans, Green and Co., 1927). Donald Tovey's letter about the Schumann violin concerto appeared in the London *Times*, September 25, 1937. The letters of Robert Schumann which appear in the novel come from *Letters of Robert Schumann*, edited by K. Storck (London, 1907).

The Ingram-Merrill Foundation kindly provided a grant for the completion of this book.

AN EVENING
OF BRAHMS

Part One

A PUZZLE

Chapter 1

THE FRIENDLY
ART

"*I*'m sorry to stop you so soon, but the opening is the most important part of the piece." The light from the window was almost gone; it was a wet February day and everyone had colds. This was what Signor Grisi hated about New York in the winter: most of them were sick. They jogged, skied, they swam in luxurious indoor pools, they ran from one engagement to the next, took mysterious pills, yet they were constantly sick, coughing and infecting more rational people like himself; furthermore, they ate too little and too early. The four young people in the studio looked as if they should be in bed. However, this advanced class in chamber music met only six times and he wasn't going to pander to them.

In teaching some thirty years at the Conservatory, Signor Grisi had developed certain stratagems. By the age of twenty-one, the little geniuses—they were all little geniuses—had developed bad habits. They could knock off concertos with gusto, but they were in danger of losing the art of listening to one another. True, they talked about responsiveness and whole textures, but this was talk. His chamber-music classes would be their first hard lessons in surrendering their egos. He chose music which particularly demanded surrender, quartets and trios with fragmented melodies, complex rhythms passed from voice to voice, unclear harmonic structures, music which meant little when each part was played alone.

He was pleased with the students in this class, who formed a piano quartet, because they gave him a chance to work on one of his favorite pieces of the genre, the Brahms piano quartet in C minor. Brahms began the quartet as a young man and worked on it for more than twenty years, pulling apart ideas, pushing together stylistic effects that didn't sound coherent unless the performers made an exceptional effort. Of the students in the class, Signor Grisi knew only the cellist, Alexander Hoff-mann, who had occasionally dated his daughter, Nicola. Alexander was a little genius who probably was a genius, at least Signor Grisi had heard him play the Schumann concerto with an authority well beyond his years; it would be interesting to see what happened to him in the third movement of the piano quartet, which has a hard cello solo. At the moment, however, Signor Grisi was worried that they would not get to this test of Alexander. The beginning was a mess.

The opening of the C minor piano quartet is a study in silence. The piano strikes C octaves and these fade away. The strings respond with a two-note figure. There is a rest, the strings sigh and rest again. A passage of dark harmonies then appears in the strings, six bars in which the players seem to be searching for a center, a place from which to begin. The piano does not help them; once more it rings out stark octaves but this time a tone lower. An announcement is being made, its gravity evoked by this mystery about where the center is and why there is silence. Brahms forces the strings to repeat their figure of sighing and emptiness three times. These repetitions increase the tension; confusion is pushed to the breaking point by a string passage of even darker harmonies which do not resolve—and then all at once the piano and the strings push forward together as if in a rage, and the piece is launched.

The pianist played the opening octaves as though she were ringing the doorbell at a crowded party. After he stopped the young people, Signor Grisi said to her,

Miss Fields, those octaves are mysterious; play them with less volume."

"Sure. By the way, I'm Susan." Since he had stepped off the boat from Genoa in 1936, Americans had been trying to disarm him with friendliness. But even though he was now obliged to call this unknown young lady by her first name, her octaves did not sound any better.

"Don't you hear?" he said to her after they did the opening a second time. "Your octaves are no anchor. You are as lost as the others, even though you make a simple sound." A third time and she still evoked no mystery, though she played with less volume. Looking at her, he thought, no matter her swollen eyes, her snuffling, and her pallor, she is too healthy to play this music.

Alexander Hoffmann began to fidget. The Japanese violinist and violist, who had introduced themselves only as Akira and Kenzo, sat patiently while Signor Grisi regarded Susan for a moment and Susan looked at the piano keys. So it was going to be that sort of class—three strong players and one weak one. At some point Signor Grisi was going to make her cry; he had done it to both boys and girls before, as though he had betrayed the first name.

Signor Grisi relented: "Let's go on." In the middle of the movement the turbulence stops. The viola plays a passage Brahms told a friend was a profession of young love, a melody which falls down a G chord and then rises up. If this profession is too passionate, it is unconvincing; the Japanese violist played it simply. The melody is then passed up to the violin, down to the viola again, and then sent into the cello, before the viola finally takes it up in more extended form. The three young men almost had it; with a little work they could make it seamless. And then, at the place marked "M" in the score, the piano enters, echoing the work of the strings in a peculiar way. Signor Grisi listened and cut them off.

"You, Susan, play precisely here but not correctly. Precise, you try to continue the strings' line by emphasizing the melody in the fourth and fifth fingers of your right hand. Incorrect, because Brahms has written a set of moving sixths for both hands, and if you play both hands with even weight, these sixths will make the melody sound hollow. Does everyone else understand me? Don't be afraid to let those double stops ring out now whenever you have them. It is something violent Brahms has done to kill the lyric passage, but you must make clear he does it, not try to be nice and cover it over."

When they repeated the music leading up to and going away from "M," the others, however, played like Susan, choppily. He had heard it so often in the orchestra in which he was assistant principal cellist: a harsh conductor browbeating the horns, say, and then the hitherto innocent strings resisting, almost instinctively, by imitating the mistake of their abused colleagues. He didn't want to pick on her, only have them all follow his directions so that they felt the chill come over the music when she entered.

Signor Grisi had certain favorite maxims. One was "Ours is a friendly art." He said this to students who were not listening to one another; he had the grace to say it to himself, who perhaps listened too intensely. So now he turned to Susan and said, "That was much better." They would come back to "M" another time.

Before they finished for the day, Signor Grisi wanted to hear Alexander play the opening of the third movement. Here the piano accompaniment also has octaves, in the left hand. They must be played delicately, but Signor Grisi was not going to insist.

Alexander glanced at Susan and said, "What tempo do you hear?" She brightened up. "Don't worry, I'll follow whatever you want to do." As they began, the octaves thumped out. But Alexander did not stop, he only continued to look at her, playing the solo without much vibrato. The clean, gentle melody made itself heard through the heavy bass, and gradually his line calmed her and her left hand became more discreet. Signor Grisi's left cheek twitched, as it always did when he had to hold himself in.

He let them go forward, to hear the differences among the boys. Akira was as solid as Alexander: there were no gooey slides between notes, no suggestion of indulgence. The cellist experimented within the boundaries of restraint, however. Suddenly there would be a slight smear from one note to the next, or an unexpected pause, details which did not draw attention to themselves but which punctuated the phrases. Kenzo's viola playing aimed at the opposite effect. The boy had phenomenal control of his right wrist, so that when the bow changed directions there was absolutely no interruption of the sound. At first this perfect fluency created a startling sense of wholeness; Kenzo's lines seemed to bind the other parts together, but after a while Signor Grisi wanted something more human, more flawed, he wanted Kenzo to breathe. Out of this mixture of young men avoiding sloppy feeling, Alexander's became the dominant voice; the Japanese watched him steadily over their music stands, and when he began to take a liberty, they gave him the time to complete the effect without trying to imitate him. Signor Grisi remembered what his daughter Nicola had said when he asked as delicately as he could about their dates: "Alex is a kid, Daddy, it's nothing serious." But then, Nicola had only taken violin lessons for a few years.

When the long chord ending the slow movement died away,

Susan turned to Alexander and blurted out, "That was fantastic!" He was short for a cellist; his face was pitted with acne scars, and his thick black hair was tangled. A blush suffused the coating of the acne, and Signor Grisi supposed he knew what his daughter meant.

They asked Signor Grisi if they could finish the last movement. This was a good sign; although it was late they wanted to hear more of each other. In this movement, more than in the previous movements, the strings tend to play as a unit against the piano. Their sound is smooth, the piano's is often rough, even abrupt; the "whole texture," which was the fashionable phrase that year at the Conservatory, is woven out of this tension. She did what pianists who are not quite in control of their fingers often do, she tried to smooth her part, so that it did not jut out but was hidden in. The movement ends with a long slide down the piano keys which Brahms intended as a final joining together between the textures that so often before had been sandpaper on wood. When they stopped, Signor Grisi said to Susan,

"Did you feel it petered out at the conclusion?"

"Yes, a little."

"That, my dear, is partly Brahms, partly because you are afraid to assert yourself throughout." It wasn't the usual problem; in the hands of a strong pianist, Brahms's dense piano sounds often overwhelm the other players. "If you had played out more against the others before, at the end you would have felt something more satisfying in finally joining them. Perhaps I can help you with that, to assert yourself."

Susan colored; Akira looked out the window, studying the view of a brick wall next door. Alexander tried to cover the embarrassment of the young people: "But Enrico, there's a lot of awkward writing in this last movement."

"Yes, that is so. Perhaps if we had more time . . . well, I was going to ask you. I usually have something at the Cafe Mauro after rehearsals. It's close by; won't you come?" Alexander and Signor Grisi had been there before; the Japanese boys politely assented. Susan hesitated, the others were so much better. "Thank you, but if I come I'd better have tea; I must shake this cold." Signor Grisi assured her that she could have whatever she wanted at the Mauro.

He had been going there almost since the day he and his wife had arrived in New York in 1936. It was the place where he relaxed with his students, listened to their dreams which were the echoes of his own, exhorted, counseled, and contradicted the young. When he received a bill for eight coffees, four Coca-Colas, and six pastries, it was a catalogue to him of just so many hours of argument, gossip, and, if he could have permitted himself the word, love. When they entered the dingy cafe today, Mauro made his usual ceremonious greeting and said he could of course produce tea. Looking at the Japanese boys he stated, "You also will have tea. I hope you like ours." Akira loved espresso, a luxury drink in Tokyo; both Kenzo and Akira hated milk in their tea. However, they were not fully acclimated New Yorkers; they believed Mauro's desire to please was more important than the exact form in which he did so, and nodded.

Signor Grisi also was ignorant about the Japanese who were beginning to flood into New York to study music. "Normally I don't talk about such things," Signor Grisi said to them when they were seated. "The music tells its own story. But with the piano quartet, personalities matter. Brahms began it when he first fell in love with Clara Schumann, and Robert Schumann was in the insane asylum. You perhaps know this?"

The Japanese nodded again.

"Well, you must forget it, in the way you probably were told. Your teachers probably made it sentimental, the death of the crazed genius, attended by his faithful wife and her devoted friend. In fact, it was very suspect."

Akira wanted things exact. "Signor Grisi, excuse me, but it was just at the time he became insane that he was working on some of his greatest music."

"No, no, I am speaking about Brahms and Clara Schumann. Schumann's death is of course tragic; the man was haunted for two years by angels. Brahms's emotions are suspect. Brahms is falling in love with Clara while Robert is locked in a cell, tormented by his angels' voices. Evidently she is a little attracted in turn, and Johannes is waiting. Maybe he lives for smelling her hair, you understand? She comes back from the hospital and he comforts her with a kiss while he smells her hair. Also Johannes was an uncertain young man and, as they told you in school, she was like a mother to him. A mother, and they turn away their eyes from each other. No, it is not a nice story. And it is during these years that Brahms began the quartet."

The waiter came up to their table. "The same for everyone?" Without asking his students, the old man nodded. He knew that students often had to choose between a second cup of espresso and money for the subway. They were embarrassed in the presence of older people by their poverty, and so they would often leave him, making excuses of work or other appointments, rather than ask for a dollar. "Since this is the first time we work together, please let the coffee for all of us be my treat."

"You think his love life affected the quartet?" Akira persisted.

"I know so. He spoke to others of the piece as a great confession of love. As Schumann dies, he starts the work, originally three movements in C-sharp minor, not C. But this he felt was no good. For twenty years he goes over his sketches, he breaks the dramatic melodies into fragments, there are new ideas, ideas which come from a man who believes he is burnt out. You know that at forty he felt that, from the impossible love of Clara, but also from just going on; you will see, after a while, how hard it is. This music begun in his youth was full of passion and then gradually in the writing there appear detours, rests, blank moments. When Brahms sent the final manuscript of the quartet to his publisher, he wrote, 'You may print on the title page the picture of a man holding a gun to his head. Now you know the truth.' "

Akira was impressed that Signor Grisi had memorized a quote; it seemed to settle the matter, and he made another attempt at the tea. Alexander had never heard the older man talk like this before. At the Grisi apartment in Greenwich Village, Nicola's father had been scrupulous in not interfering when he called for her on dates. Her father seemed just a nice old person who played the cello in the opera orchestra and had lots of students at the Conservatory.

"You know," Alexander remarked, "I was looking the other day at a drawing of Brahms when he was young. He was very thin, almost girlish."

"Yes." Signor Grisi paused for a sip of coffee. Alexander had chanced upon a favorite detail. "His youth bothered him. In his thirties he forced himself to eat to become fatter and finally succeeded in growing that beard. You see, it was a disguise, like this music, not a natural growth." Signor Grisi saw from Susan's sour expression that she wasn't having any of it. She had, indeed, never paid much attention to the stories told her as a young girl, stories designed to interest her in playing the piano. She didn't need to be fed lumps of sugar. The Brahms story she appreciated was about how he sometimes awoke in the middle of the night, driven half-insane by a chord he couldn't resolve or a melody he couldn't complete. She would have liked to know when during those twenty years Brahms woke up worrying about this quartet, exactly which measures were the gift of insomnia, but Signor Grisi was droning on about guilty love.

So he changed the subject. "You see, this quartet was the first piece I played in public. In those days, we grew up fast. There was no union to give out jobs in Rome during the 1920s; you were constantly spying for news of concerts, news which the owners of theaters treated almost as secrets. You overheard someone at the cafe by the square saying 'We have to find a cellist,' and the next morning you went to the theater and announced that you were available. If you were lucky, you were hired on the spot, you practiced perhaps once, twice with the other players, and you walked onstage." So the circumstances then meant that no one made for you the gift he was now making to Susan.

Another favorite saying of Signor Grisi's was: "My friends, never will you feel as much as you do now; ten years on the road and it will be just work." He knew that the young often sounded empty because they were afraid of the emotions flooding into their lives, their uncertainties in love, their restlessness, their ambitions. They tried to protect their music from this chaos against which they could not protect themselves. And this was really why despite the memories it brought him he liked working on the Brahms quartet, flawed as it was. The quartet forced the young to sort out expression rather than avoid it.

The fluorescent lights in the Cafe Mauro were switched on. The light was unkind to Signor Grisi; the thin strands of hair on his head were suddenly washed away, brown age-spots stood out on the white skin, his eyeballs lost their color. He looked older than fifty-eight. This sudden revelation of the light, more than the accumulating force of his words, made Susan soften, and she smiled shyly at him. Unaware of the light's work, Signor Grisi responded by folding his hand over hers on the table. After a moment, he said, "It takes time to learn to feel these things." He regretted that they could not now go back to the studio to practice, but it was too late, nearly time for their dinner.

Signor Grisi walked down from the cafe to his apartment in northern Little Italy or southern Greenwich Village, depending on where you were born. Sometimes his companions at the cafe would kid him by saying, "You are a Greenwich Village bohemian, Enrico," as though this were a great joke. He had learned here to smile at this; perhaps it was one thing America had given him, the capacity to take gentle kidding from the carpenters, plumbers, and waiters at the cafe. As he walked, he passed the clinic where Nicola had been born—an easy birth. He remembered the gingham curtains in his wife's room there, the windows open and the curtains blowing in the breeze while Flavia held the infant in her hands, resting on the bed two days after the delivery. He passed the union hall where, a year before Nicola's birth, the exile faced the immigrants who had come a generation earlier, faced them in a stormy public meeting and told them the Mussolini they loved from afar was a clown, a sadist, and a coward. He passed the bakery in which the women used to give little Nicola hot buns. He passed an abandoned synagogue, where he had gone one Saturday just after the war, out of curiosity, and he passed the Catholic church into which he never went, on principle. Finally he passed the school on Sullivan Street which Nicola first attended; from the windows of his own apartment he had often watched her playing in the school yard, frolicking and screaming at her little friends in a foreign language. To hear his daughter playing in English was the moment when he first knew that he had done something more than escape; they lived here. There seemed to be no logic to the geography of this new life, Nicola's neighborhood; he could feel no reason why the union hall, clinic, synagogue, and bakery should all be close together, whereas in Rome the visible layers of time—the Baroque church next to his parents' nineteenth-century apartment, the glimpse of the Forum he had from his old room—all seemed natural to him. If his students had accompanied him on this walk he could not have excavated these signs of the last thirty years of his life, as he could the work of ruin and love they rehearsed. He had been given no key to the secret of things he didn't love.

Three days ago he had announced his daughter's engagement, after a performance at the opera. The response of his colleagues he did understand; something like it would happen anywhere. Various bottles of liquor were produced from lockers; paper cups were handed round. Tony the prompter had wept briefly after two glasses of Scotch. Carl Trullo, his opposite number in the violas, the friend of Enrico and Flavia Grisi for twenty years, made a brief toast. Amid the sounds of scenery being shoved away for the night, the hum of voices in the singers' green room next to the bare, gymlike quarters where the orchestra changed, played cards at intermission, and gossiped after work was done, Carl shouted out an exuberant toast which ended, ". . . and so we must repeat to Enrico the American phrase, however trite also true, 'You are not losing a daughter, you are gaining a son.'" Had it been applied to Alexander, Signor Grisi might have been willing to believe him. The boy was destined for great things. Signor Grisi particularly loved the Swiss mountains; perhaps the four of them could have made summer journeys there together, the men taking long walks in the evening. . . . Carl's toast might even apply to the Japanese. But Nicola was not marrying a musician.

He knew it had been difficult for her, living in two countries. She spoke Italian without thinking about it in the house but was embarrassed to speak it in front of others. She had a genuine love of music, he could tell that, even though she had played briefly and badly. When he practiced in the mornings, she used as a little girl to sit and listen, reading her book while he played, before she walked the thirty steps to school which took her to the other land. And she had not left home; she enjoyed living with them, as of course they enjoyed her. He inserted his key into the front door.

Patrick was sprawled on the living-room sofa: tall and well fed, bland, his hair neatly brushed, his business suit perfectly pressed. Patrick was Nicola's point of arrival in America. Of course it was according to plan, the father who resents losing his little girl to another. But when Signor Grisi looked at

Patrick, as he did tonight, the evening to celebrate their engagement, it was not resentment which moved him so much as regret. The boy was decent and shared Nicola's love of reading. That was something. Now he smiled at Signor Grisi as though wanting to reassure the older man. They made small talk about apartment prices until dinner.

During the pasta course—a flamboyant concoction of Flavia's consisting of linguine, artichoke hearts, and black olives—Signor Grisi asked Patrick about his work. Patrick was happy to explain the investment strategies of insurance companies. The intricacies of this investing, the large sums of money involved, the peculiar calculations of risk, all engrossed him; he spoke in some detail. Signor Grisi was confused but, to his own surprise, fascinated.

"The debt-payment-to-bond ratio, it is as though you are hoping at the races all the horses will drop dead before the finish line?"

Why was it that when he reached out to young people they felt he was attacking them? The boy looked as if the joke were on him.

The pasta was followed by thin slices of veal seasoned with lemon. Nicola talked about growing up in the neighborhood, about how the Chinese and Italian kids would talk Chinese or Italian when they didn't want their teachers to understand them, about the school basketball team, a mixture of Negroes and Puerto Ricans as well as the Chinese and Italians, a team known in the city as the United Nations.

"You speak of this game with pleasure, my dear, but your mother and I were horrified at first by it. We were a bit wild in our youth, weren't we?" Signor Grisi asked, turning to his wife. She nodded; yes. Yes, we were not left out of life. "But we were not prepared to see you cheerlead. Our dear daughter," he said, turning to Patrick, "prancing around before a thousand people, exposing her bare legs when she jumped so that the thousand people could see up her short dress to her underwear. But no one seemed to take it amiss. This is a very tolerant neighborhood."

"Speaking of Little Italy," Patrick remarked, "Nicola and I would like to be married in a church down here. I'm sure she told you that I am also a Catholic." Flavia looked at her husband; Signor Grisi looked at his daughter; Nicola squeezed more lemon on the last few pieces of veal.

Signor Grisi could remember, as a child, watching a priest gorge himself on pasta and wine at a cafe in Trastevere; the priest's mouth never stopped moving. He could remember as a young man the voices of Flavia's parents, voices filled with rage and anguish, accusing him of casting their daughter into terrible sin by living with her before marriage. He had explained these memories to Nicola many times, but had failed to make them real.

Every exile—whether persecuted for religion or by it, whether fleeing left-wing governments or right-wing—every exile learns the meaning of loss only when in another place he finds that these injuries are not so important to other people. Much that mattered is lost in the telling, and even what is told well is only a story to others, if you have survived to tell it. Exile is over when a man can say to himself, why after all should they care about something long ago, far away? Yet though an exile is frequently forced by circumstance to act the chameleon, to pretend "I had no life before I came among you, or no life more important than you," still he will never, never lose the hope that there is one person who will learn the lessons of long ago and far away, to carry on his knowledge, if only to avoid the exile's mistakes. That person is the exile's child.

As Flavia and Enrico busied themselves preparing coffee, Flavia nodded at her husband and he merely shrugged. She would leave it at that. This was a decent young man; Enrico would come around in time, and she knew that out of sheer love for his daughter he would give himself time.

It was just before the moment of goodbyes. As Patrick finished his second cup of coffee he asked, almost casually, "May I ask how you came to America? Nicola told me you were forced to leave Rome. Why did you choose here?"

"It was purely circumstance," Signor Grisi replied. "I knew the great Koussevitzky. I had forty-eight hours to leave the country. All I could think to do was telegraph Maestro Koussevitzky in America, and he kindly telegraphed your embassy, saying I was needed in New York for a concert. This allowed them to authorize a visa. Had he been in Paris, we would have gone there. Had I not known him, I probably would be dead."

He looked intently at the young man. Patrick smiled at him, a comforting smile, neutral. Evidently the name Koussevitzky meant nothing. Why should it? But you do not, you cannot smile comfortingly at a story of desperation. It was good that Patrick's question came at the end. Signor Grisi, indeed, would need time to treat Patrick like a son.

In bed that evening Signor Grisi could not sleep. He thought about Nicola, the daughter who, whatever Carl might say, was disappearing, and about his children of hope.

He thought about the faces of Nicola and Susan. Nicola's olive, dense skin, her thick black eyebrows, her straight aristocratic nose. Susan was pale and undeveloped; she had a weak chin, a curiously grim slit of a mouth when she played. Signor Grisi had wondered at every change in Nicola's body. It amazed him to see the infant grow long legs. He could remember at the beach when first she would fit into the hollow of his arm as they dozed together under the sun, then when her head would lie on his chest and her legs would reach down to his knees, then when she was too big for them decorously to lie together. Susan's body was unknown; under her peasant costume, she appeared to be merely plump, still encased in baby fat.

Yes, he knew. Had Nicola chosen Alexander instead of the

bland young man, Alexander would have passed the Kousse-vitzky hurdle but Signor Grisi would have found some other test for him to fail. Once safe, the survivor sets high standards for admission to his history.

Over the years, however, Signor Grisi had erased the explanation he had made of the dark side of his care for his students, his hurting them. When he first came to New York, exile had been his excuse; he didn't know foreign manners, at home the young would not have taken his passion so personally. Now he knew this was not true, because these young people he taught were not like children in a family. The young musicians have a choice—anywhere. They could leave if his exclaiming "You ruined the opening" hurt too much, if stories about what was hidden in the music bored them, if they were frightened by an old man saying, "Perhaps I can teach you to assert yourself." Or they could accept these things as the price of his hope for what they might become.

Indeed, there was a certain sense in which exile was good for music. Signor Grisi's own teacher had once said to him something like, "I never wake up in the morning without wishing I will play better today than yesterday." Signor Grisi felt that too, for himself and for others. Exile had strengthened this desire in him, the desire of a man to throw down roots in other people's lives, helping them to play better, through a friendly art.

Signor Grisi switched off the reading lamp next to his bed.

Chapter 2

THE DARK SIDE

Three years later, Alexander sat in his studio trying to choose among the letters of Clara Schumann and Brahms. He could already feel people cheapening him and Susan: such a good marriage, two young people with everything going for them, a tragic accident. To counter these half-truths, he wanted something which would suggest the gravity of their life together. Perhaps he should start at the beginning. He would choose something from that time to explain what had happened.

In the twenty-two days since Susan had been run over by the taxi he had been in a confused state, sometimes drinking too much, sometimes overexcited, although to the others who were already cheapening them he seemed admirably in control. He had been straightforward with the doctors, and organized the flow of visitors to Susan's room. The day she finally succumbed to her injuries undid him, which the others also expected, and the Ethical Culture Society leader who would conduct the funeral service said he could provide a commemorative text, but Alexander had wanted to make sure it was absolutely right. That had been part of their problem.

There were the famous passages from Clara Schumann's diaries about Robert Schumann's last three days:

I saw him between 6 and 7 in the evening of 27th July 1856. He smiled, and put his arm round me with a great effort, for he can no longer control his limbs. I shall never forget it.

Not all the treasures in the world could equal this embrace. My Robert, it was thus that we had to see each other again, how painfully I had to trace out your beloved features! What a sorrowful sight it was!

Two and a half years ago you were torn from me without any farewell, though your heart must have been full, and now I lay silent at your feet hardly daring to breathe; only now and then I received a look clouded as it were, but unspeakably gentle. . . .

On Monday, the 28th, Johannes Brahms and I spent the whole day out there, going in and out of his room, but often only looking at him through the little window in the wall. He suffered dreadfully and he often spoke vehemently. Ah! I could only pray God to release him, because I loved him so dearly. . . .

On Tuesday, the 29th, he was to be released from his suffering. At 4 o'clock in the afternoon he fell peacefully asleep. His last hours were quiet, and he passed away in his sleep without its being noticed; no one was with him at the moment. I did not see him till half an hour later. His head was beautiful, the forehead so transparent and slightly arched. I stood by the body of my passionately loved husband, and was calm.

The lie this contained might serve—or rather the secret Clara Schumann left out, since no one could doubt the genuine love she felt for her husband. Though Susan might have scoffed that evening when Enrico had told them the story, while Alexander was intrigued, neither of them had taken it personally. In time, each of them knew the other carried some acid secret. The diary, however, was not a copy of their own lives: Robert Schumann had suspected nothing.

It seemed much longer than a day since he had watched Susan sleep. Sleep was difficult for her, and in his excited moments he imagined it was like an emissary coming from far away. Its soft, heavy wings lay over her eyes, shutting out the light; its heart lay against her mouth, and gradually its beating heart grew calm and regular, calling from her an answering rhythm. Alexander had made sure yesterday that she had succumbed to sleep and then he had gone out to forget.

At moments of great stress throughout his life, Alexander's stomach muscles tightened like a vise around him. Last night he had gone out to forget the sight of his sleeping, dying wife, but his muscles wouldn't let him. Over the years he had tried everything—exercise, pills, drinks. None of them really did much good. He had gone last night to Sim's Bar, close to where he and Susan lived and where their friends had often joined them. It was a friendly, rather grimy place. He'd had a few drinks, but his stomach was still knotted up.

Enrico Grisi had found him there. "Nothing," Signor Grisi had said, motioning the bartender away. "Alexander, Flavia has just telephoned me from the hospital. You must return at once." It was nearly midnight, the bar was crowded, but the patrons, guided by their radar to avoid people who were no fun, had left the barstools on either side of Alexander empty.

We say about the dying, "Let them be released from their misery," which often means, "Let their death release us." Unrelieved compassion is too demanding. Indeed, how could

Alexander tell if he did not wish this dark emissary to be seeking a permanent home? The soft, heavy wings of the angel would seal her eyes, the heart beating in its round, furry body would stop up her mouth, like a cork in a bottle, and so lead her away forever.

In the hospital, Alexander had made a discovery. There was one language the healthy spoke to the sick, another to themselves. In the private rooms or on the wards, the healthy comforted the very ill by declaring, "I will never forget." In the hospital coffee shop, those bringing comfort occasionally betrayed other thoughts; suddenly a person in the coffee shop would announce to a stranger, "She's been sick two months already," as though the illness were the fault of the person who was ill.

Just before her accident, Alexander had blown up at Susan. He had imagined, during her first days in the hospital, that the sudden flushes of anger he felt were echoes of the interrupted explosion, and of course these angry moments made him ashamed. But by the second week of Susan's confinement, it was clear that other comforters also spoke to themselves in these bursts. People who declared to him they had spent thirty years without a fight, people whose loved ones had fallen ill slowly— these people could occasionally be seen standing by the bedside of the drugged loved one, their mouths formed in angry slits. "Why are you abandoning me? Do something, get better, you could if you wanted!" This shaming anger was also missing from Clara Schumann's diary.

In the bar, Alexander turned slowly to face Signor Grisi, who asked, "Alexander, how much have you had to drink?" Not very much. "The end is approaching; you must return with me to the hospital. Do it for her; she would want you there."

In the weeks before her accident Susan did nothing but accuse him of being self-centered. In fact he had struck back about this favorite subject just before she had run out into the middle of the street. On the other hand, he was not neurotic, unstable, or unreasonable. Conductors liked working with him because he was amenable to suggestion, players because he didn't display temperament. He was just the person he was supposed to be. "Do it for her"; at least this one last thing. His stomach grew even tighter.

Alexander and Susan had lived for three years in Carnegie Towers, built on top of Carnegie Hall. It is a skyscraper of artists' studios, apartments with thick walls, and suites of offices inhabited, for the most part, by agents, violin makers, and recording companies on the edge of failure. Normally, real estate entrepreneurs buy up bits of Bohemia in the city, sell their charms to companies with fat bank balances, or, if the Bohemia is residential, to businessmen whose spouses have a taste for the arts. Rents go up, the artists leave, the violin makers retire, and the new inhabitants dwell in the memory of what was. In the 1960s, Carnegie Hall was in trouble. Smart money expected it to go bust, the building to be torn down or renovated. So they forgot about it for the time being and it was affordable.

The young couple lived next to an instrument insurance broker and across the hall from a mysterious operation called Diva International. They could never make sense of the original purpose of their own apartment. It was three stories high, but minute, the three floors connected by a shaky circular staircase. The cats were happy there and spent a great deal of time sleeping on the staircase; because they were overweight, Susan had put their food dish on the bottom floor and their litter box on the top floor, to force them to exercise.

Alexander and Susan were also happy living in Carnegie Towers. The piano was on the bottom floor, next to the door. The secretary from Diva International often rang the bell to tell Susan that she was playing one of the secretary's favorite pieces. Alexander practiced on the top floor, the bedroom, his practice chair next to the cat box. When Alexander and Susan were together in New York, their days followed a strict routine. They woke at eight, dressed, and went down to the coffee shop on the corner of the building; the apartment had no kitchen. Eight in the morning was too early for the hustlers, who started doing business in the coffee shop at about noon. In the morning, other bleary-eyed regulars from the Towers also had breakfast; the agents began to crank up the word machinery they would use during the day for a deal involving double-bass recitals in Omaha or the purchase of a dubious Stradivarius viola. The waitress knew the needs of the regulars; bagels, juice, and coffee came without the young couple having to ask.

After breakfast, Susan and Alexander would return to the studio. The cats were fed four tablespoons each of Diet Kitty, the telephone answering machine was switched on, Susan opened the piano, Alexander ascended to the living-room floor, sorted the mail, paid what bills he could, then climbed up to the top floor. Both Susan and Alexander practiced all morning. The cats, whom Susan hated, nestled against her on the piano bench, the cat box caressed Alexander with its various odors. Alexander loved the cats; no matter how long he had been on the road, he would always pet the cats as soon as he could when he came home.

A practical observer could have made a simple explanation of what ruined this domestic life. In the last three years Alexander's career had taken off. Often a review of a concert or news of a prize will cause an agent to try out a young artist by sending him or her on tour. If the tour works out, the agent may then try to move the musician from giving concerts in obscure recital halls in New York to larger halls, places in which there are patrons who subscribe for a season rather than individual concerts; the change would be from the little room at Carnegie Hall, for instance, to a recital in one of the Metropolitan Museum's concert series. During the first year, Alexander had toured and changed halls.

The next move can be in various directions: more recitals, a concerto engagement with a major orchestra, a recording contract with a minor company. The economy during the last few years had been forcing out little record firms, so a major orchestra engagement was easier, though less valuable. A clever agent could use a record, made up into a package with copies of reviews and glossy photos, as an effective way of advertising that the young artist was already "someone," and so the agent could secure more engagements, and more income, than a single concerto date would yield. During the second year, Alexander had signed his recording contract.

There comes a point in every musician's career when the momentum is word-of-mouth. People begin talking: just out of conservatory and already making records. He's busy now; if you want him, you ought to call his agent soon. The telephone calls to the agent increase; the clever manager might set dates six or eight months in advance, even though the concert could be arranged for almost any time after four months. Alexander's agent was booking him satisfactorily for eight months ahead. Talk to the artist also gives momentum. At a concert by a big name, people ask him, as they always have, "What did you think?" But now he's not as free with his opinions as he used to be; he might soon be playing with the big name; his agent warns, don't gossip any more. And the friends who have asked him, "What do you think?" hear in his necessary restraint a further signal that his career is taking off. Never chatty in public, Alexander now seemed to be noncommittal at concerts because he was on the inside.

Susan, after three years, was still playing, when she could, at the little recital halls. She had decided to stay on at the Conservatory for an advanced degree, which meant she could eventually get a teaching job. A doctorate in music never earned an artist a concert booking; in fact, it makes managers suspicious: what is someone doing in school when he or she should be out touring? Failure to take off is mitigated by numbers in New York; there were over two thousand professional pianists in the city when Susan and Alexander graduated from the Conservatory. Everybody knows that accident and chance rule among so many; still, few people want to leave, hoping that somehow they will be one of the few whom fortune favors. Her years in New York had made clear to her the level of her talents. She was a solid, reliable musician—therefore unlikely to be noticed. Candor with herself dampened her jealousy of Alexander when his career began to flourish; still, he was her husband.

Their instincts as a couple were evasive. Since it was too much for her to stay backstage in the green room after a concert while he signed programs and received compliments, they made one of their arrangements: she would leave after the concert and meet him and their friends at a chosen restaurant later, once he had completed the ritual of the green room. The practical observer would have pointed out that such evasions cannot cope with the powerful effect of one partner taking off while the other remains grounded. For instance, at home she became more critical of his domestic habits: his clothes, his cooking, his strategy for paying bills. He always took her criticisms very seriously, which only made her feel petty.

Alexander knew she hurt. "Career conflict" was one step up from "perfect marriage," but it took no account of the following: when he was in front of an audience his stomach was in knots, he was scared, and so, in a different way, were they. Anything could go wrong; gradually over the course of an evening they reassured each other. He would never drive them wild in the aisles, but he would make them feel that they could have access to something very precious, that there was a reason for sitting still and listening; their trust would gradually loosen his muscles. Critics liked to describe him as quietly compelling or sincere, yet these were qualities he did not bring to a concert but rather happened during it. He didn't play as well when he was rehearsing; indeed, one of his worries before a concert was that he never quite felt prepared, and it was hard, when he started recording, until he began to treat the engineers as an audience. He came home from these acts of completion, of reassurance by other people, and she was there, resenting.

He tried at first to push the world away from them. He spoke of his successes in a flat tone of voice, and sought to keep his agent, who tended to be effusive, out of their tower refuge. Suppressing his own pleasure in a good review or satisfying performance did not, however, lead him to understand her failure. At a dinner party she was the outgoing one, telling jokes or gossiping; she loved to do post-mortems on the dinner party later on the telephone. But once at the piano she held back. After four rehearsals of the Brahms piano quartet she still could not perform the speaking silence at the opening, nor at the end could she make the piano sandpaper the strings. Enrico often called music a friendly art, but, evidently, it depended on something other than being friendly.

In his anger at her dying were folded in many other rages held in check before: the sight of her smiling sardonically when she caught him stroking the cover of his first record, the time she turned abruptly from his father when he said, "You must be so proud of him." Alexander was angry, and he was also puzzled: once, after one of her concerts, he had gone backstage and found her crying. When you play badly you shouldn't feel sorry for yourself, and if he had challenged her, this could have been a moment of connection between them, but he let it go. Another time she said to him, "You should stand up to me more." You should have, you shouldn't have. . . . He had kept his anger secret and she in turn was disappearing without revealing to him what had paralyzed her art.

People imagine that when the chips are down and there is a great life-and-death crisis, you rise above the stresses of the past; they seem minor in the light of this ultimate threat. Not at all: the accident just made him see clearly. They'd spent three years hurting each other. The worse it got, the more they had pretended: they made a point of being a couple when they were out socially, responding to each other's jokes, each making sure at a party that the other had enough to eat or drink. Why had they bothered?

Signor Grisi had paid the bill last night at Sim's, led Alexander outside, and was hailing a cab to take them back to the hospital when Alexander suddenly turned to him at the curb and said, "I won't go back with you." Signor Grisi looked confused. They couldn't stand on the curb while Alexander tried to explain, even if he could, so the young husband only added, "I couldn't face it." The muscles squeezing his stomach relaxed. Signor Grisi sympathized; the boy was of course unprepared to lose her.

If Clara Schumann's picture of Robert Schumann's death was unusable, perhaps something from her late letters to Brahms. The phone kept ringing; he'd taken a couple of calls, but already he had twinges about his final absence which none of the callers knew about, and there was, in any event, nothing to say. So he let the phone ring. These late letters were curious; Signor Grisi had told Alexander about them while they were all still working on the quartet. "You see," he said, "so Victorian, thirty years later all they worried about was what people would say after they died." The late letters approached the subject innocently; in May of 1886 Clara Schumann asked for her letters back, a year later Brahms asked for his. Then Clara Schumann began to worry. In a letter of July 23, 1887, she wrote to Brahms, "For what seemed good and at times sad to ourselves belongs to us alone, nobody need know anything about it." In August of that year Brahms too began to worry; he had sent her the letters she wanted, she had returned nothing.

This was because Marie Schumann, Clara's daughter, had taken a hand. She prevented Clara from sending many of Brahms's personal letters back to him, and made Clara preserve many of her own. But in rereading the final, bitter letter Clara Schumann wrote to Brahms on this subject, Alexander found that both Clara Schumann's daughter and Signor Grisi had missed the point; burning the letters was the last step in a war that the two lovers had been conducting for a very long time. This revelation occurred on September 17, 1892:

If, however, I offended you, you should have told me at once quite openly and not have given free rein to the base suspicion that I did not like to see your name connected with Robert Schumann's. Such a thought could only have occurred to you in an evil hour, and after so many years of artistic association, it is utterly incomprehensible to me how you could suspect me of such a thing. Surely it is quite out of keeping with my attitude of reverence towards you all these years, and also with what you say to me at the end of your letter. If your suspicion were well founded surely I could not be reckoned among the most pleasant recollections of your life! You are certainly right in saying that personal intercourse with you is often difficult, and yet my friendship for you has always helped me rise superior to your vagaries. Unfortunately, on the occasion of your last visit, I was unable to rid my heart of the bitterest feeling that it harbored against you.

It had always been Alexander's fantasy, to share his life with someone who shared his music, the two loves intertwined. Once he had said to Akira, "It must be marvelous, living with someone you can practice with," and Akira rather shyly agreed; he and Kenzo often took pleasure in playing music together. At first Alexander thought this would be true for Susan and himself as well, but it disturbed Susan too much. They always had to talk about what she should do differently. On the other hand, Alexander's father had once suggested, when his son confessed to marital troubles, "Why don't you play with her in public?" and Alexander had replied, "She's not good enough." His father had been taken aback. "So what?" It was difficult to explain to a nonmusician that it was harder to hear your wife play badly than a stranger.

Love, as it will, had gone in a different direction from fantasy—toward his wife's humor, her messy nesting around the house, the way she smiled, their good times traveling, going to restaurants, buying odds and ends. All his life he had hated his puny body; when acne began to ravage his face he had wanted to hide from the sight of others. She liked holding him.

His parents had taught him to suspect people who excused everything because of artistic temperament, but beneath a surface mildness he was as unyielding as a prima donna. The recording people, for instance, at first found him a pleasure to work with, but by the end, after obsessive retakes with Alexander asking if they'd just change this microphone a little, or sit in front of him once more, not moving behind the glass, they were glad to see him go. His body after one of these sessions felt wrung like a twisted cloth.

This was surely part of what went wrong. The recording technicians never felt he was angry with them, but a wife subject to "You are still playing those notes too slowly, Susan" for the tenth time is justified in thinking that her husband is putting a little extra something into his precision. Yet he did not mean to hurt her; at least, he did not mean to hurt her music.

Considered objectively, there is no great crime in a man seeing his wife for the last time while she is only asleep. And it is only normal for flickers of guilt to twitch at the survivor after a loved one has died—one remembers all the things one might have done differently. But there was nothing he and Susan could have done to lead the life of colleague-lovers.

Happiness in the house, pleasure in bed, shared interests in travel, in restaurants, do not make up for unequal musical gifts. The fantasy lovers had had decades of writing to each other about work and colleagues, learning from each other—a whole lifetime together, equal—even if at the end they were settling the scores of accumulated bitterness.

Alexander went to the ground floor of the studio to make himself some coffee. As the water boiled on the hot-plate, on which they had finally learned to produce entire meals for guests, he looked at one of their earliest purchases. It was a print of a Poussin landscape, the one in which small figures flee from a snake in the foreground. The light blue clouds and dark greens of the landscape are luminous, almost too pretty, because the restorer has scraped off every trace of dirt and old varnish from the canvas. In this gleaming landscape, the drama of flight from the snake in the foreground seems nearly unbelievable; there is no reason to be afraid in the midst of such radiance.

Safe in the tower, wrapped in the money that was now flowing in, surrounded by friends, she had also become afraid, a fear more profound than "What will posterity think," or "It was your fault." By the end, she said she preferred performing only for friends. No, there was no memorial possible in the music which brought them together, no explanation of the end in the beginning.

After leaving Alexander, Signor Grisi had hailed a cab and told the driver, "Uptown, Lenox Hill Hospital." The driver began to talk about his own operation last year. Floating on the sea of words, Signor Grisi considered: should he have forced Alexander to come with him?

". . . the fault of the colored. Four-fifty."

Signor Grisi paid the taxi driver, forgot to tip him, and entered the hospital.

At two a.m. the halls of hospitals take on a special character. The noise of possibility—talk of things to do, places to go later, the television blaring away in rooms of patients recuperating— this noise of possibility has ceased. In the night silence, the hospital gets down to business. Signor Grisi found a large group assembled outside Susan's room. On one plastic armchair sat Susan's mother; across from her on a plastic couch sat Susan's father and stepmother. Flavia Grisi was reading a magazine, perched on a wooden chair. Akira was standing, his back leaning against the wall next to Susan's door. The door was closed. Signor Grisi asked Akira, "Where is Kenzo?"

"He had to go to Boston tonight; there is an early rehearsal. Where is Alexander?"

Mother, father, stepmother, his wife, turned to look at him. Signor Grisi said, "I couldn't find him."

The two doctors came out of Susan's room. They were surprised at the number of people outside. The older one, a man in his fifties, had thrown a white coat over his dinner jacket; his black tie and diamond shirt studs peeped through the uniform. He must have been called in while Signor Grisi was away. He looked to the woman in the armchair and then at Akira.

"I'm sorry, but hospital rules don't permit anyone but immediate family here after visiting hours. Could you please go downstairs to the main lounge?"

"I'm Susan's mother. I stay."

She had only come yesterday. Susan's mother had been divorced by Susan's father the year after Susan came to music school in New York, and she had decided, Susan had said, to confuse the two events in her mind; father and daughter had shut her out. But there are moments in life, Signor Grisi thought while watching her rigid in the armchair, when one must leave the fortress one has built for oneself.

Signor Grisi took the hand of the second Mrs. Fields. Akira escorted Mrs. Grisi. The four of them walked toward the elevator, leaving the parents of the dying girl to sit in silence across from each other on the plastic furniture, waiting for the end.

The end came an hour later. The elder doctor came down to the large lobby. He had removed his black tie, his diamond studs; this was his homage to death. He asked the four of them to come into a small office.

"We did everything we could. You should know that she died in no pain. There were unforeseen complications during the course of treatment; for the last two days all we could do was try to make Susan comfortable. That's all we could do."

The four in waiting and the doctor came out of the little office just as the parents emerged from the elevator. They were not touching. Mr. Fields collapsed in the arms of his new wife. Susan's mother walked very erect, very slowly. Signor Grisi came up to her. He wanted to say something to her, to comfort her—she was alone in a strange city which she hated, she knew no one—but she brushed past him, walked through the hospital doors, and disappeared into the night.

In the taxi home, Signor Grisi told his wife the truth about the scene in the bar, concluding, "Perhaps at such moments one cannot insist on the proprieties."

Flavia Grisi had always been the cooler of the two of them. "And yet," she said, "you blame this woman who is the mother for coming only yesterday."

"I do. This woman is filled with rage."

At the funeral home, there were students from the Conservatory, there were people from the jury which had awarded Susan an honorable mention at a contest last year, Alexander's agent had brought all of his own family, the Grisis stood talking quietly with Susan's father just inside the door, many members of the chamber orchestra with which Susan played, even occasional players like the harpist, seemed to be there.

A man in a black suit motioned them to enter. Susan's mother was already seated in the front row, staring at the coffin. Susan's father and Alexander walked in together, the Grisis behind them. Once the mourners had assembled, the leader from the Ethical Culture Society stood to face the audience.

"I have been asked on this sad occasion, by Alexander Hoffmann, the husband of Susan Fields Hoffmann, for whose passing we today grieve, if we might alter the service of mourning. Mr. Hoffmann would like to read a short passage to you." He sat down and Alexander walked to the front of the room. He took a few sheets of paper from his pocket and calmly faced the mourners.

"First, I want to thank all of you who have sent so many kind messages of condolence. It is a tribute to Susan, who had a unique gift for friendship. I hope you will forgive me for skipping the usual ritual, because I want to pay a tribute to Susan's greatest love, greater than her love for all of you, greater than her love for me: her music.

"I wanted to read something from the lives of Clara Schumann and Johannes Brahms, because it was the piano quartet which Brahms wrote for Clara Schumann which first brought us together. But I found in their diaries and letters nothing which expresses Susan's love for music. You all know that Clara Schumann and Brahms had a tangled life together lasting nearly forty years, yet they could get over their difficult moments, sometimes rise above themselves, because pieces of music came out of these trials. Finally they both retired to the solitude of their own rooms to write.

"Our teacher, Enrico Grisi, who was Susan's devoted friend, taught us to think of music in a different way: to reach out to others. But our music lasts only a few moments, it lives a precarious life in the memory, a music less solitary than a composer's, and less enduring. So I have been thinking, the last few days, of how this fragile art is part of the fragility of life."

Alexander looked over his papers out into the room. At least half the people in it knew that he and Susan had been on the verge of divorce.

"A few months ago, Susan and I were at a restaurant with a friend of ours who had just played a concert. He still had the bandages on his fingertips which he had put on before the concert. He blamed the bandages on Liszt, the Liszt split his fingernails. These bandages bothered me. Most of us have thick calluses, we need them to play. A plastic bandage instead seemed like cheating, losing contact with the keys. In fact I thought that if someone played as well as our friend, there must come a time when you want to give just one concert unbandaged, just the exposed hands making the music. But the plastic is protection, so that you can play tomorrow, again.

"Susan was someone who lacked this protection. I wouldn't do her memory a service by saying she was so great a pianist she didn't need it. If anything, it was the other way around, she was too vulnerable, her hands alone weren't enough to make the music she loved."

Alexander turned to his last page. "Many of you know the fear I am speaking of. In our kind of music we can't be solitary, and when we are needy we are likely to be hurt, by audiences, by each other, or by ourselves. So many people have said to me that her accident is unfair, which it was. All I want you to know, and to remember of Susan, is that long before it she accepted the risks of our kind of life, and her love of music never waned." Alexander put down the paper; his voice became a little more hesitant. "I want to thank you for the kindness you've shown Susan's family and me these last weeks. People have asked us if there is some memorial they could make to her, and we'd like it if you gave something to her school. I think—I'm sure—she'd also appreciate that."

The mourners filed out of the funeral home into the bright sunshine on the street. It was difficult to know what to say to Alexander; many felt he had been compelled to unburden himself of some private sentiments about his marital problems, upon which it wasn't anyone else's business to comment. He seemed to have himself in hand, they said. Alexander looked around. Where were his own parents? He'd seen them just a moment ago. All the parents had gone. Flavia Grisi came up to him as he made small talk with a little knot of people. "The others left to deal with Mrs. Fields," she told him. The Grisis would take him back to Carnegie Towers: "We're ready whenever you are." At last the crowd dispersed. Alexander didn't want Signor Grisi, he wanted to be alone, but the older man was beside him and grasped Alexander's hand. "My friend, perhaps I understand."

The trucks on Columbus Avenue were deafening. "Do you really?" Alexander replied. Signor Grisi could barely hear Alexander, who had turned away from him slightly, which was perhaps as well. Someone was going to pay. But Alexander was just able, for a moment more, to perform the better words outside himself. He moved closer to Signor Grisi; his stomach was killing him. He smiled and said, "Then explain it to me: what was wrong with us? We meant well. It was the music, wasn't it?" Signor Grisi couldn't hear anything. When the traffic was like this, you might as well be deaf.

Part Two

LEARNING TO
REACH OUT

Chapter 3

TOUCH

"Samuel Gregorovich, I've been thinking," Abraham Zilker said to his son-in-law just before Alexander turned six. Samuel's full name was in fact Samuel Gregory Hoffmann, but Alexander's grandfather considered it impolite not to use the patronymic of adults he knew well, even if they lacked a proper patronym. He spoke at the end of a grueling afternoon in which the two men had completed a deal in tin, always a tricky metal.

"I'm sure the price will hold firm."

"Not about that. About the piano in my living room. I want to give it to little Sasha."

"Alexander? He could barely touch the keys standing up. And where would we put a grand piano?"

"I want to say to you, take this piano, please, it is something you can do for me. It would make me happy, I don't know why but it would."

As a boy, Abraham Zilker sometimes, when scavenging in St. Petersburg, had been able to hear music coming from the great houses which threw out more or less valuable refuse. The thumping bass, the melodies muffled by glass, and the barely audible applause gave him a comforting feeling of life within. Abraham bought his piano, an enormous grand unsuitable for a home, as soon as he started making real money in America, though neither he nor his wife nor their daughter Gerda could play. He bought it before he purchased the automobile, the canopied bed, or the etchings of America's Great Presidents (Washington, Jefferson, Lincoln, and Grover Cleveland). The piano sat in the Zilker living room like an ebony monument; it was conscientiously tuned, the ivories highly polished.

Samuel responded to the pleading behind Abraham's words, although the old man said nothing of the past, nor of his discovery that a piano is sad in the home of a widower. It seemed a little extravagant, but Samuel liked music and hoped Alexander would learn to play. Alexander was delighted that such a big object was all for him. Until he was six, his principal excitement had been the back yard which served as parlor, whorehouse, and promenade for the neighborhood cats. The piano arrived one Saturday morning, the movers struggling to get it up the narrow stairs. They positioned it in the small living room away from the radiator; all the furniture had to be shifted. The result of this tugging and pushing was that the tuning gave, which Samuel noticed when he played a few chords. He said, "The sound is a mess."

"Don't worry, it's not your money," Abraham assured him. After conducting the movers he was glowing. "I pay for the tuning, too—it's part of the deal."

The Hoffmanns now had in their living room a bulky lesson they had learned in other ways before: be careful of his gifts, there will always be a little twist of the knife. Samuel went to work for Abraham when no one else would give him a job. His father-in-law had regularly increased his salary; first, on

Gerda's birthday each year, then, after Alexander was born, on the grandson's birthday. Abraham trusted his son-in-law with all the secrets of the business; on the other hand, he frequently answered telephone calls made to Samuel. Samuel said to his wife, "I can't complain," which in one way was true. He could pay his bills. Moreover, six months before Alexander was born the Hoffmanns were able to move from their cold, mouse-infested apartment on the north side of Chicago to the neighborhood they loved, Hyde Park, next to the university. Abraham had made it all possible. A little subservience, a few moments of dull anger: Samuel could bear it.

The neighborhood around the University of Chicago was, during the Second World War, one of the most beautiful in the city. Everything in Chicago happens fast; the oldest people in Hyde Park could remember when it was mostly single homes with wide stretches of lawn between the houses, a neighborhood of small English estates. At the end of the nineteenth century great families like the Rockefellers gave money to build the university, whose buildings were copies of medieval quadrangles and cathedrals. Ancient Oxford, coming to Chicago after the Augustan age, was succeeded by a riot of history at the time of the First World War. Apartment houses were built as everything from Jacobean mansions to Florentine palazzos—but the medieval note dominated, because the university was the center of Hyde Park's life. The neighborhood was a haven for lawyers, doctors, and cultivated businessmen as well as for professors, a place in a different time from that of the slaughterhouses and factories established to the north and east. But since the smoke from the factories was often visible through the trees, and on bad days a faint smell of the slaughterhouse might taint the air, people had to explain away this incongruity, and they did so by invoking the children. It was good for the children of an industrial city to grow up in a neighborhood of recent medieval buildings.

Certain ramshackle wooden buildings untouched by the great

Chicago fire of 1871 were preserved. They housed the second-hand bookstores, where students had their first adult taste of buying and selling. The Hoffmanns lived in one of these wooden buildings, the one next to the coffee shop. On the ground floor was a good bookstore, the yard in the back of the apartment was filled with trees, the street in front was lined with trees, there were flowers in the window boxes; it was a clean Bohemia.

When Alexander was born, early in 1947, the Hoffmanns believed that the place perfectly suited their child. Alexander was a happy baby, if not a distinguished one. He learned neither to walk nor talk earlier than other children; teething, toilet-training, and the capacity for mischief arrived on schedule. He loved going into the shops in Hyde Park with his mother, sweeping all merchandise within reach to the floor; he played happily with other children in the park called the Midway. At first, his parents thought the grand piano was, if anything, another folly of Abraham's, akin to the baseball bat for Alexander's third birthday which the child could barely lift, or the train set last year which had nearly electrocuted him.

He couldn't play the tunes he heard on the radio, or when Gerda would sing a song to him, he would play something totally different. He sat on the piano bench, his legs dangling, striking notes over and over; indeed, he spent a great deal of time at the piano worrying. By the time he was seven, his hands had spread out enough to play simple chords, and these, like the notes he first picked out, worried him.

The Hoffmanns, not being musical, were afraid this meant something might be wrong with Alexander; perhaps he would have a problem reading as well. They didn't understand that musical curiosity is closer to anxiety than to pleasure. A child strikes notes on the piano the way he scratches at a sore. There is an itch teasing under the scab; there is a mystery in the sound. The child repeats the note or chord, trying to get underneath. A musical child hears the rainbow of overtones contained in any note, and feels a melody as a possibility. A melody can be moved up or down, new notes can be added to it, a song grows or shrinks. This curiosity often makes musical children poor mimics. Gerda once saw a look of disgust pass across the face of her six-year-old boy while he was listening to some children's records Abraham had bought him. He went to the piano and played one of the melodies backwards.

After the piano had been in the house a year, it was clear to the Hoffmanns that their son had an affinity for music, even if he had no gift for it. They found a teacher for him, a young woman who had given up her concert career when she married a professor of botany. After the first lesson, the young woman drew Gerda aside.

"How long has he been toying with the piano?"

"So you think it strange, too?" Gerda said. "Well, we do want him to continue. He likes it and not everyone has to have talent."

"Mrs. Hoffmann, you don't understand. He is amazing for a seven-year-old."

Gerda heard these words with a mixture of surprise, deep pleasure, and anxiety.

"Why?"

"He has worked out the basic principles of harmony for himself; little kids don't do that. When I showed him how to tuck his thumb under his palm, which is a hard motion for a small hand, he imitated me instantly."

"That's funny, because he can't imitate tunes at all."

"He's way beyond that."

As the young woman explained to her, the surprise wore off, but not the mixture of pleasure and anxiety. Samuel had the same reaction that evening. "We won't push him, Samuel," she repeated like a litany, "we won't make him feel he is a freak." Already he was a genius.

• • •

In some ways the piano is a cruel instrument for the young. Parents start their children on it because by simply banging or poking, the child can produce a sound. Once a child takes to music, he or she finds in playing the piano an unfurling frustration; the more you know, the harder it is to play. After a year of suffering for all concerned, a child can play for its parents long tunes on a violin; as a child goes forward on the piano each new combination of hands, each new movement for the fingers, is like starting all over again. The whole world in ten fingers—too much possibility.

It was exactly this cruelty of possibility which absorbed Alexander. He was fortunate in the young woman who first taught him. She also subscribed to the principle of not pushing him, but she understood by this maxim not to insist on easy victories over the instrument. If Alexander wanted to spend two months playing scales badly by experimenting with different combinations of fingers, that was better than insisting he play in one given way to achieve quick results. The young woman explained to him how chords work, why one chord dissolves into another, why the building blocks of each chord could be arranged in so many forms, in order to teach him how to make them himself. He was progressing, the Hoffmanns thought, very slowly; other children by the age of eight seemed to be able to play whole little pieces, while he was still frowning at fragments.

Alexander continued to be easy with his playmates, but Gerda could see that in the afternoons he was often eager to get home. Although the Hoffmanns knew nothing about music, they did know something about little boys—the young piano teacher was childless—and they knew that withdrawal was not a good sign. Gerda therefore had a long talk with the principal of perhaps the greatest institution of organized hope in the United States after the Second World War, the University of Chicago Laboratory School, whose child victims came mostly from the immediate community around the university. The principal agreed with Gerda: the piano was an "a-social" instrument. For growth to occur, children must play together. The principal and Gerda decided to place him in the school orchestra, although at eight he would be the youngest player. His asocial piano lessons could continue, and orchestra would be an "integrative, interactive" experience. The choice of instrument was dictated by his size; he was given a cello because the school happened to own a half-scale one. A new orchestra teacher came to the Laboratory School the year Alexander was put in the orchestra and this young teacher, a bearded enthusiast for the social virtues of music, also knew how to play the cello; he was engaged to give Alexander lessons.

At first Alexander didn't care; it was a new toy. In one room of the Laboratory School there were fifteen child guitarists singing work songs from *The Socialist Song Book*, in another were twenty members of the orchestra hacking through *Eine Kleine Nachtmusik*, both rooms full of noise, everyone having a good time. The cello teacher told him to hold his left hand in four basic positions on the strings, to hold the bow firmly but flexibly, and not to practice at home more than fifteen minutes a day. He would "learn by doing" with others. Against this mindless freedom Alexander could set a deeper one; after practicing his positions on the cello as though he were performing athletic exercises, he would move to the piano, where now he was exploring the mystery of repeated blurring chords in a Chopin prelude, the blur somewhere between an echo and a drum-beat.

One day, Joyce, the serious young teacher who asked what-if and why about his piano playing, broke a piece of bad news. "My husband is moving to a new job." This meant nothing to Alexander. "I . . . well, I didn't want to tell you before. We're moving quite soon. In fact, next week." This did mean something to him; he and the piano would be lonely. "But I've arranged for a new teacher for you, Alexander. Oh yes you can. I'm not the only person in the world who knows how to play the piano, and Rita is very good. You will like her. Now don't look like that." The young woman suddenly turned away; she hadn't realized how much she was going to miss the little boy who had said about a fantastic chord they built together with twenty fingers, "Joyce, listen, listen to it!" All she could think of to add was, "Now until Rita comes, I want you to practice your cello."

Samuel Hoffmann too had news. They were leaving Hyde Park; nearly thirty years of family disorder had come to a head. He also counseled work on the cello while the piano was being packed and shipped, even though they were only moving across town and the piano would only be in storage for a few days until their new apartment was ready.

The scrap metal business is not for the faint of heart. A dealer in scrap is buying from people who may have only the most dubious right to sell what they sell; for instance, a used-car dealer may suddenly have twenty broken-down sedans available which must be transported to the dealer's yard and pounded down beyond recognition as soon as possible. The scrap dealer must have a wide range of potential customers eager to buy whatever he has; the stock is so costly to process and to warehouse that you lose money if you have a large inventory. These customers are usually respectable minor manufacturers. A dealer in scrap is thus not a crook, but may well know many crooks (not only suppliers, but police inspectors on the take or trucking-union officials who make their men work for less than union scale in return for a little something on the side), and on the other hand a dealer in scrap must be able to talk comfortably to the respectable minor manufacturers in their offices, even in their clubs, about tonnage deliveries and the injustices of the tax system of the country in which dealer and industrialist have nonetheless somehow managed to become rich. The bigger the scrap dealer, the more agile he must be; although a heavy man, Abraham Zilker knew how to move. Yet to describe him as either a crook or a profiteer would have been a gross injustice.

"Patriotism" would inadequately evoke Abraham Zilker's love affair with America, despite the fact that he continued to employ Russian courtesies, eat Russian food whenever possible (in dining at the industrialists' club he would pass up lobster for meatloaf, if that simple dish happened to be on the menu, as it reminded him of a recipe from the old country) and despite, of course, his implacable hatred of the government tax men. One government fought the Second World War, another taxed him. He could have become even richer between 1941 and 1945 had he manipulated scrap inventories, as some of his acquaintances in the trade did, in order to up the price. An order from an armaments factory, an aircraft plant, or a shipyard he considered a sacred trust and filled as rapidly as possible. However, as he often said, a man in scrap during the war would have to be sleeping not to make a dollar, "And I have insomnia bad."

Like most other self-made men (he was peddling from a cart when he was nine years old), Abraham Zilker made a sharp distinction between the family, which was a garden, and the world outside, which was a jungle. "Anything and everything for you," he said to his only daughter. He said it more often after his wife died, with a trace of regret, and repeated this declaration of love after Gerda married, with a trace of disappointment.

Samuel Hoffmann was not the son-in-law Abraham would have chosen, but in America a father didn't choose. Samuel was quiet and modest. On the other hand, Samuel had worked ten hours a day for five years to put himself through the University of Chicago, where he had studied French and Italian. These were not quite the languages for a rabbi, but Abraham could make sense of his son-in-law by thinking of him as someone like a rabbi. Eventually, he was sure, he would be allowed to help the young couple; the rabbis all took money when they settled down. But they didn't settle down, they joined the Communist Party.

They thought: from rags to riches in America (by 1931, when they joined, he was already rich); a contributor to the Republican Party, one of the first Jews in Chicago to be one; a man whose chauffeur wears a fur coat. They thought: he will be furious, but they had no access to his nightmares—to the nightmare memory of the young man rooting around in the garbage cans, of the uncle who did the young boy's parents a favor by buying him a passage to America when he was thirteen years old, a passage he made before the obligatory bar mitzvah he never had, the young boy thinking, as he retched across the Atlantic, "I am one less mouth to feed." Nor did they have access to the nightmare of remembering other young men chop off their thumbs, to render themselves unfit for the twenty-five years of service the Tsar extracted from those in his armies. Abraham Zilker's joke was true; he did have bad insomnia, he feared the gates of memory that sleep can open.

He said to them, "You are going to see, it's a mistake, but *geh gesund.*" When his industrialist friends said that any man in America who really wanted to could find work, he kept silent. He knew too much about the jungle, he knew that most of the creatures in it, Depression or boom, were there to be eaten. However, he had no impulse to give away his wealth to the poor; generosity belonged in the garden of his family. So he waited for his children to come back.

Up until 1929, a girl could grow up in Chicago without any knowledge of the poor, if the parents were careful. The chauffeur must drive from the South Shore to the shops, concerts, and restaurants downtown only by taking the Lakeshore Drive; a man thought twice about which business associates he invited home. The city was vast, but in those days it hadn't quite filled out, so that the poor, the factories, the warehouses did not crowd up against the rich who lived alongside Lake Michigan; there were empty fields or ruins or parks that still made a barrier. I am your father and I will protect you from my nightmares.

When Samuel met Gerda, he took her to Halstead Street, one of the toughest and reddest parts of the city. His own father was a tailor who had protected Samuel in a different way. For fifty years the Germans in Chicago had been at the center of the socialist community; they were the victims of the Haymarket massacre, they fought Pullman, they were Chicago's Wobblies, which they pronounced "Vobliess," but people still knew who they were. A family affair, a faith passed down through three generations, their radicalism gave them not only solidarity but a sense of being safe. People knew they could count on *die Brüder* to lend them money, to take care of their children if they were in jail, to take on the older ones as apprentices. In 1929 it seemed that the doom they had prophesied had arrived, revolution was at hand. When Samuel walked Gerda past the lines of men waiting for a cup of soup, when he showed her the radical newspaper for which his father wrote "Tailor's World" (a column she couldn't read because it, like the rest of the paper, was in German), when he introduced her to older women who shook hands with her and she was caught short for a moment in realizing that, on the South Shore, you never shook hands with a seamstress, she felt she touched reality and she felt relief in touching it. A child always knows when a parent is holding something back.

At first it seemed an adventure, then it became a nightmare. In 1933, he began organizing electrical workers; she made coffee for the organizers. In 1935 he moved to the bottom rung of the central committee of the Illinois Communist Party; she also moved to the central office to stuff envelopes. In 1936 both of them began to have doubts at the time of the show trials in Moscow; he was sent back to the electrical workers, she was sent back to the coffee machine. In 1937 the Party found a way to convert their doubts into disloyalty; they were accused of

Trotskyite sympathies, and they fell into the trap. Samuel spent twelve hours a day rather than ten on the job, to prove he was not a turn-coat; Gerda donated the last of the money Abraham had given her as a girl to the Party's strike fund. In 1939, when the Hitler-Stalin pact was signed, both the Hoffmanns quit the Party.

Samuel thereafter found that the phrase "all doors were closed to him" could be literally true. People did not return his calls, they had never heard of him. By 1940, all the odd jobs— typing, running errands—were over. In 1940 Samuel was a messenger for a printing firm, and he kept telling himself, "Labor of any sort is dignified," as he bicycled around the city delivering packages. At the end of one week early in 1941 he was told he needn't return next Monday. Broke, exhausted, the Hoffmanns had only the one connection left. Samuel went to work for his father-in-law. Abraham had waited a decade.

Abraham Zilker trusted no one but himself to negotiate deals; Samuel would learn to do the bookkeeping. But the books had constantly to be "revised" because of the nature of the deals. Often in the 1930s Samuel had spoken about "criminal capitalism" at meetings; now he was working in its shadows. He had also spoken at meetings about the relationship between capitalism and the war machine of the First World War. The family business was an excellent example of this alliance in the new world war.

As soon as Samuel went to work for Abraham, the subject came up. "Now, my dear, we are together, now you are ready for a family." It was not a request; there must be children, otherwise what was the business, their business, for? Like many of their friends, the Hoffmanns had deferred children under the press of their political work. When he first went to work for Abraham, Samuel was afraid that he could not take care of a child, that something would go wrong now, because something always did. But the Hoffmanns soon were as anxious for a family as Abraham Zilker; family would substitute for the decade of mailings, meetings, and lies. Gerda discovered, however, that a woman does not always conceive easily; she had almost given up hope when Alexander was finally in the making, and the birth was difficult.

During the halcyon years of the cats in the back yard, the piano in the living room, the pageant of evolution at school, they could tell themselves that things were better. For ten years, Gerda had felt the lash of retributive guilt—you're soft, you came from a rich family, prove yourself. Her son's only demand was love. For ten years, Samuel also had been tested—are you tough enough, do you have discipline, are you your father's son? His infant boy had no reason to ask these questions. All this molecule of a family required was that Samuel agree when Abraham at work said, "Samuel Gregorovich, let me handle it, it's complicated."

The Jew's belief in the child-genius—Joyce had not used the word "genius," she had simply said that Alexander had unusual ability—has something to do with lacking a redeemer. Each generation mothers and fathers its redemption, called the little genius, a stock figure of fun only if you are already furnished with the divine version. But precisely the appearance from your own body of someone whose gifts promise to take him beyond the circle of your own sorrows can cause great anxiety as well. When Samuel said, "We won't push him," he meant, "Let's not tempt fate." The chances are so slim. This fear of tempting fate expresses the Jew's world-fear: the knowledge that God abandoned man to the jungle of men, no sweet stories of salvation to make it all come out nicely if only you are good, the fear of that jungle, and yet perhaps the possibility that someone you create may find a way out. But that someone must be very special. And since you have made a mess of your own life, why shouldn't you infect this special creature you have made, infect him with the disease of your own lost hopes? "No, we mustn't push him."

Samuel had reserved some small region of hope within himself from which he found the energy to keep resenting the slights that Abraham did not know he was inflicting. In 1957 circumstances offered Samuel the possibility of drawing on this reserve. One man who did not treat Samuel as invisible after he left the Party became, in 1957, the general administrator of Washington Homes, a project built on the near West Side after the war for Negroes who couldn't find decent shelter elsewhere. Washington Homes was more than a place to live; it was an experiment in mixing the races, poor blacks with liberal, mostly Jewish, whites, the only people willing to try. The buildings looked like prisons—squat brick piles surrounded by metal fencing, concrete paving instead of grass. But to the Negroes who had lived in metal huts during the war, Washington Homes seemed palatial.

The administrator offered Samuel a job as "general assistant," an ill-defined status somewhere between janitor and landlord, with one ironclad condition: Samuel and his family must live in the project where he worked. Samuel immediately turned the job down. "My son has a scholarship to the Laboratory School of the University of Chicago."

"So do four other children, although your Alexander would be the only white from Washington Homes. We could hire a bus service to the university."

"He takes piano lessons once a week downtown."

"How old is he?"

"Ten."

"Ten is old enough to take his own bus downtown. It's up to you, Sammy. I can make it possible."

Samuel broached the matter tentatively to Gerda.

"Half your current salary?"

"He will throw in the apartment for free."

"He really wants you?"

"Yes, he really does."

"I could work."

Abraham Zilker was stunned. 1957 was not 1931. In twenty-six years he had fired many people more competent than Samuel, which was to say that Samuel was the only person he had left whom he trusted. Despite the notion that the business was "anything and everything for you," Abraham didn't want to sell it when he retired, he wanted it to go on, to survive him. And then the deal: less money, living with the shvartzes, his grandson pushed into the mire, and for what? Fixing broken windows was more dignified than trading scrap?

"You talk about leading your own life, doing some good. What about doing your child some good? What about doing your father-in-law some good? Look, I am a simple man. All I know, I helped you when no one else would, when you needed me. Look at me, both of you, look at me; I am sixty-three years old, you are what I have. All right, Samuel Gregorovich, you tell me I could have been more delicate with you. I am sorry, that is what I can say. But now you do the same, you do more; it is not my feelings you are hurting, you are saying goodbye to our life. Each other, that's all we have, and you tell me you want to be free?"

"I'm sorry, Abraham, I'm sorry, too."

Abraham Zilker stood up, took out from his breast pocket one of his silk handkerchiefs monogrammed "AFZ"; he began to raise it to wipe his nose, suddenly stared at it as though he were holding a foreign object, dropped the silk handkerchief onto the floor, and walked out of the Hoffmanns' apartment.

Alexander sat in their new apartment in Washington Homes waiting for the piano tuner. The piano had been the hardest object to move; they found it would only fit through the bedroom door of the ground-floor rooms. The big bedroom became Alexander's; his parents slept in the little room. The place was noisy, as it gave on the Washington Homes playground; they had to keep the shades drawn for privacy from the screaming children. The piano didn't belong here.

Alexander sat waiting for the piano tuner, and after a while he took out the cello to help pass the time. He began to tune it; the children outside ran to the window and knocked, wanting to come in or have him come out and show them. He stayed in the darkened room, concentrating on his own tuning, while the light filtered through the slats of the wooden blinds.

Fingers can press down the strings of a cello in two ways: head on—that is, the hand held at an exact right angle to the strings—or sloped, the wrist broken like a violinist's, the strings touching the sides of the fingertips. Alexander had been taught the seemingly logical way, the hand meeting the strings square, as though fingers and strings formed two sides of a box. Teachers who like this neat join of body and instrument usually prefer an exact distance between the fingers. Once the open strings are tuned, each finger is taught to the millimeter how far away it should be from the next when it presses down. This logic produces sour sound. No one had ever explained to Alexander about "Pythagoras' Comma," the reason for the flaw in this logic, but his ears told him that this squared-off way of playing produced notes which set his teeth on edge. One reason he had always liked to move from cello practice to the piano was that suddenly the sound came clear and he could stop wincing.

Waiting for the piano tuner who would make him a gift of clear sound, he tried, just to see, what it was like to defy his teacher's instructions and flop his hand to the side, as he had thought he had seen a cellist do. The result startled him. The box-method has to treat all the fingers as if they were the same length; there is always tension at the knuckle of the longest, middle finger when the cellist is pretending that the hand is not naturally shaped in an arc. Now, when he flopped his hand to the side, this tension disappeared.

The children screamed at each other outside, a basketball bounced off the outer wall of the apartment, and Alexander pursued his discovery. Now that the knuckles of the left hand were free, he found he could adjust the distance between his fingers without straining; the sour sound could be erased. There were no calluses on the sides of his fingertips, the string bit into the flesh, but for the first time he was enjoying what he heard.

The piano tuner arrived and set to work, with the children in the playground imitating the pings they heard coming from the apartment of the new tenants who kept the shades drawn. "How do you get a piano in tune?" Alexander asked the man, who was made a little nervous by the mimicry going on outside.

"I do it just the way you do on your cello—not from note to note, but harmonically, through shading chords and octaves."

The bearded enthusiast had said nothing about this at school. Alexander took the cello into his parents' bedroom while the tuner went on working. He began to play the notes of chords using his new hand, trying to hear the sounds in relation to each other and making his fingers go to those sounds, rather than thinking about the distance between the fingers on the black fingerboard. Breaking the old habit was not easy. The children outside were even more stimulated by the cacophony coming from the new tenants inside; they began pounding on the walls.

When the piano tuner finished, he was in a hurry to leave. Alexander saw him out the door and went back to the cello. The possibilities for clear notes seemed endless if he could break his training. The children outside had become bored, and the shouting and thumping ceased.

What Samuel hoped for himself happened. Most of the Negroes in the Washington Homes came from backward rural areas. They applied the logic of country people to city things; a few even considered the toilets as wells. Samuel found he had the talent to explain the proper use of the sanitation without making the residents feel ashamed of themselves. He organized the part of the housing project under his control into little brigades—for garbage pick-up, coal delivery, night security.

Although never a hard taskmaster, he found that this quasi-military routine made daily life easier; the presence among his residents of five Negroes and one white who had fought in the war meant there were others who understood. A deserter and a failure in the eyes of his father-in-law, he now felt himself useful.

Gerda did find a job, as a typist in a nearby hospital. She had to lie to get it, saying she had never belonged to a subversive organization, but the FBI search for Communist infiltrators of hospitals had not yet gathered steam in Chicago; the witch-hunting was still centered on smaller cities in the Midwest. Her job was at a quarter of Samuel's old salary, so with his half and the free apartment they weren't doing too badly. They tried to see Abraham Zilker, but for six months he said he wasn't interested.

The two years Alexander passed at Washington Homes were happy in one way. He and four Negro friends took the bus every weekday to the temple of hope. One of the other boys was brilliant in mathematics, and he and Alexander became friends. Alexander often practiced on the school piano or played the cello after classes while his brilliant friend received extra tuition in math and other Washington Homes children were treated to supervised play time, virtually indistinguishable from the hours they spent in class. The bus collected them all at around five in the afternoon, and they chattered their way through the slow rush-hour ride home.

By 1959 Alexander and the other schoolmates in the Washington Homes were in danger. The Negro adults in Samuel's brigades treated him with affection and Gerda, whom they saw less of, with respect. The Negro children were not so easily assuaged. The move to the North unleashed generations of fury long buried; gradually these children gave vent to the hatred too dangerous to speak its name. Their parents would slap them when the terrifying words of racial hate poured out of the young mouths, but silence reigned only until the children were alone. The four Negro scholarship students were classed by the other children as no better than whites; Alexander's mathematician friend was beaten senseless twice.

Hatred erupted finally in the great glass war of 1959. This pitted two bands against each other, the "niggers" versus the "kikes"; the children in Washington Homes were not offered the luxury of declining to join in. The leaders of both sides said it would be a war to the death, and chose as a battlefield two abandoned buildings which faced each other just outside the metal fence surrounding the housing project. The children had already found it easy enough to get into the buildings; there were plenty of broken panes of glass inside. The battle was set for dusk one day in April; Alexander and his mathematician friend Clarence sat silently in the school bus on the way home that day. They briefly held hands until one of the other boys turned around and started chanting, "Fairies, fairies," a singsong from G to D which Alexander could not help noticing was perfectly in tune. As the bus deposited them outside the project, they looked at each other in silence. They were twelve years old; this meant they were honor-bound to fight. Clarence, perhaps more than Alexander, felt that fighting would redeem him in the eyes of the other children, who did not understand what it was to be already possessed by a force that ignored the fact you were only a child. As the sun set on a beautiful, cloudless day, the two gangs entered their fortresses, which immigrants who were no longer poor had once called home. The boys took up positions at the sides of the windows, and a rain of glass began to fall across the street.

It was a serious war. If a boy did not get away from the window fast enough, he could get cut by a pane of glass; the other side had then scored a "direct hit." Even if he moved away in time, the splintering of glass inside the room of his fortress sent showers of slivers all around. The warriors slung the panes with the same motion that one skips stones over water. Alexander broke panes across his kneecaps for the warriors to throw. After five minutes, one of the boys in his room suffered a direct hit on the arm. There was blood; the boy tried to keep going in silence. Suddenly the boys heard scratching and little whimperings on the floor. Rats in the dust were also frightened.

The warriors were oblivious to time, but it could have been no more than ten minutes after they began that the police arrived. First the police saw the Negro children in their fortress and one of the policemen shook his head in disgust. Then the officers saw the wounded white warrior in Alexander's room. They jumped from their squad cars, drew their guns, and shouted to the children to come out. As though a light switch were flicked, the war stopped. Alexander could hear the boots of the policemen crunching on the broken glass in the street. Twenty trembling boys came down; there had been three direct hits. One Negro boy was especially badly cut across the leg. Alexander looked for Clarence and saw, with a wave of relief, that his friend was safe.

The disgusted policeman, on seeing the badly cut Negro boy, surprised himself by putting his arms around the bleeding child; he spoke soft words of comfort, he looked at the white boys with anger. The parents ran out from the project; two ambulances arrived. Samuel looked at his son's hands and saw splinters in them. He shouted at Alexander, one of the rare times he ever did, angry words of love. The police filed no charges because there were too many parents in this chaotic rage of love; the officers had enough to do packing the wounded boys into the ambulances. One of the fathers in Samuel's garbage brigade looked the white man in the eye, and both of them knew: by moving north the black man had not escaped.

When Gerda came home from work, she found Samuel bathing Alexander's hands in the sink. Neither man nor boy spoke at first and she misunderstood; she was touched by the sight of a father gently washing his boy, although Alexander seemed a little old for this. After Samuel was satisfied that he had soaked all the splinters out of Alexander's hand, he came out of the bathroom and explained.

In the trial of those we love there sometimes appears a terrible opportunity. Like the policeman who did not know he could feel compassion for a Negro, Gerda was surprised by Alexander's hands into deciding to end the search for Samuel's self-respect. For herself, she had sealed perhaps fifty thousand envelopes of propaganda in her life, and made perhaps twenty thousand cups of coffee for male revolutionaries. People said it required a strong woman to cope with a beaten man. She would have phrased it differently. Life, that is, life outside the Zilker fortress, had allotted her tasks, and she had so far performed them.

A whole lifetime of worrying. Had he been some self-pitying sensitive little flower, she would have left Samuel after a few years. But Samuel was driven. When Samuel was hit by a hired thug during a strike in 1934, Gerda was worried and proud. When Samuel stood up to the Central Committee she was proud and afraid; by then she had seen the Party make vicious use of its own thugs. When they went back to the electrical union, she was worried and confused; why were they trying to prove themselves to people whose acts falsified the noble words? When the Hoffmanns resigned in protest over the Hitler-Stalin Pact in 1939, she felt an immense surge of relief; now it was over, they could settle down. There was no money for a baby, and she next worried that they would soon be out on the breadlines themselves. Her girlhood had fitted her for nothing; during the Party days all people thought she was good for, really, was a loan from her dwindling savings. In the early Forties she worried about whether Samuel would save them, and then her father did, and finally Alexander was born. Now they could stop worrying.

But they couldn't, they were immigrants to a new land of care. When would Abraham learn to treat Samuel with respect? When could Samuel find a job of his own? It was worse because her husband spoke matter-of-fact words about his humiliations. If only he had complained bitterly, wept in her arms—then she could have done something, or the tears would have purified him. But no, he was steady, he kept it in and like her father he lay awake at nights staring at the ceiling. So that worry hung over them.

Now her son was also falling into the pit. She had had enough. She just wanted them to live, back in the apartment over the bookstore, in their own garden filled with promenading cats, a good enough life. Samuel would have to do this for her. He owed her just this one thing—relief. She would make him do it.

While Samuel dried his hands at the sink, Gerda said, "We're taking him away."

"What do you mean? We live here, we have to work this through."

"Not any more."

"Gerda, calm down. It's Alexander who's had a scare; don't upset him again."

No, you're not going to get away with it, not any more. I deserve to wake up and say, today I'm going to enjoy walking, reading a book, talking to friends. I deserve to be able to open the shades of our house, free of sitting in half-darkness, no more project children are going to make me spend a day in shadows. Free of doing good, free of making you feel better.

"It's not discussable, Samuel. We're moving."

Gerda called her father; the family would go to his house temporarily. Abraham Zilker hesitated. Of course they could come back to the silent mansion where all the rooms but his bedroom and the living room were closed up, of course they could come back, but. . . . "You are fighting with your husband?"

"No, I just want a safe place for Alexander to stay until we can find another apartment near the university."

"Samuel Gregorovich does not agree?"

"No."

"Let me talk to him."

Samuel took the telephone from his wife and said in his ordinary, quiet voice, "Yes, Abraham, I'm on."

"The boy is not hurt? Good, now listen to me. I will do what you want, do you understand me? This is not like before. I will do what you want. If you say, take care of us, I'll take care of you; if you say no, I will tell her she cannot come to me without your permission."

Samuel felt the echo of an old surprise, his surprise at Abraham's understanding when he had joined the Party. The morals of a patriarch he could no more fathom than the nightmares of poverty which the old man had kept from him long ago.

"You don't have to tell me now," Abraham whispered. After a pause, he cleared his throat and said, in a stronger voice, "You tell Gerda Ivanovna that she must have your permission."

Samuel hung up and told her. She was stunned; hadn't her father sung over and over again, "Anything and everything for you"? Half an hour ago, images of a boy's cut hands had struck her like whips across the face, but now all that seemed far away. She wanted to be free, yet her father was deserting her in her moment of need, her father who had promised.

Alexander was in his room, confused. The boy in him thought it was his fault his parents were fighting; events had moved so rapidly that they had momentarily forgotten him. Angry, meaningless words about his grandfather, who was not there when it happened, came through the thin walls. In his solitude he thought they were rejecting him. The man in Alexander looked at his hands. When they had worked on the Chopin prelude with the repeated chords, Joyce had said to him, "Make bear-paws when you play them, Alexander, pretend you are a bear flopping your paws in front of you." He had learned since then to express this truth more abstractly: the hands have a life of their own. The trunk of the body does not need to rise and fall to play repeated chords, not even the arms do, just the flopping paws. And yet these independent hands cannot live cut off from the body.

Since his discovery about the position of the left hand on the strings, both hands had more life, each finger on its own. The bearded enthusiast at school was a little taken aback when Alexander explained what he had discovered. "It's one way to do it," he said, as if he had known. Fairness prompted him to add, "The cello isn't really my instrument. When you're a little farther along, we'll get you a professional." Unlike the announcement of Joyce's move, this caused Alexander no grief. "Go ahead and play that way if it makes you feel better." So his hands on the cello for the last two years had run free. Rita, the new piano teacher, was good, but she was stricter than Joyce; this only made his cello playing more of a private freedom—not at all what the Laboratory School had anticipated.

His hands were still stinging from the strong soap his father had used to bathe them. They were the most precious things he had; left to themselves, the accidents of school, neighborhood, other people could hurt them. Sitting in his bedroom, staring at his hands while Samuel and Gerda argued about decades of failure and worry, Alexander thought, "I've got to be careful."

The day after she saw what Abraham's promise to protect her was worth, Gerda said to Samuel, "There's no reason why you can't keep your job." She did not say, "I'm leaving you." It wasn't that simple. They began to reason, within the limits of her unshakable determination to move, which, having lasted only twenty-four hours, ravished her in wave after wave of relief. Samuel protested that by now poor blacks were crowding around the University of Chicago. He pointed out that there was a housing shortage; their wonderful apartment above the bookstore would surely be beyond their means, and they had little chance of regaining it or anything like it. Gerda was certain they could find something; she was certain she could find a good job at the university hospital doing something. She was going to make it work.

Gerda took the first apartment she could find. She signed the lease, then took Samuel to see it. All he could say to her when he saw the apartment, close to the university's cathedral, was that the piano wouldn't fit.

"Then it can go back to his grandfather's house. Alexander lives only a block from school now."

By 1959, Samuel had so established himself as an indispensable presence at Washington Homes that the administrator made no objection when told "My wife insists we move back to the university; it's closer to Alexander's school." The Negro residents also accepted this fiction. Despite the fact that he had been obliged to teach them the principles of modern sanitation, they were too worldly to blame him. The black children were for the most part indifferent to Alexander's departure. Clarence said, "I'll move there soon, I'll get my dad to move us." A brilliant mathematician and a brilliant musician—but they were only twelve years old; impossibility did not yet exist as a category.

The white adults to whom they returned in Hyde Park also understood; poor Samuel, strong Gerda. Yet Gerda was only humanly strong. She told Alexander that all these disruptions were for his sake; the moving, the lost friend, the piano he could no longer play whenever he felt like it. She did not tell him she had reached the end of her rope, that "I am in my own way as desperate as your father." Moreover, she could not explain about the favors of chance. A job at Billings Hospital as a counselor became available, and though she was without credentials, Gerda was able to convince the hospital, through sheer persistence, that she could advise the families of polio cases. The pit of worries; at forty-six she knew enough to find the right words for these families. But her time was not her own; frequently she would be at the hospital until midnight.

All Alexander knew was that, after Gerda had taken him home, she was seldom seen in that place. Because of the great glass war, she had abandoned him even as she said it was all for his sake. And Samuel was not the sort of man to hold a job and forget about it when his day was finished. He began to linger at the housing project after hours, passing the time with his former neighbors.

Now that they were all safe, and seeing so little of his parents, Alexander spent late afternoons and early evenings at school. Clarence was his only link to Washington Homes. School was silly as always, but it was a neutral place where he could work, alone in a practice room, strengthening his hands. The palm of his right hand began to spread out, the muscles running from the palm under each knuckle grew supple, and thick calluses began to form on the side of each fingertip. The teachers at the Laboratory School said to each other that because of his parents' troubles he was becoming withdrawn. Abraham Zilker also watched this garden of family wither and he stepped in, though not to interfere, not to arrange. He was old and often ate alone. Now, again, he could taste the pleasure of family meals, with the boy who was also often alone.

On those nights the chauffeur called for the grandson when the school doors closed and janitors began cleaning. The boy riding in front, the cello perched like a passenger in the back, servant and scion picked up grandfather at his office. Grandfather walked slowly down the steps of the office building with the aid of a cane; he never let the chauffeur touch him until he stepped onto the pavement. Then the chauffeur held the door open for the old man, Alexander moved to the back seat, and they rode south along Lakeshore Drive, the cello nestled between them.

Sometimes when they arrived at Grandfather's house, Alexander practiced on his old piano, so much better than the school's grand piano with its loose action. Or he did schoolwork while Abraham read the paper. Then the two of them sat down to eat. The maid brought in the good kind of food from the old country, and Alexander talked excitedly about school, the old man often falling into a dream-trance at the boy's prattle, rousing himself occasionally to speak about times and places very far away. When Alexander spoke more seriously about music, Abraham tried to understand, but it was beyond him. The generation between them was seldom mentioned. The dishes were cleared, the old man kissed his grandson on both cheeks, and the chauffeur drove the boy and cello back to the other place called home.

As this became the rhythm of his early adolescent years, Alexander played the piano less and less at Grandfather's house. The piano, too, seemed to belong to times and places very far away. He could make music no one could ever take away; he could carry the cello with him no matter where his parents moved. And if he were tired or lonely, Grandfather's chauffeur would always come to carry it for him. Then he stopped playing the piano at school, although he would occasionally perform in a school recital. He was ceasing to be a child, he became absorbed in the cello; it was his responsibility.

Chapter 4

TENSION

*T*he finger of the left hand should press the string down just hard enough for the string to touch the fingerboard. All the other fingers should float, the thumb brushing the wood underneath lightly. The left arm can then begin gently to pulsate forward and back; the motion starts at the elbow, passes through the wrist, which does not break under the rocking but transmits the pulse solidly into the hand and down to the finger. The elbow thus makes the finger roll on the string. When the other arm draws the bow across a string held this way, the rocking finger creates a little rainbow of tones around the center note: the sound seems to undulate in waves. This caress is a cellist's vibrato.

The peculiar thing about vibrato is how it tests the cellist's inner ease or anxiety. Nerves can be masked somewhat in the bow arm by squeezing the bow hard with the thumb; the energy is then buried. Anxiety cannot be covered over when the cellist tries to vibrate a note. The nervous player shakes his arm too fast and too hard, hoping to discharge his energy, but this hard and fast motion fails to get rid of the tension. A strand of muscles in the forearm, linked to the fan of the muscles in the palm, always tightens up. The thumb then grips the underside of the fingerboard like a vise. The sound no longer undulates and the rainbow of near tones evaporates. The cellist thus tells his audience through the locked vibrato that he is afraid.

Unfortunately, vibrato reports on fear anywhere in the body. For almost every musician, raised shoulders are a common and deadly form of tension. When a cellist hunches up his shoulders, both arms move on an unnatural pivot. The bow arm will strike the strings at a slant; after a while the cellist will feel cramped in his bow arm, and there is no remedy but to rest or to force the shoulder down. But hunched shoulders immediately make themselves known through the vibrato, since the elbow is displaced from hanging naturally and so rocking easily. The vibrato immediately reports on other tensions which do not show themselves so boldly but hide in the body; stomach tension, tense back, the feet twisted around a chair like prisoners grabbing at the bars.

A cellist can acquire vibrato in one of two ways. In twenty minutes, by instinct, or in two to three years, by a hard struggle which teaches the body to relax. To call someone a "natural" cellist means, physically, that the vibrato makes intuitive sense and that the cellist's body shows itself clear immediately when he wants to caress the sound. Immediate access to vibrato is a clue that the natural cellist, like other natural musicians, will find playing before two thousand people relaxing, before three thousand even more enjoyable. For most musicians, however, the crowd of two or three thousand people is a threat. They must learn to assume the poise the natural musician possesses as if by right; they must learn to forget the audience in order to play to it. This discipline of forgetting others, forgetting one-self, just making music, begins in the mastery of the left arm. Most cellists have to work hard, learning to vibrate anywhere in front of anyone.

While he was studying with the teacher at the Laboratory School, Alexander went through the motions of making vibrato but he could not produce a good sound. He thought at first, it's just an adornment, nothing serious. Then his pride was touched; this was his first check in playing the cello since he had dis-covered for himself how to tilt the hand. Now no experiment seemed to work. The bearded instructor was also baffled. With the other children, sound quality was just one element of dis-order amidst their sour intonation and their inability to play all the notes. But because Alexander was so much better than the others, the flaw stood out; the time for the promised change of teachers had evidently come. The bearded instructor had an idea. He would call Claude Simon, the best cellist in the city, and get someone's name. Claude Simon said, "What's the matter with me?" If the teacher had begun, "I know how busy you are, Mr. Simon, and I'm only calling to ask for the name of someone for my best student . . . ," Mr. Simon would have given the name. But the schoolteacher was in a hurry the day he called and asked bluntly, "Who is the best cellist for my best pupil?" Mr. Simon countered with, "What's the matter with me?" and an audition was arranged.

At the audition, Alexander played the first three movements of the Bach suite in G. After he finished the first movement, Mr. Simon said simply, "Go on." Alexander played the second, then the third piece.

"Sweet Jesus, what have they been teaching you? Your left hand is a mess. Your tone is awful. In tune, O.K., but pinched, pinched, pinched."

Alexander began to loosen up his bow the moment Mr. Simon began barking. The boy reached for his cello case.

"Here, what are you doing, why are you putting the cello away?"

"I thought . . . you don't want to teach me."

"Look, sonny, did you hear me say anything like that? I said your left hand is terrible. Your vibrato stinks."

Alexander was confused. Mr. Simon was evidently taking him on as a student, but not paying attention to his feelings.

Mr. Simon produced a tennis ball.

"The first thing you do is buy one of these. They come in cans of three; get the hairy kind. Now, squeeze the ball hard. Harder. Your knuckles aren't white yet, harder! Good, now drop the ball, put your hand on the fingerboard with the fingers curved the way they were around the ball. Quickly, hurry up before the strength comes back. Play any note, quick, that's it. Now you see, you squeezed all the tension out of your hand, your thumb didn't lock on the neck of the cello."

Claude Simon circled around and around Alexander's chair, unrelenting.

"Squeeze the ball again, drop it, hand on the string, vibrate. No! No! Don't hunch your shoulders, you should be too tired, sink into it. Here," Mr. Simon grabbed Alexander's cello, "listen to me." He played five measures of the opening movement of the Bach. "Why do I sound so beautiful? Because my shoulder is down, I'm totally relaxed. Try again."

Alexander picked up his cello, concentrating on feeling tired.

"Better. A little."

Alexander tried the measures once more, just to be sure.

"What happened? That sounded like before. I told you, loosen up on that tennis ball first, then play. I'm hard on you, no?"

The possibility did not seem to perturb Mr. Simon.

Claude Simon was famous and fat. He was famous enough

not to need to live in New York, where the merely good had to struggle. He was beyond all that, and his wife worked in Chicago as a dentist, and the airport was the best in the world. Incidentally he was the most famous musician in Chicago, not counting the conductor of the orchestra and its first cellist, with neither of whom he was on speaking terms. He wore fat man's clothes, mostly emphatic suits made for him in Italy by a tailor who charged him double the prices extracted from his Italian clients; he lived in an apartment with fat man's furniture: overstuffed chairs, lace doilies on every inch of bare wood, and a gleaming steel and tile kitchen. The studio was in the child's bedroom because there were no children, there was always Coca-Cola laid out on a little side table if the students were under sixteen, beer if they were of drinking age, but more often Coca-Cola than beer because Mr. Simon liked to take his students on young so he could fully control their development. He had two ironclad rules: he never kept anyone more than four years, "because after four years with me either they can do it for themselves or they can't"; and he never did any of his ex-pupils any favors, "because I don't like competition." Most people who knew him well saw through him; like an optimistic bear living in a paradise of berries and trout, he believed that the fortunate always make their way, and any pupil of his was by definition fortunate.

"Now about your vibrato. Certainly the raised shoulders are one reason it is so tight. But I notice that whenever a phrase reaches a climax in a sustained note, your vibrato hardens because you are overexcited. In that low D in the first movement, for instance, you underline how important it is the way old ladies used to underline important words when they wrote letters. Just take it easy, okay? Don't feel so much."

This cunning little speech Mr. Simon produced for almost all his new pupils. The discovery that they can feel usually means to adolescents that nobody has ever felt anything before. "My God, how much I'm feeling." There were two standard reactions to the command, "Don't get excited." The natural musicians quickly perceived that the music was better the less self-conscious they were. "Amazing that Bach doesn't need you to do his work for him," Mr. Simon would say, reaching for the student's Coca-Cola or beer. The other musicians were often affronted. "He doesn't understand me, no one does." With these Mr. Simon kept chipping away cheerfully until they relaxed.

It was a lengthy investigation. Claude Simon wanted to find out what happened to the body of a young man who, when he let go, produced such long unified lines. Alexander wanted to find out why he was a tense person. They started with the cello sonata by Samuel Barber. The piece was too sentimental for Mr. Simon's taste, but its melodies required a wide variety of vibratos, from slow, undulating waves to slight colorings of the pure tone. Alexander quickly learned the notes.

"So that's out of the way," Mr. Simon remarked nonchalantly at their next lesson.

Undulating seemed to be the boy's problem. The slow movement of the Barber requires absolutely steady pressure on the bow to make an exposed melody cohere; the piano part is spare. A climax builds up from the first long strokes at which the penultimate tones must ring out, confident and composed. As Alexander approached the climax his shoulders began to rise. Mr. Simon could see the vibrato becoming faster, the bow begin to slant off the string.

"What are you doing? You look like Jesus Christ rising from the tomb."

Alexander looked blankly at this teacher, today wearing a three-piece, black-and-white-checked suit.

"I'm sorry."

"Sonny, I'm going to stand behind you. You play the opening again, and I'm going to hold down your shoulders, O.K.? Play it over and over again until you don't feel my hands pressing down."

Usually, this was an efficient technique. The shoulders of the pupil, pushing up as the intensity of a piece of music mounts, are surprised at encountering the resistance of a foreign body. Sometimes a pupil would suddenly pull away as if Mr. Simon had pinched him, sometimes indeed Mr. Simon would pinch him. After two or three rounds of pushing down and pinching, the shoulders would begin to receive the message of the foreign fingers and stay in place. Alexander felt his shoulders hunch up uncontrollably the first time against Mr. Simon's greasy hands. The usual magic didn't take. The third time his shoulders stayed down, but the music stayed down too, limp.

"Louder!"

The shoulders went up again.

They spent nearly half an hour working this way. Mr. Simon sweated through the underarms of his suit. At last, there was one short moment in which the boy's tone rang out beyond his body. "I knew it was in there," Mr. Simon exclaimed. This oblique comment filled Alexander with a wave of pride.

Alexander also knew for the first time that "it" was in there. Most child musicians think tension happens to them, arriving like an unwelcome visitor. At twelve Alexander had not imagined that he issued an invitation; all he thought, looking at his hands after the great glass war, was that they could have been hurt. Now the hard work of body knowledge was beginning; hunched over the cello, tense, shutting the world out, he made a gesture of protection and this gesture hurt the music. At fourteen, a boy still needs his body to be explained by the outside, the outside against which he is also protecting himself. For instance, Alexander often dreamed he was sitting with Clarence at the edge of a lake. They were tired of swimming. The sun went behind a cloud for a moment, Alexander looked up, and his father was standing over them. Samuel said to both of them, "Come"; they rose and followed him through the woods. They left their towels and luncheon basket by the lake and they walked nowhere, through trees, clearings, more trees, the light filtering through the leaves, and the woods were beautiful. They walked forward, but the boys became cold in their bathing shorts. Alexander began to shiver uncontrollably. It was so simple, the dream went on even when Alexander was awake: Mr. Simon was watching Alexander shiver when he played vibrato. Someone older might have said, "There it is, I get frightened sometimes." Alexander wanted Mr. Simon to know without being told.

The boys and girls at the Laboratory School were just now making their first forays into each other's bodies. Alexander's face had taken its adult form, thin, high forehead, bushy eyebrows; his beard began to grow, as did his acne. Abraham Zilker was buying him old man's clothes, or rather, an old man's version of young clothes—pants which were cut full and which needed to be pressed every night, cotton shirts which also needed regular attention. On the nights Alexander spent with his mother, these attentions were not forthcoming; Gerda was too tired. So her son was sometimes rumpled and baggy at school, then on days after his grandfather's maid worked on his clothes, neat and baggy. The girls preferred boys in jeans and workshirts.

Frequently at his lessons Alexander looked haggard. Despite his fat man's manner, there was a spirit in Claude Simon that did the listening, conceived the tennis ball and shoulder exercises, and was no fool. But Mr. Simon was interested in producing a musician. The best way for the kid to get a hold on himself was to do some work.

They left the Barber and learned repertoire. There are two schools of thought about how to do it. One says, start with the earliest cello music and go up to the present; go through the literature fairly fast, so that the student knows what the history of the cello contains. Later in his life he can go back and concentrate on perfecting particular pieces. The other school believes the student should work from the simpler to the more complex pieces, without regard for chronology, but with great care about technique and musical expression. Mr. Simon decided to take the historical, rather sloppy approach with Alexander. It was more likely to build the boy's confidence.

It was a fortunate method in that the demands of most eighteenth-century cello literature—with the exception of Bach —did not seem to rub open the wound of Alexander's vulnerability. He played the slow movements of Baroque sonatas tight, but it didn't sound too bad. During Alexander's first two years, Mr. Simon made rather a specialty of Baroque pieces, especially the sonatas of Bréval and Francoeur, and found hearing the boy's mistakes and limits helpful in showing him by contrast what he might do. He said as much to Alexander.

"Neat and tight-assed in that sarabande—that's what you like? Well, I don't. I'm going to open it up next month. You know I'm playing the Bréval E major in San Francisco? I wish you could be there." Somehow these comments comforted Alexander. They were partners, even if he showed Mr. Simon what to avoid. He also learned how to pay Mr. Simon compliments on his clothes—"That's a beautiful leather jacket" about a leather sport coat made of squares of different-colored leather like a patchwork quilt—compliments which Mr. Simon would take seriously, reinforcing his belief in his own good taste and faith in his Italian tailor, compliments which gave Alexander pleasure because he didn't believe a word of what he said.

The lessons occurred anywhere and any time, arranged for Mr. Simon's convenience. Once Alexander went out to the airport to work for two hours with Mr. Simon in a VIP lounge, canned airport music gently filling the room. Once they had an exhausting three-hour session just before Mr. Simon was to play a solo recital in Chicago. They finished a half-hour before the concert, Mr. Simon struggled into his Italian tuxedo and sauntered out onstage as though he had just woken from a nap. Abraham Zilker's chauffeur would sometimes drive the boy to these odd rendezvous, and although the black limousine gave

Mr. Simon endless opportunity to chide Alexander for being a poor little rich boy, the truth is that Mr. Simon would occasionally boast to others that "I leave the hall in my limousine and my pupil leaves in his limousine."

Their progress stopped at early Beethoven. This was "basic stuff" and Mr. Simon wasn't going to let Alexander coast through it. "You've got to play loose." In the second Beethoven sonata, the fear of exposed emotion appeared in the introduction, technically one of the simplest pieces in the whole literature, musically one of the hardest. The back and forth between cello and piano is subtle; the instruments don't imitate each other but rather make small changes in playing the same line to each other, which gives the piece texture. The cellist has to surrender, to listen to his partner, as he does in no previous music except Bach. Mr. Simon played the piano, a little spinet crammed into the childless child's room, and made it sound like a Napoleonic pianoforte. Alexander sounded like his old self. "No give, no give! I wouldn't pay a dime to hear you play this."

"I wish, dear, you could show your feelings more." Gerda had started saying this to him even before they left Washington Homes. The teachers had only given her confirmation when they reported that he was becoming withdrawn. But it was no more possible to instruct someone to open up than to order him to relax. However, Mr. Simon had an idea.

"Kid, today you're going to play the introduction five, maybe ten times over, without me. I'll just sit here. I want to look at the stock market prices in the paper anyway. You just go ahead and play it until you're sure of it. Then we'll work on it."

Mr. Simon settled himself into an armchair, reached for Alexander's Coca-Cola, and started to read the paper. Alexander interrupted him.

"You mean I should just play as though you aren't here?"

Alexander, at first hunched and tight, began shutting Mr. Simon out. But the older man seemed genuinely absorbed in his paper, the light glinted off his greasy forehead, and so Alexander did gradually forget about him. In fact Mr. Simon was listening intently, while rather enjoying his own pantomime with the stock pages (in any event, he had already called his broker that morning and made a modest killing). The first few times Alexander was thrilled privately as always; by the fifth repetition he was beginning to get bored. He stopped.

"No, keep going," Mr. Simon commanded. "How can I concentrate on the stock prices unless I hear noise in the background?"

By the eighth repetition Alexander thought he would go crazy. Nothing was left of his first surge of emotion, the lines for the missing piano part were the only thing in his mind which seemed fresh, but Mr. Simon's gold pencil, underlining now this stock, now that one, commanded him to play it all again and again.

After the eleventh repetition, his teacher looked up.

"Well, you may make me a rich man. Now let's get to work. Play it with me."

"But Mr. Simon, I've played it until I'm sick to death of it."

"Too bad."

Alexander started the piece once more, in a rage. He played with his shoulders down, his vibrato was slow, and his wrist in the bowing picked up the inflections of phrasing Mr. Simon made on the piano.

"Bravo!"

"You really think you're something, don't you?" Alexander lashed out. But Mr. Simon was so used to displays of temper at lessons, rehearsals, and performances that he never bothered about them.

"Now let's just take a look at that finger exchange at 'B' . . ."

It became something of a game with them. Mr. Simon would greet Alexander at the door with, "I wonder how A T & T is doing today," or, "Who knows, this morning I might become as rich as you," and the lesson might in fact begin with a little reading while the boy warmed up. Alexander was supposed to choose the passages where he thought he would most likely become tense and repeat them until they felt dead. Then the two of them would begin working together on the dead passages. If other points in the Beethoven sonatas produced unexpected tension, Mr. Simon would make as if to reach for the paper, and if Alexander couldn't stop himself, Mr. Simon would actually begin to read.

To his cronies, Claude Simon said, "The craziest experience teaching I've ever had in my life." He said it with pride; he liked the way the boy was beginning to sound. To Alexander he said, "You ought to be in a mental home." Alexander was getting stronger; coming from Mr. Simon, it was just noise.

By the time they arrived at the Beethoven, Alexander had taken sides in his parents' separation, which occurred just after his sixteenth birthday; Gerda Hoffmann was now cast as the villain responsible for his tension. The separation aged Abraham Zilker ten years. There was no reason to have kept the business running at all—except for Alexander, who was going to become a great artist, not a dealer in scrap. Neither Alexander nor Abraham was getting honest answers from Samuel. He had delayed telling a very simple truth: he was having an affair with a married woman at Washington Homes. The hours of passion snatched between tenant meetings, the lies to the respective betrayed partners over three months, the day he had to hide in his lover's broom closet for an hour when her husband came home unexpectedly from the factory with a headache, all had taken their toll. Samuel was feeling lesser emotions than despair: physical lust, for the first time; and shame, for the first time. In middle age these ordinary desires and fears seized him unprepared. He told Gerda only when he and his lover finally decided to live together.

The flame of being there for Samuel had long since gone

out—long before the great glass war, she realized. People said Gerda was becoming hard; she used a lot of make-up these days, and smoked nonstop. Her voice, once so girlish, coarsened in her throat because of the cigarettes. But what did "hard" mean? She was giving comfort to people every day, people in great need, and she did it well because she acted professionally. Some of the pleasures of her youth now appeared to her as genuine; it was absurd, all those years of pretending to loathe comfortable restaurants or bourgeois vacations and clothes. She no longer wanted to possess either Samuel or his world.

Who will tell Alexander? Samuel asked. We both will; it will be easier for him. This meant Gerda did most of the talking, Samuel sitting in a chair in the living room nodding agreement while Gerda broke the news that they thought it would be best if they lived apart. She did not say they were doing it for Alexander and she omitted mentioning her husband's new mistress. Samuel was not entirely passive, he never was—he took Alexander aside afterwards and confided to him that there was "someone else." But it was difficult at first for Alexander to take this in, and in any case Samuel diverted the discussion to Alexander's own future. That was what the boy possessed. Gerda also spoke of his future.

The evening his parents told him about their separation, Alexander sat in a chair thumbing through the family scrapbook. There were pictures of Abraham Zilker's first car, the house on the South Shore, news clippings of an electrical workers' strike, photos of the baby Alexander in his bath, the toddler chasing pigeons, the child at his first piano lesson—Joyce looked younger than he remembered—a picture of the school orchestra with Alexander frowning at the conductor. His eyes fell on another news photograph of Samuel seated at a table in front of a microphone, the family lawyer looking uncomfortable at his side. Underneath the photo was the caption "A commie's challenge: 'People were starving then. I was proud to be a Communist. Where were you, Senator?' " Samuel had denied nothing about himself and told nothing about others. Gerda Hoffmann watched her son studying this relic of the past and said to him, "You know, my dear, I was also part of that struggle." Alexander closed the scrapbook on fifty thousand stuffed envelopes and twenty thousand cups of coffee.

The cruelty of adolescence is that fixing blame, naming the villains and heroes of domestic life (or inventing them), is so immensely liberating. Suddenly there is reason for the suffering within, a mechanics of pain. Gerda understood Alexander's turning against her—somewhat. The record in the scrapbook also was no lie. Perhaps Alexander didn't want her evidence, it would have made things just too confusing for him. At least she could be consistent now. She would make rules which could be logically explained, about how late Alexander could stay out, when he could use the car, or what he could spend. She would avoid the humiliation of trying to caress his hair at night, when she came home from the hospital, and feeling him turn rigid. But she had no idea this rejection would be useful to him musically.

In adolescence, unlike childhood, the sufferer once having identified the enemy can strike back: I don't belong to you any more. You can't get at me by saying "I wish you were more affectionate." It had been three years of hard struggle, but Claude Simon was well pleased with himself; he'd made a success of this one. When Alexander told Claude Simon that his parents were divorcing, Mr. Simon thought they were in for a bout of hand cramps, but the Beethoven got better and better. True, the boy sometimes bit into the strings so deeply that the sound grated harshly, but what did this matter? His shoulders were down, the vibrating hand was released, the boy was fueling his energy into the music.

Or, almost. Just as throughout our lives our dreams migrate from scene to scene, so the ghosts in the body migrate from place to place, looking for a home in which the old terrors can settle in and flourish. The last place they tried to make a home in Alexander was his stomach.

"Sonny, I played for the governor last night. I threw a scene, there were waiters moving around in the back of the room rattling glasses. Do you know what I did? I stopped in the middle of a piece; never before in my life. The governor made them jump, let me tell you. Now let's hear the Chopin."

Alexander played the first movement.

"You look good but sound bad. Why aren't you biting into the string with the bow? You sound like some lisping fairy."

"Where?"

"The whole movement. If you have to play it ten times, I'll miss my lunch. Do the sixteenth-note runs for me."

Alexander tried to play them with a heavier weight on the bow, but this made him slow down.

"You know, Mr. Simon, it may be the beer. I have a stomachache."

"Too young to drink. Let it go."

The next lesson, Alexander avoided the beer, but still his groin tensed.

"Let me feel your stomach. Not much there for the ladies to grab on to. Your mother a bad cook?" Alexander winced.

Mr. Simon went back to working on Alexander physically. "What I'd like to do is punch you in the stomach, but you might sue me, and you haven't earned me enough money on the stock market yet to pay. Start playing. I'm just going to jab a finger in your ribs, but I won't tell you when."

"But that will only make me more tense."

"Probably."

For the next three lessons, Mr. Simon stood behind Alexander, talking over the boy's shoulder, listening to him play, and occasionally poking him hard in the ribs. He defeated the ghost's expectation by not poking only when the music was feverish and the boy worked up. Sometimes he poked when

Alexander was merely accompanying the piano and could relax. The effect of these random assaults on the stomach was excellent: Alexander stopped squeezing. The reason that jabbing someone has such a healthy effect is simple: the musician should feel that even an inert part of the body like the stomach is implicated in his playing; the parts are independent, but the entire body plays. The random jabbing made Alexander constantly aware that his trunk was connected to the rest of him.

Neither teacher nor student anticipated one benefit produced by this exercise. Cellists often have a hard time breathing, holding the breath in, then suddenly sniffing for air through the nose. It may be that the light pressure of the cello resting on the chest creates difficulty in drawing breath, or it may be that the position of the arms speaks in some obscure way to the lungs. This common mystery afflicted not only Alexander but to some extent Mr. Simon. Alexander discovered that the jabs in the stomach loosened up his breathing.

One day, when his whole body at last seemed unlocked, Mr. Simon ventured to say, "Kid, why don't you help me a little with this?" Teacher and student looked at each other, disconcerted. "Well, maybe not." Mr. Simon had slipped for a moment. "They always erase the breathing on recordings, and no one's complained yet at a concert. Let's get to work. The last movement of the Debussy sounds dreadful." Neither of them quite believed it. After four years of browbeating, insults, and frustration, their work was done.

Alexander had ten months to go before leaving for a conservatory. Abraham Zilker marked them off on his office calendar, Alexander in his mind. Nothing more could happen here; his parents could not get farther apart, he could not get closer to his music, despite the occasional set-back. Abraham once said to him, "You have filled the last years with such joy"; another time, "You've grown up so fast." The energy his intense grandson had acquired in the last few months was, however, a victory of youth, a triumph of muscles.

Claude Simon had been mesmerized by this victory; they had spent so long preparing. Of course he had given a great deal of purely musical advice—his own bowings, tips on ritards and dynamics—but the boy seemed one of those who would go his own way; for instance, Alexander had the annoying habit of erasing the pencil markings Claude Simon made in his music. What Claude Simon believed he had really done was to set a musician free. The kid had one step to go; he'd played in student recitals, now, before he left Chicago, he needed to make a proper debut.

Chapter 5

CONNECTION

Alexander finished school two weeks early so that he could prepare for his recital debut on the day after graduation. He missed the last dance at the school, the tearful farewells at which everyone promises to write and to remember forever, the forty-five minutes of graduation speech from the principal. Alexander asked his friends to come backstage for their farewells.

Claude Simon, who never did any favors for his pupils, had been rather clever about arranging the event. A solo recital by a seventeen-year-old boy who had only appeared in public with school orchestras would be an affair of family and friends. Mr. Simon decided to make the evening a chamber-music program. He would play the Handel two-cello sonata with Alexander to begin; then Alexander would play the Bach unaccompanied suite in C. After an intermission, Mr. Simon would play the

Ravel sonata for violin and cello with a good violinist from the Chicago Symphony, then the evening would conclude with Alexander playing the Chopin sonata with the violinist's wife, a mousy but competent pianist. This way there were two big names on the program to draw the public, but once there, both public and reviewers would have to pay attention to the featured player, Alexander.

"I can't thank you enough," Alexander had stammered when they discussed the program many months before.

"Well, it will get you out of my hair for good," Mr. Simon shot back. He was a bottomless well for praise of his playing, but personal gratitude made him nervous.

After four years, Alexander knew him. The young man was determined to go on, although the speech he had in his mind made him nervous too. "But I want you to know that you've helped me so much. More than music, and it's meant so much to me. . . ."

"You are a good boy, Alexander—crazy, but a good boy. Enough; let's talk about the program some more. You understand how it works? You can only look good in the first half; the Handel is easy to listen to, it makes people happy. The Bach is a nice contrast, more dramatic, but also comfortable. Then after the intermission, Jimmy and I are playing something special. If we bring off the Ravel right, we'll stun them; if we don't click, people will be bored. Either way, you have to make a big impression with the Chopin. Jimmy's wife will be background noise, but I couldn't get him to do this without giving her something."

"How much will we get for it?"

"You mean you want to be paid?" Rich people never let an opportunity slip, but this was outrageous—the boy should be paying, if anything.

"No, no, I mean you and the others."

"Oh, that. Don't worry, there will be enough from the tickets. But the money is going to me and Jimmy; our managers only agreed to it on that condition. You won't see a penny, nothing for your chauffeur."

"You misunderstood, I only wondered . . ."

"You wonder too much. Let's work on the Chopin." What Mr. Simon did not tell Alexander was that the concert also got him out of a bad spot. Mr. Simon's wife was a trustee of a dental clinic for the poor. For months she had been after him to give a benefit concert; he had resisted because, he said, at benefits people usually don't listen to the music. He swaggered but she was tough. He needed an excuse for himself whenever he gave in to her; this time it was Alexander.

"You can play one encore. How about the Fauré 'Après un rêve'? But that's it. I don't want you stealing the show."

A month before the concert, patriarch descended upon teacher. Abraham Zilker's limousine pulled to a stop in front of Symphony Hall, where Alexander and Mr. Simon were going to practice in one of the studios. As Abraham made his slow, majestic progress from limousine to artist's entrance, people on the street paused. Here surely was a great artist; his young assistant held his cello. On the spur of the moment, a woman came up to ask for Abraham's autograph; he waved her aside without disabusing her. At the door of the studio Alexander presented Abraham to Claude Simon.

"I am delighted to meet you. So you are the grandfather of this person who has given me nothing but trouble for four years."

"I happened to be in the car when Alexander was on the way to his lesson." "Happened" was good; for two weeks Abraham had been planning this visit. "I would like to know about the concert."

"Sure, come in, of course. Now, we are going to play four pieces, one together, one Alexander all by himself, one me and a violinist, the last Alexander and a pianist."

"You mean there will be a time when Alexander is not present before the public?"

Mr. Simon's reply suggested that if four years before, Alexander had told him about his dream of shivering, Mr. Simon would have understood.

"It's only to give the boy a chance to rest, Mr. Zilker. We have to consider his strength."

Abraham nodded. This was logical.

"And the other musicians? I know, of course, of your worldwide fame."

"They are famous as well. It's so important an event that we are staging it as a benefit, for only the best society."

The old man smiled. It was just what he imagined as proper.

"Now, my dear Mr. Simon, I will not take up your time further except to enquire of one detail. Even for so illustrious an evening as this, there may possibly be a few tickets unsold?"

Mr. Simon could barely hold back a smile as he thought of the frantic efforts of his wife and her committee to flog twenty-dollar tickets to Chicago dentists, their spouses, and dental philanthropists for an evening of cello music.

"As a matter of fact, because it is society women arranging that end of things, and because they aren't too skilled in the concert business, there are still a fair number of tickets to be sold."

"Good. I will take care of it."

"Excuse me?"

"I will buy the rest. Here is my card; please ask one of the ladies to call my office this afternoon."

Thus it came about that Alexander's debut was to a full house of a thousand people. Approximately half the crowd were dentists, dental spouses, and dental philanthropists; the other half were all the dealers in scrap metal in Chicago, the passably respectable among scrap suppliers, many minor manufacturers, and twenty of Alexander's schoolmates. Alexander had been given his tickets to distribute the day before. Abraham Zilker sat alone in the front row of the best box; behind him in the box sat his maid and his chauffeur. Alexander's parents sat together, uncomfortably, in choice orchestra seats.

Alexander Hoffmann and Claude Simon were seated on the stage with their chairs turned slightly toward each other. They were in front of the pianist, whose part in the Handel double sonata was a figured-bass background, and so the lid of the piano was down. The stage lights at the Lyric Theatre were hot, much hotter than those of the school auditorium and more sharply focused. The musicians played in a pool of bright white.

The two cellists had walked onstage to tepid applause, seated themselves, and opened their music on the music stands. Then Claude Simon surprised Alexander; from the moment they began to play, he never took his eyes off Alexander's face. Alexander, who of course also had the music memorized, found that he was returning Mr. Simon's hypnotic stare. So that the public saw a huge, middle-aged man locked in profile with a thin young man, their dark red cellos gleaming in front of them, then the face of the pianist, naturally in profile but fainter in the background, the ebony piano melting into the blackness.

At first Alexander was disconcerted by Claude Simon's stare: did his teacher think he was doing something wrong? But Alexander had played the opening measures of the grave perfectly. Then Alexander understood. Claude Simon was listening to him by looking at him. Mr. Simon's concentration was absolute; he heard every inflection Alexander made, and responded —now imitating, now contrasting. Alexander found that by staring back, he played back. There was no one else there.

The grave is a lyrical duet. The following allegro is in an older contrapuntal style; it is thought by some to have been written several years earlier than the rest of the sonata. Alexander was annoyed by Mr. Simon's unwavering stare during this movement; he wanted to play his own part more independently, as the style seemed to demand. But Claude Simon wouldn't let him go. In the slow third movement, Mr. Simon had a big solo beginning, and for the first time he turned away. He stared out over the audience with his eyes as he had held Alexander. When the other cello entered, the fat, greasy head glistening beneath the lights swiveled again, and Mr. Simon watched Alexander take up the theme. Then at the end of the final allegro, he broke into a broad smile as he and Alexander completed a bravura passage of double stops added by an enthusiastic editor to juice up the sonata's conclusion. Alexander suddenly smiled back.

The roar of "Bravo!" from the grandfatherly box—grandfather, chauffeur, and maid in unison—was deserved. The audience was surprised into listening by what they were seeing. The dental benefit made into a financial success by the scrap-metal circles of Chicago had become a real concert; that is, the audience wanted to hear more. The performers walked offstage in a warm bath of applause, they reappeared. They could have come out a third time, except that Claude Simon knew what he was doing and didn't want the enthusiasm to wear itself out. A local music critic, dragooned by him from the pleasant prospect of putting his feet up for an evening into yet one more debut, began scribbling notes.

In the wings Claude Simon said to Alexander, "Not bad, not bad."

"I didn't expect you to keep looking at me like that."

"Like what?"

"Staring at me."

"No, no, you looked fine. Now, sonny, you've got to be a little smart with your timing. Give them a few moments to chatter, at these damn benefits all they want to do is flash their clothes at their friends, and just when they are wondering 'Where's the musician?' you'll walk out and play right away. Tune up now, before you go on. Just a minute more, Mrs. Smith and Mrs. Jones are still blabbing. Okay, now!" Claude Simon gave Alexander a little push, and suddenly the boy was alone onstage in front of a thousand people.

It started wonderfully. The third Bach suite opens with a descending C major scale, and Alexander played it as a trumpet fanfare. In the middle of the prelude, there is a different metal color, a pedal-point passage which should sound like the ringing of bells, and it did. What kept Alexander's confidence up was the silence in the audience—no coughing, no rustling programs; he had them. He had them in the allemande, in the courante. And then, in the sarabande, when there is peace after the fireworks of the first three movements, his stomach had him. He could feel it tightening as he played the D major seventh double stop in measure six, the richest chord you can make on the cello; he got to the top of it and he tightened. To chase away the ghost he decided to repeat the opening, something perfectly correct though he hadn't planned to. Again at the rich chord he tightened.

Now it became a nightmare. He went on with the sarabande, there were no mistakes, but the stomach muscles were grabbing him every time he played a double stop. He looked out into the audience; he knew his grandfather was in a box somewhere—he wanted to lock his eyes on Grandfather and get back into control—but it was dark, no grandfather, and he was afraid he would see instead his father and mother sitting together; maybe his father's woman was also somewhere in the hall, but he didn't know what she looked like. He couldn't see anyone, even though his neck, curved upward like a swan hissing, set his head forward so that his eyes could scan the darkness. He finished the sarabande, and decided to tune the cello; it would break the tension. Programs began to rattle.

In the two bourrées, to his surprise, he did regain control. He had always thought of these pieces as the music he would like to dance to at a ball. They were among the first Bach works he had ever learned, and the friendliness long memory inspires released him. He thought there was nothing to worry about now in the final gigue, he would just keep going, and he did, playing gracefully until he came to the G which closes the middle of the piece. It is a big note, and has to vibrate out. Alexander's stomach muscles grabbed him again, and his vibrato locked. He felt that he was locked on the note forever, that he would never be able to remove his hand from the ghost's vise, but somehow he got going again after what sounded to the audience like a ritard, went on through the piece, playing hard, almost with anger now rather than pleasure, reached the end, another big chord, and strangled the neck of the cello with his hand again.

There was a moment of silence, then a wave of applause. They hadn't noticed anything! Alexander stumbled to his feet, the applause swelled, he leaned over slightly to bow, and a wave of nausea swept over him; all at once his forehead was coated with sweat. He straightened up, smiled wanly, walked quickly off the stage. The moment he was safely into the wing, he vomited over the front of his cello. Red-yellow fluid dripped over the fingerboard onto the front plate, a piece of something undigested—but he had only eaten a bun before the concert—dropped through the F holes into the cello's own belly. The stagehands, the violinist, and Claude Simon stood absolutely still as the vomit fumes spread through the wings.

The audience went on clapping even more loudly. The dramatic shift in the last movement had jolted and aroused them, the music critic scribbled more notes on his pad—and besides, the musician needed to come out once more before they could have their intermission.

Claude Simon took matters into his own hands. He walked out onstage, and gestured to the audience to be quiet.

"Unaccustomed as I am to public speaking—" the stale joke came to him mechanically and produced the usual mechanical titter among his listeners—"I would like to say just a few words to you about the Chicago Dental Hygiene Foundation. This worthy organization provides free teeth care for those who can't afford it in our city; thanks to you, poor people are healthier." Mr. Simon was indeed unaccustomed to public speaking about healthy teeth. He paused, and then added, "On behalf of all musicians playing tonight, we would like to thank you, and are glad to lend our support to your good work."

There was a flutter of applause. In the lobby of the Lyric

Theatre, members of the benefit committee looked rather grim; Simon had given the impression he was donating his services, when only that nice boy was playing for free. Other members of the audience, particularly those in scrap who were there because of Abe's grandson, were disappointed that the young man wasn't allowed his due number of bows. Gerda stood next to her father; he beamed at each compliment, and pressed hard the hand or shoulder of the person who gave it. Gerda was also pleased, but her attention was divided. Tonight she would get a glimpse of the other woman. She had asked Samuel, rather brightly, "Is your friend here?" when they first sat down. He said nothing, which meant yes. So her eyes roamed the lobby, looking for her ex-husband. Samuel and his lover stood in a side hall. The woman was black, and the few patrons who remarked them assumed a donor was speaking to one of the needy beneficiaries of the Chicago Dental Hygiene Foundation; how nice that she had been given a ticket, how nice of him to pay attention to her, and how discreet he was about it.

Samuel's attention was divided too. His lover was the only black woman at the concert; she was trying to talk to him about this. "We must be careful." And yet the whole record of his earlier carefulness was proving irrelevant; his son was a success, fate had not been tempted, and there was nothing more Samuel could do. Rather than pure relief, however, Samuel was feeling another emotion that, coming so late to a middle-aged man, was confusing. He was jealous of Alexander. One thousand people had just taken notice of him; no one had ever paid that much attention to Samuel, except when he had testified, but then few people had applauded. His son didn't need him, he no longer had a wife, and his lover had a problem with the color of her skin which would always keep him at a distance. Of course he didn't want his son to fail, but, this new voice insinuated, it seemed unfair that the boy should be exempt. Father and mistress remained in the corridor throughout the intermission, she talking, he half-responding. Gerda never did get to see her.

Backstage there was chaos. Alexander was slumped on a sofa in the green room. The stagehands were cleaning up the mess on the floor, Claude Simon was attempting to clean up Alexander's cello. But it was no use. The vomit had soaked into the strings, washing off the rosin, so that a whole new set would have to be put on, and new strings never stay in tune. Some of the liquid vomit had also dripped inside the belly of the cello; the instrument smelled hideously.

Mr. Simon went into the green room and sat down on a chair next to Alexander. He took the young man's hand, and spoke softly.

"Your cello is ruined. Not forever—the inside can be cleaned, and the stains on the front revarnished—but you will not play that cello again tonight. You will play mine."

"I can't go out there again."

"How long have I known you?"

"What? Four years, I suppose."

"When you first came to me, that very first day, did you ever think you would come back?"

"Well, no, I didn't."

"Each time in the beginning, when you got tense, did you ever think you'd get over it?"

"No."

"Yet you did. You came back, you got over it, you are here. Now I have to play, Alexander. It's not quite as easy for me as you think; sometime, perhaps, I'll tell you why. But now I have to play. And when I finish, I'll come offstage, I will give you my cello, and you will go on. Now rest, or come hear me if you like. I'd like it, Alexander, I'd like you to hear me play."

Claude Simon pressed Alexander's hand, rose, and left the room. After a moment, Alexander rose too. He went up to the wings, where people asked him how he was doing, and he said quietly, "I'm doing all right." He was dreadfully tired from his purge.

Mr. Simon was entirely correct about the Ravel violin and cello sonata. It is very difficult. Two instruments are written to sound like an orchestra, but not an ordinary orchestra, more like a huge gypsy band. Yet there are moments, like the opening of the slow movement, where suddenly each instrument is totally exposed, having to sound almost withdrawn into itself, as though it is being played in a faraway house. Great technique does not solve the problem of this alternation between mass and isolation; the only way the players can make it work is by an absolute concentration on each other. The Ravel contains the same problem as the Handel double-cello sonata, but the problem is much more difficult.

Claude Simon and James Whitman, the violinist, looked onstage the way Mr. Simon and Alexander had appeared, two men facing each other rather than the public, although the music was so demanding that their eyes frequently broke contact to glance down at their music stands. The magic of connection didn't work. James Whitman as well as Claude Simon was shaken by the scene at intermission: violence perpetrated against an instrument. Over the years you develop so many little ways of petting it; rubbing off the rosin underneath the strings every morning, a special cloth you're convinced does a particularly good job of shining the back, little rituals about where to place the bow when you set it down—never on the edge of a table, for instance. Now faint acrid fumes hung in the air that the votaries of these rites were breathing. All the notes in the Ravel fell properly in place, all the markings were observed, but in their minds the musicians still played the scene of vomit dripping inside an instrument. As the Ravel droned on, coughing started up in the audience.

It is to the credit of the two men that when they walked offstage to sporadic applause, they didn't begin to blame Alexander. They were professionals; if they didn't produce, excuses didn't matter. Mr. Simon handed Alexander his cello.

"You've played on it before. Remember, my bridge is cut a little higher than yours; there may be a slight woof on the middle E. Use your own bow; it's unharmed and sounds fine with my cello. Mrs. Whitman, are you set? O.K., I suggest you both go on quickly."

They did. Alexander was met again by the surprising, warm applause. Mrs. Whitman sat down behind him; the cello chair was positioned full front.

Exhaustion made Alexander a gift. There was no point in struggling; there was nothing you could do. Four years of work, and the demon had contrived his most cunning revenge, a bomb planted in the motor. Alexander had his own moment of professionalism: the name of the demon didn't matter. He would at least try to get through the piece; he wouldn't humiliate Mr. Simon in public. Thus he began the Chopin from very far away, the opening theme evoking regret, the only emotion left to him in his exhaustion; the range from loud to soft shrank so that he made only small changes in shading his volume. The Chopin spoke who was dying while composing the sonata, rather than the Chopin of the salons. In the slow movement, Alexander's exhaustion made him slide across big leaps; slides are considered sloppily sentimental by modern cellists, but they are what people heard in the composer's time. Since the boy was too tired to emphasize, these slides between notes struck his audience as strange, affecting wails, rather than as sugary gestures. It was all over, he could barely hold the bow in the last movement, the last movement of music he thought he would ever play in public or private again. "He was dying all his life," Berlioz said of Chopin. Perhaps if Alexander had read this funeral notice he would have been comforted during these final moments of his debut. But then if he had known the words, perhaps he would have been blocked from breathing their spirit into the music.

Alexander stopped. A moment of silence, and then a storm

of applause. Mrs. Whitman came around from the piano and pressed his hand. Mr. Whitman and Mr. Simon were applauding; a tear had formed at the edge of his teacher's eye. But this storm did not revive Alexander; he could barely hear it. They had already won: whenever he would attempt to get outside, they would find some vicious way to call him back. "You belong to us." Alexander walked slowly off the stage, he was afraid to bow; what if he destroyed Mr. Simon's cello too? His one wish was to get the precious instrument out of his hands, make it safe. He walked into the wings and handed over the cello. "Go back out, get out there!" his teacher commanded. Tightly holding onto the hand of the elderly, comforting Mrs. Whitman, he walked out onstage. The applause began to warm him —just a little, just enough to risk a bow. Nothing happened. He straightened up and smiled. He heard shouts of "Encore! Encore!" But he wasn't going to attempt it. He wasn't going to offer them another chance to strike.

Abraham Zilker got backstage remarkably quickly for an old man. He started moving the moment Alexander stopped playing. His grandson came offstage, collapsed crying into his arms, and begged his grandfather, "Get me out of here, get me out of here."

The notice of the concert which appeared in the Chicago morning paper two days later ran as follows:

The Lyric Theatre was the scene, June 10, of a remarkable debut. The young cellist Alexander Hoffmann appeared with his teacher, Claude Simon, in a benefit program for the Chicago Dental Hygiene Foundation. At benefits, the music is usually incidental to social encounters among the audience, but young Mr. Hoffmann made us listen.

The program opened with the Handel double-cello sonata in G minor, a transcription of a work originally for two violins. Teacher and student played together as equals.

Claude Simon is famous for his big, warm sound; young Mr. Hoffmann cannot hope to match him in this department, but showed himself a sensitive partner.

The fireworks began when Mr. Hoffmann played the Bach suite in C for solo cello. From the opening notes the audience knew they were in the presence of a mature and distinctive artist. There were odd shadings, unusual pauses and ritards, but the work held together as a whole. The bourrée dance movements were airy, and the final gigue was a masterpiece of theatre, beginning in the spirit of a dance, ending with a passion, a fierceness even, which recalled the drama of the opening movement.

After intermission, I am sorry to say, the senior musicians did not match the artistic integrity of their junior colleague. Claude Simon and James Whitman, of the Chicago Symphony, played the Ravel sonata for cello and violin. It requires subtlety and mutual understanding to be convincing; the two musicians gave a merely workmanlike performance.

With young Mr. Hoffmann back on stage for the final piece, the Chopin cello sonata (partnered by Ruth Whitman, a familiar pianist to Chicago audiences), the evening revived. Again, Mr. Hoffmann gave us an unusual interpretation. This was not a flashy performance. Indeed, it was in some ways a scholarly one; the slides (portamenti) with which cellists of Chopin's time played were employed by Mr. Hoffmann to great effect. Great care went into this historical recreation. Mr. Hoffmann limited his dynamic range so that the music did not sound sloppy, as Chopin should never sound. Instead, we were privileged to hear a Chopin of pathos and dignity.

Alexander Hoffmann is a young man with a great future ahead of him, judging from this debut. He is a natural musician, wiser than his years.

This long review was given a prominent place on the arts page of the newspaper. There was a photograph of Alexander taking his final bow.

Alexander and Claude Simon had arranged to have lunch the day after the review appeared, but at the last minute Mr. Simon canceled; something had come up, he had to go out of town. He would look Alexander up in New York.

Alexander was to leave shortly after his debut. He had been accepted as an advanced student at a conservatory in New York, and Abraham Zilker had settled a surprisingly modest amount of money on him for his first four years in New York—the school fees could be paid, a decent apartment rented, but there wouldn't be much left over for frills. Gerda thanked her father, but said nothing about the amount of money he had provided; he brought the subject up himself when they were alone together.

"I decided at the debut. Yes, he was worked up, but this is perfectly natural. I am so glad we did not know about the accident to his cello, but our boy, he has courage. I decided at the debut; he is a young man who needs to find his own way. I say this as your father, you know me; you found your own way too late. Perhaps it is my fault. You, when you were a little girl, I wanted you so much to have the best of everything. I still remembered the ship, the cans. Perhaps it is my fault it took so long for you. There are many things I will never understand. I did not want to hurt you, but I did. And you hurt the boy in your turn—I know, I know, you were tired of the life Samuel Gregorovich gave you. We can only be ourselves, him too, you know. He could have had the business, he could be a rich man now, covered with respect, but he did not find it in him to be so.

"All I can say to you about Sasha is that I will go differently than I went with you. In thirty years you will see, you will want to make the gift the right way. And I will tell you something strange. I once knew a man who dreamed of enough money to buy his children a wooden cradle; this man came across the year behind me but was not fortunate in America. He dreamed of just enough extra money to buy the most beautiful cradle for his children, and I asked him, 'Do you not dream of clothes, of good shoes for them?' and he said, 'No, I dream of their cradle which will rock me to sleep.' And it is somewhat this way when I hear Sasha play his cello.

"So I am not making perhaps the gift you think generous enough. I will give him the money which will start him in life, only that, and this is the best I can do for him. You must make a different gift. I knew another man from St. Petersburg. He had five sons. Four were fools, one an angel, a fine boy who became a rabbi and made the family proud. This rabbi son said to an older rabbi, 'I have so much to thank my father for,' and the rabbi replied, 'But your father has not yet thanked you. He has not loved your brothers.' You have yet to thank Sasha, to tell him you love him, that it is you who are his mother."

Had Alexander overheard this conversation, he might have been confused at Gerda's reaction. Her father's grave words made her think that she should call Samuel; perhaps they should discuss trying to live together again. We only have what we have been.

"You want to see me again because Alexander is going away? I don't understand. What is there to discuss? You think it would be better for him? But he is leaving, Gerda, he is on his own now. Yes, I feel that too, we didn't pay him enough attention in the last few years. Now it's too late. What you say is irrational. It's over. You want me to call him? Yes, yes, I'm planning to. I know he leaves in five days. I've told you, I'll be calling him. Yes, goodbye."

"He was dying all his life." Some men in this condition became masters of evasion; like tubercular patients in the time of Louis the Great, they never open the windows which would let in the fresh air that might cure them. Samuel called Alexander; they discussed arrangements. Samuel wanted to know with whom Alexander would be staying when he first landed in New York. Alexander told him: a Japanese boy named Kenzo Sarumi. Samuel asked if Alexander was financially "settled"; Alexander didn't return the evasion and replied directly that Grandfather had given him enough money. Samuel wanted to know how Alexander would spend the summer. His son replied, "As I told you before, I'm going to practice, and look around the city." Samuel informed Alexander that the Seventh Avenue line was both an express and a local. When Samuel asked where Alexander was going to be staying, what he really wanted to say was, "Would you like to look up any of my old friends?" When he asked about Alexander being "settled," he wanted to say, "I can't give you much, but I'd be glad to give you something." When he repeated his question about the summer, he was wanting to ask another question: "Would you like me to come visit you?" And when he gave Alexander the information about the Seventh Avenue subway, he wanted Alexander to understand that he knew the city a little and they could explore it together.

Why was it so hard for him to say these simple things? A son becomes a man when a father fears his rejection—not the child's rage of "I hate you," but the man's polite refusal, "Thanks, but I don't need you." Every father recognizes the man in his son when he hears that polite refusal. In families where there is love, there must be this loss. But a father can avoid asking the question whose answer is, "No, thank you." He thinks he can avoid losing by not risking: neutral words, practical connections, information exchanged instead. This is the father who has been dying all his life.

On the plane, Alexander's mind wandered. It was peaceful up here, and the stewardess had served him a martini, his first. His parents had been good about things like that—wine at dinner, cigarettes; try it out for yourself, Alexander, and see what you like, in moderation. Other people had envied him his parents. It was part of the mystery, why his body rebelled. During the last two weeks he had played the scene at intermission over and over again, a broken record. When the cello went to the restorer, he thought it was gone for good; he would play the piano, conduct, perhaps give music up altogether. It would be strange if he wound up as president of Zilker Metal Industries, Inc. Then the cello came back from the repairer; there were no traces of the stains, no smell save new varnish. Just to keep his fingers in shape he began to practice again.

The plane was over Ohio now. Would Mr. Simon call him in New York, would he ever write? Alexander doubted it. On a set of scales, four years of work lay in one dish; in the other lay "After intermission, I am sorry to say, the senior musicians did not match the artistic integrity of their junior colleague." The scale balanced.

Eighteen, launched on a new life. The flesh-and-blood creatures who were his parents were left behind. "Wiser than his years"; perhaps only in that he knew they were traveling with him by other means. The sanitary cello contained all of them, not just one at a time—mother when he was tense, himself when he was free, it held a whole family history. Yet it spoke of other matters to those who knew nothing. Yesterday he had played the debut program over to himself, including Claude Simon's part in the Ravel. The critic was quite right to say the slides in the Chopin were interesting. He packed the cello afterwards in its new, hard traveling-case, carefully stuffing underwear and socks into the spaces between instrument and case. Perhaps the restorer had been too successful. The stains, too, were part of its history.

On the plane, people made jokes about the cello nestled in the seat beside him: does it want lunch, a drink? He should have traveled more when he was younger; perhaps that was part of the trouble, he had so little experience of playing in public. He could make himself do that now, even if he could not be master. He had gotten through it once; the worst that could happen would be more restoration.

Alexander had his first moment of adult love for a flawed thing in itself. The captain instructed the passengers to put their seats in an upright position, to fold away their tray-tables, to extinguish all cigarettes. As the plane lowered toward New York, Alexander looked over the strapped-in cello, out the window to the smog halo over the city in the distance; he would use those slides again.

Part Three

ALCHEMY

Chapter 6

THE NATURAL MUSICIAN

Alexander did not imagine that the struggle with his body had anything to do with marriage or home decoration. After two years in New York, domesticity still seemed a separate compartment of life, one which remained bare. The day he met Susan at the first rehearsal of the Brahms piano quartet, all he thought was that the group had not played well together. The four young people watched Signor Grisi's back recede up the street after he left them at the Cafe Mauro; standing outside while the wind blew hard, they made various suggestions about dinner or just meeting at the next rehearsal.

Akira thought of a restaurant in Chinatown, then began to cough from deep down in his chest. Kenzo put his arm around him and said quietly to Susan and Alexander, "Akira should not stay up late. We'll see you in a few days." And, still with his arm around Akira, Kenzo led his friend away.

"I guess that leaves us," Alexander said.

"They are queers."

"I suppose so."

"It doesn't bother you?"

"Where did you grow up?" Alexander replied.

Susan colored; even after two years in New York she worried about seeming provincial. "In Iowa."

"Would you like to have dinner just with me? There must be something good nearby."

"Come to my house," she offered, although "house" did not really fit her room. Few children played on Susan's street: old, handsome mansions had been divided into tiny apartments rented by women who made careers rather than families, artists with a little money of their own, or couples who traveled. There were usually a few good pieces of furniture, a Turkish carpet, and some carefully tended plants which were the owners' principal objects of domestic affection. West Tenth Street was empty until six, when, sagging from a day at the office, people crammed into the Jefferson Market for the food they would need that evening, or into the little flower store for something to bring to the dinner party of others who were shopping at the market. The lights went on in the apartments a half-hour later, and you could see through the windows middle-aged women holding a drink in one hand and a watering can in the other, giving the adored household plants their daily cocktail. In spring and summer, the sounds coming through the windows at night were of discreet laughter, Maria Callas on scratched records, or, if the evening was especially still, the tinkling of ice.

If Susan stretched out her arms, she could nearly touch the opposite walls of her apartment, little more than a long corridor carved out along the stairs of an old house. The first thing she did after moving in was to paint the room light blue, all the walls up to the ceiling. She spent her savings on an upright piano, a brass bed, and a narrow French country table. Her savings gone, she shopped carefully in the flea market on Fourteenth Street for a set of four white plates, two china mugs, and some old silverware. This was all she needed. No mother would enter here without knocking.

Susan and Alexander sat at her table, chatting about the rehearsal, drinking red wine from the coffee mugs. She had bought a chicken from the market on the way home, and they'd almost finished it, and the evening, when they discovered that each other's parents had recently divorced. The Hoffmanns had fought about money which didn't belong to either of them— Abraham Zilker's trust fund for Alexander. In case Abraham Zilker died before Alexander turned twenty-one, who would administer the trust, who was the responsible party? For the first time in his life Abraham Zilker was disgusted by money talk and he kept out of it; the judge solved the problem in divorce court, appointing himself trustee. Alexander told Susan about it as all three had told it to him, a little operetta of recrimination.

"I was on my father's side too—"

"I didn't say that," Alexander protested.

She poured him more wine. A few months ago her parents had also tried to put into dollars, in court, the exact sum of their grievances against each other. "My mother said to the judge that my father was incapable of providing me with a happy home, and the night I was accepted at the Conservatory she sat at the dinner table, going on endlessly about how I didn't know how to be a good daughter."

About prominent families in small towns there are certain rules. You don't discuss some troubles with them, because they may think you're asking for money, and you expect the people in these families to maintain standards, especially the girls. Susan's mother had suffocated within the cage of her prominence. To her credit, Susan said, her mother wasn't bitchy to others, nor a gossip. She was a respected lady in a small town she hated, and she was frequently unwell. Only Susan was fair game.

"Around the time they were divorcing, she began attacking

me, saying I was a cold person . . ." Alexander looked up from his wine. "Of not showing my feelings enough . . . and the music only made it worse."

Susan also listened well, her feet curled up under her, smoking and sniffling, the pile of chicken bones on a plate and the jug of bad California wine between them. The children of arty left-wing Jewish families have a homing instinct; Alexander's friends in New York his first two years were other people who had the *Socialist Song Book* and the *Little Lenin Library* as childhood relics in their apartments. Susan wanted to know what was so bad about being a Trotskyite, and she asked how his parents reconciled the family money with the family politics, which required more explanation.

She was surprised that he, too, listened well. An endless, empty horizon of wheatfields surrounded her town; the sky was too big. Alexander's idea of Nature was Central Park. She had seen him look confused earlier in the evening when she had said, about her troubles with her mother, "We'll make it up. We have to sometime." So she had to explain about the pressure for reconciliation when people live together in the same routine, year after year; had she stayed, she couldn't have avoided her mother.

It was early in the morning. More wine, more life story, and they were in bed. In the inner recess of each of her armpits there seemed to be too many nerves, and, if she was touched there, her whole body recoiled. Alexander came upon this place by accident, as had other men before, but their hands kept moving back, as though hypnotized by her secret, unable to leave it alone. After Alexander discovered these nerve centers, he was careful to keep from touching them; he put his hands around the outside of her arms and protected her from being shocked.

There were still traces of acne on Alexander's face. Susan caressed these eruptions, thinking that they were more battle scars than the last signs of immaturity. After he had known her longer he let her spread a cream over the acne, a service she performed gently, as gently as from the first he had held her by the outside of her arms.

They lay in bed and he confessed, "I, well, I have to tell you, I haven't really done this before."

Without thinking Susan said, "Lucky for me." He didn't draw away, but moved his hands gently over her breasts, massaging them. She could always tell if a man liked their weight; Alexander did. As she stroked around his buttocks and then reached a hand below them she realized he wasn't erect. This didn't seem to bother him; maybe he didn't know he was supposed to be. He continued to caress her lightly, all over her body. Very gently he began to stroke her pubic hair, rubbing his hand between her legs. Now she felt the way she did when she made herself come, his hand moving between her legs. He did this for what seemed a very long time; occasionally she heard the sound of a truck outside.

She could feel that the bed was sopping wet. Had she looked beneath her, she would have seen that the sheet was stained with a faint brown film; Alexander had loosened her all over. Throughout what seemed the hours of their love-making Alexander had not once become rigid, but she could feel sperm lining the insides of her thighs.

As he fell asleep in the strange, quiet apartment it occurred to him that, whatever people might say in the abstract, a body making love is a different creature from a body playing music. She had performed without much feeling twelve hours ago, but her hands seemed like little animals when she touched him. He had imagined out of ignorance that you were transported into a frenzy when you made love; instead it was simple, just holding and moving at the same time.

Enrico must have scared her, he thought the next morning. He wanted to hear her play again, already testing the clear distinction that had come to him just before sleep. She was working on Schumann's *Scenes from Childhood*; she said, yes, she'd like to play for him.

Schumann once remarked to Carl Reinecke that the *Scenes* "are reflections of adults and for adults." They form a journey in twelve vignettes, passing from dreaminess to nervous excitement to a moment of peace to troubled sleep after a sustained nightmare. Only in a final, thirteenth scene, which Schumann added later, is the ear released from this drama.

Susan played the opening, dreaming scene, "From Strange Lands and People," with no rubato; the simple melody moved steadily over the rolled chords. But some little inflection, perhaps in the fifth bar when the line is repeated a third time, is necessary to keep the ear alert. When a child singsongs, the pleasure comes in repeating over and over again. Because this was a singsong by an adult for adults, there must be a pause, as though in renewing the melody, suddenly a very old memory— perhaps watching the rain in the afternoon through the window of a school-room—returns to the mind and checks the hand.

In the second half of the scene the bass plays a duet with the treble. The bass darkens what was first the sweetness of the treble line and ultimately pulls it apart. The little drama in this scene is that the treble melody then sings again, for the last time, as though nothing had happened. Susan balanced the volume of the lines, so that there was no drama.

After one of the happiest nights of his life he was frowning— about the missing pause and the wrong volume. She stopped.

"What's the matter?"

"You hear it, too?"

Susan played a scale to get back in contact with the keys. "But that was beautiful," Alexander said to her. Their teachers had warned them: amateurs doggedly practice scales and arpeggios and then hope as though switching on a light suddenly to play with expression when the scales and arpeggios appear in a composition. "Do it again," Alexander said, and she spread the notes out like cream.

So it was Enrico, or perhaps this kind of music. Each of the *Scenes* is a moment called back with longing, passing through the lens of memory, a very distant cousin to the evocations of the Brahms quartet but still in the family. Perhaps, Alexander thought, regret was not important to her. She switched gears and played a Haydn sonata.

"Who wrote the ornaments?"

Now Susan was really pleased. "They're mine. I've made sort of a study of ornament, so, well actually I improvise a bit, the way people did then." What she did not tell him was why the little twists and stutters of melody she invented pleased her so much. An ornament is more than the decoration of a musical surface; it's a comment on what is printed on the page. When you are in control enough to comment, you can step back, no longer a slave to the notes. When she added a trill, or rolled a mordant, she smiled slightly, almost contemptuously. It was so easy. Alexander never felt confident unless he wrote his ornaments out beforehand.

When she was a little girl, Susan said, she took to the piano quickly and began to accompany the church choir. When she was ten, her minister arranged for her to play with the choir in the next town, a few miles away, a town pretty much like her own, but at ten it was a great adventure. The worse things got at home, the more she toured. There was a circuit of church choirs in her part of Iowa, and early on Sundays her father would drive her to a church, she'd play at the service tunes she'd played with a choir somewhere else before, and they'd come back in the late afternoon to a darkened house; her mother went to bed early.

"So you don't get nervous playing."

"Not much. In a church you're lucky if half of them are awake, so there's really no need to worry as long as you keep going. The real problem is the people you've left behind; they resent you and you don't feel you fit in." When she was thirteen, not fitting in meant that her breasts were too big and her hips too thick. At night she would stand in front of her mirror and practice squeezing her shoulders, to make her breasts contract;

the moment she stopped squeezing they flopped down. She didn't know what she might do for her thighs and she didn't want to do anything about the overdeveloped part within her. It was her visa.

Alexander seldom now talked about his debut. People were full of sympathy when they heard his story, which was a good story they could tell to others who in turn could tell it at dinner parties, or just to fill a lull in conversation during an intermission. This devalued coin did not produce respect, certainly not love. Susan, however, hearing it now, did not say, "Poor wounded you." She said, "Well, you certainly got over it."

This was almost true. Alexander had spent his first three months in New York virtually alone, found his studio through an advertisement in the *New York Times*, and then had little to occupy himself with other than practicing and reading. But he had, even in those days of boredom, a plan. He would spend two years at the Conservatory forcing himself to do one thing—to play in public without vomiting. He played in old-age homes, in schools, anywhere in the city which offered him the chance to test himself.

The first time was a nightmare; he could feel the vomit rise almost to his mouth. Then it got a little easier, each time a little easier. The old-age homes were especially good for him: as in Susan's churches, half the audience slept, the other half was amazed that a young person would bother with them at all; he only had to get through whatever program he had chosen. After two years, he was reasonably in control; he felt nauseated both before the concert and afterwards, but he shut it out while he played. He had succeeded in keeping his nerves to himself.

It was now early afternoon, twenty-four hours after they had begun to rehearse, and for the moment they had exhausted their stories, themselves, and each other. The test at such a moment is how specific people are when they say, "We must see each other soon." Susan and Alexander were quite precise. Alexander invited her to come the next day at seven to his house. The three-story studio was palatial by the standards of Manhattan in the middle 1960s. When Susan entered, she was stunned. "This must cost you a fortune."

"It does."

She was pleased. Susan's parents, like all leading families, feared spending money; they didn't want to attract attention to themselves. They had resisted buying her a grand piano, which might appear ostentatious since there already was a perfectly good upright piano in the house. Abraham Zilker had made his money a generation after Susan's great-grandfather and was foreign, for both reasons therefore *nouveau-riche*; he had evidently not instilled in his grandson the fear of using money for pleasure. There was wonderful recording equipment, an enormous grand piano (Abraham Zilker's), and many hardcover books. On the other hand, there were few signs of nesting —no madras bedspread, the walls were peeling, there was a metal bed on the top floor, one practice chair, and a cheap plastic table littered with dirty coffee cups. Above all, there was a pervading smell of cat; Max and Pierre had emitted along the walls for the sake of lady cats who were unlikely to take the elevator to the seventeenth floor, and their litter box, although capacious, contained the souvenir-remains of many visits. Susan had her work cut out for her.

They went out to dinner. It seemed the only thing to do, as he stared uncertainly into the chipped white cabinet filled with cans of expensive cat food.

About a month after they met, Alexander went to Susan's first concert. She said it was "little to medium," at a college in upstate New York where Darius Milhaud had taught, once, for a few weeks, a fact the college mentioned to everyone it invited to play. They boarded a dirty train which had no dining car and no working toilets, emerged six hours later, begrimed, at a small station where they were met by a very clean man in a suit who said, "I was afraid you wouldn't make it." It was six in the afternoon, the train two hours late on its supposedly normal four-hour run, and the concert was at eight-thirty.

"I imagine you'd like to tidy up," the neat man said in his best welcome-to-our-college tone. "You can do it at the reception."

"A reception before the concert?" Alexander couldn't believe it. Darius Milhaud must have intimated that performers require inner preparation.

"Yes, it's just a little gathering to meet some of our students that Chuck and I arranged." Chuck, it developed, was the other music teacher. As they drove through endless shopping developments, cash-and-carry lumberyards, and windowless factories, the reception committee of one told Susan and Alexander about Chuck and the problems of the music department in detail.

"Here we are," their host said, pulling up to a glass-and-cedar house that was shaped somewhat like a ship. He opened the door and they were in a room filled with people their own age, who looked surprised that the artist and her boyfriend were so young. On a table were glasses of wine in clear plastic cups and waxed-paper buckets of fried shrimp, fried chicken, and barbecued spare-ribs. These waxed-paper buckets were set in a circle around a large silver bowl—"My own tomato sauce," the host said.

Susan had immediately disappeared into the bathroom to scrub off the grime and to change. Emerging, she sailed straight to the table. "I'm starving," she said, as she picked up one of the frilly cocktail tooth-picks on which the crustaceans had been impaled.

"My own sauce."

"Delicious." Susan winked at Alexander. However, she went on wolfing down shrimp, chicken, and spare-ribs as she chatted to the music students. This she did very well. Within ten minutes, they were calling her Sue, talking about hiking, clothes, and New York. Alexander sat in a corner with Chuck discussing

Milhaud, except when Chuck left him for another "filling" of food.

It was eight o'clock and the host broke things up saying that they shouldn't monopolize their artist for the evening; he would drive Susan and Alexander to the auditorium. On the way out to the car, Alexander said to her, "You'd make the perfect older sister," not entirely in good humor. At the auditorium, there was a practice room instead of a green room, and Susan began to play through the program she would repeat in a few minutes on stage. He always spent the last few minutes before going on tuning his cello and playing chords; it had become in the last year a sacred injunction that on the evening of a concert, the music would happen when the concert began. "You're not afraid of dispelling the energy?" he asked her in the practice room.

"Shut up. I'm getting rid of my energy. Weren't those shrimp awful?" She went back to her run-through.

Susan ambled onstage like Claude Simon. Tonight she was playing Haydn, Mozart, and Schumann. It was the same Haydn sonata she had played when they met. Tonight, the trills and mordants were even more florid, as if she were dancing over the musical lines. At one point she tossed off a long trill in thirds, a virtuoso feat at the end of which she smiled broadly. It was the first time Alexander had heard her play in public, and it was going to be a triumph. The Mozart continued in the same vein, however.

The A minor sonata is one of the darkest and most dramatic Mozart wrote. The mood depends on the sound of the minor chords which support the opening melody. In the days when Alexander was making bear-paws with Joyce, he once tried to get the sense of these repeated chords and gave it up. They exist somewhere between hard and ugly. Susan played them simply as an accompaniment rather than a disturbing intrusion on the melodic line. In the middle of the first movement, when the left hand erupts into a rolling bass rumble, she repressed that too. Only an exhibitionist would decorate this movement freely, and she knew how to hold back. Everything was in good taste. The opening of her slow movement sounded delicate, the extraordinarily pained middle section was crisp—its death-rattle trills were exactly in time—and then the music went back from crisp to delicate. The last movement of the sonata is like the last movement of the G minor string quintet, not relief so much as a gathering-in and summary of the unhappiness which has come before. She played the last movement with almost no weight in the hand. It was a performance with its own integrity: Susan's Mozart looked backward in time, back to the grace of Haydn, rather than forward to the string quintet or the drama of *Don Giovanni.* Except that Mozart wrote this sonata just after the death of his mother.

She walked offstage and asked Alexander, "What did you think?"

"I never heard it like that before," he replied truthfully.

They sat and talked in the rehearsal room, interrupted only once by one of the girls from the reception, who stuck her head in the door to say, "We're rooting for you, Susan."

The Schumann continued the temperate mood of the first half of the concert. When it came time for encores, Susan did something Claude Simon also liked to do. Instead of playing without identifying the encore, she actually spoke to the audience. "This is from the first book of Debussy etudes. . . . This is an old war-horse by Moskowski." She could, he felt, have chatted with pleasure about each of her pieces, and the audience felt it too. Even from the wings, Alexander could hear the affectionate little ohs and ahs as Susan announced each of her three encores. It was a friendly concert.

The next day in the city Susan asked him what he really thought. What he really thought was that it was too easy.

"That doesn't mean anything to me." After a month, Alexander had begun to hear the limits of her naturalness. "O.K., I'll be concrete."

Between the fourth and fifth movements of *Scenes from*

Childhood there is a question. "Pleading Child" ends on an A major seventh; "Happy Enough" could be interpreted as the response to this ending, since by the third bar it is firmly seated in the resolving key of D major. But should the movements be connected this way?

Schumann named "Pleading Child" well; the line is searching and nervous; the unresolved A major seventh might well serve as a summary for this plea. "Happy Enough" uses some of the same melody, turned around. After the A major seventh, which is marked with a long-hold sign, Schumann has written in a rest; the pianist who believes this last chord is an end rather than a lead into "Happy Enough" must hold the pause longer than the chord, to indicate by silence that the child's plea has no answer.

"I'm not saying do it one way or the other. I'm just saying you've got a choice. Rest or make it smooth."

"It's more logical smooth."

"I thought you'd say that."

I thought you'd say that: knowing what a person's answer will be takes her freedom away. But it wasn't Alexander's nasty little demon niggling over a detail, paying her back for the fried shrimp and the ooh-ah encores. All he wanted to say was that ease can be a defense against music—this music, "reflections of adults and for adults." Indeed, Schumann was a meticulous craftsman about the words he used as well as the notes he wrote; it is no accident that at the end of a piece called "Pleading Child" there is a musical question mark, asking whether the mood can be resolved into "Happy Enough."

I thought you'd say that: perhaps she shouldn't have asked him. They'd hashed the other side out a couple of weeks ago. "I'm sorry you go through the wringer before you play," she had told him then, "but it isn't my problem. Oh yes you do. You talk about how wonderful it must be to be so spontaneous and free, which means poor you, the suffering genius. I know you don't complain, or you do every time you tell me how wonderful it must be to be so relaxed. Just stop it, Alexander, it's got nothing to do with me." Which was true enough, but this didn't work in reverse. The only music a person can get right the first time, spontaneously, is boring music. She had to be interested when he suggested that maybe the rest was longer than the hold because she made suggestions to herself all the time, and rehearsing was nothing but a give-and-take of suggestions.

So she tried making the break which she hadn't thought of before, and it was possible; more, it was interesting. He listened to her play with the child's question answered by silence and commented, "Yes, that's what I hear." A harmony of violation: on the low notes Signor Grisi is nagging what-are-you-doing, the middle note is Alexander's complacent I-thought-you'd-say-that, the high note his earnest that's-what-I-hear. Susan banged the piano lid shut and snapped, "You can listen to me practice if you want, but leave me alone to work in my own way."

Every couple devises rituals to counter its little frictions and jealousies. Susan and Alexander began shopping. Carnegie Towers now acquired signs of West Tenth Street coziness. They bought an old horsehair sofa. Alexander decided to learn to cook, doing it his way. He bought a *Larousse Gastronomique*, which looked the most authoritative volume in the bookshop, and was working on possible dishes, given no refrigerator and a hot-plate. They bought the Poussin print. The landscape in the background was so vivid, the frame so attractive on the wall, that the flight from the snake in the foreground seemed just a flourish. They were making a home together.

The bond between them tightened as the bonds of their far-away families loosened. In March of 1968, three years after Susan's father had left her mother, Father announced that he was remarrying. Holding the letter in her hand, Susan thought back to the day when she was fifteen. Father had come into her room and sat on the edge of her bed; all he said was, "Your mother has not been my friend for a long time." Yet this letter announcing his remarriage—"I know she cannot be like a mother, but I think you will find her a reliable older friend"— seemed a betrayal.

She went out for a walk, the letter in her handbag. She walked north, not meaning to go to Alexander's until much later. She walked toward the East Side in the Thirties, where there were many small restaurants which specialized in providing romantic dinners in discreet settings, the scenes of many evenings which Susan had enjoyed before Alexander, in the company of men with distinguished gray at the temples. Red plush on the walls, the walls hung with pleasantly impressionistic pictures of Paris; there were always fresh flowers on the tables and usually candles or little lamps which made each table an island of soft light in a pool of shadows. Occasionally it was necessary to raise the curtain of darkness for a moment when a table ordered flaming crepes; some of the suddenly illuminated diners at nearby tables would smile into the flames, while other couples would quite gracefully but efficiently shade their eyes and so their faces from view. At four o'clock on a raw March afternoon, the façades of these restaurants did not make promises of passion; the sidewalks were piled high with plastic bags of refuse.

Now she was on Park Avenue in the low Fifties. Many of the distinguished graying men had offices here. Behind the walls of glass and steel they made the deals they dreamed over the dinners of forgetting with her. Father, a pillar of the local church choir, was ludicrous ordering crepes Suzette. Alexander was also inconceivable in the red plush restaurants. The few times they went on a binge, he did it properly. He dressed in his one good suit, they went to a French restaurant where most of the patrons were regular and elderly. She chided him for bourgeois taste and he smiled.

Now she was at Carnegie Hall. There was something she might do as a favor but she couldn't remember what. She stood indecisively in the front of the Towers entrance until it came to her: the Diet Kitty. The cats were now on Diet Kitty and their owner was always running out. She went down the block to the pet shop unfortunately close by, since Alexander had acquired his animals on an impulse when he was wandering alone around his neighborhood the first summer. As she reached into her purse for money to pay for the Diet Kitty, she saw her father's letter. The pet-store owner must have noticed her distress, for he said, "They are very sick? Don't worry, this is the best food you can give them."

That night she made vehement love to Alexander; she made him force his hands into her armpits. He did just what she wanted, and when they lay back exhausted asked, "Please tell me what it's about." Instead of telling him, she gave him the letter. He read it, said nothing but that he would make some tea. He went downstairs. The hypochondriac cats lay at the foot of the bed watching her. Alexander returned with the tea.

"Would he have been happier living alone all his life?"

"No, of course not."

"So what are you going to do?"

"There's nothing I can do."

"Susan, what happens when someone writes you with a great piece of news?"

"You . . . I suppose you write them back. Don't be so sensible. What if your father wrote you a letter like that? Wouldn't you be upset?"

"Yes, I would."

There was a silence.

"Well, I suppose I should write."

"Do it now. I'll keep you company." Alexander picked up his book.

It was hard at first, but somehow Alexander reading without further comment, the pampered cats sleeping at the foot of the bed, made it possible to write words she did not feel but which she knew Father would want to read. "I'm happy for you, because you deserve to be happy." When Alexander really got engrossed in something, he had a tendency to sniff through his nose. "Don't do that," she commanded and went back to writing. "Anyone who makes your life better certainly will be my friend." It was a book on germ warfare. Once they had been to a peace demonstration in Central Park and Alexander had insisted that the flier of "Musicians for Peace" state explicitly that the group was disloyal to the American government. He wouldn't listen to reason, she wound up marching without him and they had a screaming match later at the meat counter of the Jefferson Market. "I know that the last years I was home were difficult for all of us, Mother included. I hope, and also believe, that your new life will encourage her to get herself together and find her own happiness. For myself, I am very happy with my school, with Alexander, and feel that New York is where I belong." She wrote herself into believing all of it.

Zilker Metal Industries had recently been sold. Over seventy, Abraham Zilker couldn't move fast enough on the day-to-day trading, and he had no successor. He sold the inventory, the good-will, and the name during a boomlet. Now, because he had time on his hands, Alexander invited him to New York for a visit. The day Susan met him he was itching to make a deal, for her sake. In Alexander's studio she stared at him while he telephoned the opera.

"Manager's office, please. Is this the manager? No? Tell him Abraham Zilker wishes to speak to him. No, he does not know me, not yet. I need three tickets this evening, to bring two extraordinary young artists to listen to your *Boris*. Yes, I have already been told that you have nothing, by a lower functionary. It is why I appeal to you. May I ask, what is your name? So, you are Jewish. Listen, my friend, it is not a matter of whether but how, you understand? These are great young artists; in a few years it will be an honor to your house to have introduced them to *Boris*. Yes, yes, I understand the difficulty, but you must understand the obligation. May I ask, how old are you? Do not laugh, Abraham Zilker never asks silly questions. Well, that is quite old enough to understand the duty we have toward artists, although you sound a much younger woman. Now do this for me, please."

It was not a question, nor, oddly, was it a demand, simply a declaration of the responsibility owed by the unnamed lady of a certain age. There was a pause on the other end of the line. Abraham Zilker, without covering the phone, said to the two young people: "It always pays to go right to the top. Yes, yes," he said into the receiver, "a box will do. I have to pay for all of it? I would not have telephoned if I were not prepared to. Good, I will send an assistant for the tickets. Thank you, *geh gesund*, my dear."

The old man set down the telephone with an air of modest satisfaction.

"Sasha, you will appear at the opera house in an hour to pick up the tickets. Identify yourself only as the messenger for Mr. Zilker."

"But you are amazing, Mr. Zilker. How did you manage it?"

"Long ago, I learned that the word 'no' is only a beginning which may result in some sort of 'yes.' As it happened, the guest box next to the manager's is vacant tonight, or so I heard him say. The nice Miss Feinstein requested it for me, her distant relative."

"Is she?"

"Perhaps. We would have to meet and discuss the matter. Sasha, also send a dozen roses to this Miss Feinstein."

That evening the three of them sat in a box big enough for eight, which was just as well. Abraham Zilker corrected the Russian pronunciation of the singers in a barely lowered voice when they made errors, and he wept profusely during Boris' death scene. After the final act, he swept them off to the Russian Tea Room, where they had arrranged to join the Grisis for supper. Abraham Zilker had arrived in New York just as Alexander was going to a rehearsal with Signor Grisi. "Ah, the teacher who has become your friend. I should very much like to meet him. He works at the opera? Then let us go to the opera tomorrow, tonight is just for us; after his performance, ask him to join us."

So the five of them sat down. Menus were produced by the waiter and waved away by Abraham Zilker. He gave a few short orders in Russian and they began eating food which had not been listed for many years. After ordering, Abraham Zilker turned to Enrico Grisi and announced, "I believe I could hear you quite distinctly from our box. It was a beautiful evening."

Signor Grisi had over the years had a thorough education in Russians—taxi drivers, visiting cellists, and his dry cleaner. He knew what to do.

"I am delighted we played well, and I thought the boxes were particularly attentive tonight." Alexander told the story of how Abraham Zilker had acquired the box. Signor Grisi was not surprised; the dry cleaner had once subjected him to an impromptu audition of a budding-violinist-son-genius, the boy playing behind the counter while his adoring father held Signor Grisi's concert tux firmly in one hand.

"Now tell me, my dear," Abraham Zilker said, turning to Susan, "why do you call him so formally? Why is he not Sasha to you also?"

"I didn't know that was Alexander's nickname."

"His what? Well, all Alexanders are Sashas to those who love them. You ask me why I am so happy, and I will tell you I did not expect to be. The first thing I asked Sasha is whether she is one of us. Unfortunately not, and so the children will not be Jewish."

Alexander was inexperienced about emotions which didn't involve work. It seemed only natural that two people in love eventually married, yet whenever he said "marriage" she grew uncomfortable. Susan's first two years in New York had been a great surprise to her. Those men incarcerated in the advertising agencies and publishing houses, suffering the usual mid-life torments, saw in her a young woman who could take care of herself. She saw in them people who were established, who knew interesting stories and good restaurants—safe men, who, because of their families, did not pull. But after a few months they always did. They began to think of leaving the family web and fleeing with her, the ex-publisher writing his cherished novel in the country house while his young mistress played Bach in the studio in the barn. The moment the men started fantasizing in the expensive restaurants about the farmhouse and the novel and the barn, warning bells rang immediately in her head and no matter how much she liked them she withdrew.

Alexander was the first lover her own age, the first musician, and she was taken by a new surprise. She was pulling on him. She wanted his approval for what she did, and when he took her seriously he hurt her. In the last few weeks she had caught him repeating the ornaments he had heard her play; for instance, he took a little arabesque she had made one morning and worked on it in the afternoon until it sounded so perfect that a listener might imagine the composer had written it in the score. He had said nothing to her about it; she sat downstairs, immobile, listening to him practice the arabesque to death. They were talking less about their work, and she wanted his approval more. Thus, when he said "marriage" the old warnings of claustrophobia rang out in the Iowa of the mind, along with the new warning, "You aren't good enough." If only they could forget the work. The evening Alexander was practicing cassoulet he said to her, "Susan, here's how to do it. Take the bowls of stuff I'll first need to the top floor. Go up and guard them. I'll put the later bowls closer to me. When I tell you, bring down a bowl; remember, the cats never scratch, or hardly ever. Just keep shooing them away. By the time you've arrived at the bottom floor, the cassoulet will be done. What's the matter? It's perfectly logical."

Now Alexander said to his grandfather, "We haven't quite gotten that far."

"A man makes an automobile; he does not sit waiting for the car to happen, or the metal rusts. As I was saying, the children cannot be Jewish, it is the law. Then I thought," now turning to Susan, "you will convert. I do not wish to intrude here; that is a matter of faith."

Flavia Grisi interposed, "Young people have different ideas than we did."

"And your daughter," Abraham Zilker asked, "she was recently married, Sasha tell me, in a synagogue?"

"No, in a church."

Abraham Zilker had spent a lifetime interpreting hesitation in other people's voices. "If I may pose a delicate question— you are new friends—this setting, it was agreeable to you?"

"I was brought up a Catholic," Signor Grisi said, "in a neighborhood of starving people where the priests ate, drank, and counseled fortitude. No, it was not agreeable, but my daughter wished it."

The two old men regarded each other for a moment. "Then I will tell you a story. I knew a man in St. Petersburg who was blessed with a great fortune. I went to this man to ask for money; I was a boy, and I was going away, I also would starve if I remained. This man refused me. He said, 'I will give you advice more precious than gold. You think the wild ones who want to kill become rich. It is not so. They run forward, but they do not look carefully to the side or behind. They trip if more cautious men stick out a leg. Look everywhere, do not run. It is more profitable.' I was angry with this rich man at the time. I could not eat advice, although it was good advice which I have since followed in business all my life. But this rich man was counseling me to follow his own example, and marry outside the faith. Unfortunately," Abraham Zilker concluded with a slight smile, "this man was later shot."

Both the Grisis also smiled slightly. Susan looked at Alexander. He eyed his grandfather, whom he had heard tell this story many times, as if the old man had just brought out a good bottle of wine. She had caught herself just in time from saying, "But how awful for you, Mr. Zilker, that he wouldn't lend you money."

That evening Susan asked Alexander, just before they went to sleep, "Does your grandfather have a cruel streak?"

"Whatever makes you say that? He's the kindest person I know."

When Abraham Zilker left the city, giving her a big kiss as he entered the limousine to the airport and saying softly to her, "Take care of him," they went on diets to work off the effects of a week of elaborate restaurant food. Her father's marriage was celebrated in Iowa.

Within a few months Susan had to decide; she had known Alexander nearly a year. She could not go back to where she had been. Susan's town in Iowa was filled with men out of work, hoping to start over farther west or moving to a big city where there were jobs in factories. This economic uprooting made people at home dream of stability—white church spires and neat wooden homes, the swing in the deep back garden where the children played. Everyone paid tribute to this dream of what once had been, of what should have been, even those who were packing. She too would be crushed by nostalgia if she went back. She could remain stationary, as she was before she met Alexander—free, with more older men and no engagement. Or she could go forward, into the world of exiles and exile-heirs. She would need to become tougher and more wary if she went forward.

Alexander's career advanced its first big step while she was de-bating with herself. Signor Grisi introduced him to an agent, not the sort who used the coffee shop downstairs as an office. Sorokin had secretaries and assistants. His flat, sagging face gave an impression of permanent mourning which evaporated as soon as he began speaking. The creases became smiles—

Lincoln Center next year, why not, everything was possible. The moment he stopped speaking the face dropped back into its wrinkled mask of gloom. Alexander sent Sorokin a tape, Sorokin called. "Let's get together, someplace relaxed, there's a lot to talk about." Alexander invited him around the corner to the Towers.

One of their good rules was to be free together. That meant they made a point of spending certain evenings alone, or of making no dinner or concert dates without consulting each other. When Sorokin arrived, therefore, Alexander was to take him up to the second floor while Susan stayed below working on the piano. Her only concession to the big event was to make the men coffee, from the complicated espresso machine that Alexander had recently purchased and which tended to blow fuses when excited. "Let me do it, you can talk to him while I make repairs." The despondent Sorokin arrived, ascended, Susan brought them coffee while he was saying "May 16th is free; it's only five hundred for the concert but . . ." and a half-hour later they both descended, Alexander smiling and Sorokin seeming on the brink of suicide. So she was off-guard when the agent said to her, "Alex tells me you are a fine pianist. I'd like to hear you play."

"Sure." Susan thought he meant now. She sat down at the piano, Sorokin off-guard stood, Alexander stood, and she began to play, not the Haydn, which would certainly have made a good impression, but the more demanding Schumann.

"Knight of the Hobby Horse" is an ancient singsong, set by Schumann in the bass underneath a jerky treble rhythm, the whole flying at demonic speed; by the twelfth measure the sound is enormous; no child could shout it. The piece abruptly snaps shut in the last measure on colorless octaves. "Almost Too Serious" is no relief. The restlessness which appeared in the midst of earlier pieces returns. A syncopated melody is set over harmonies which keep shifting as they roll down into the bass; the syncopation moves the piece inexorably forward, not to resolutions, but to four questions. At each, a chord lies over its weakest element; the movement has stopped, but the weak underpinning means the ear does not hear the search fulfilled.

Her "Knight of the Hobby Horse" rocked happily. She made "Almost Too Serious" dramatic, playing the stopping-points full volume, so they were not questions.

The scenes of childhood now turn into a nightmare. "Frightening" begins with a melody that works itself into G major, seeming to put an end to the unrest which has filled the child's memory before. But just as the ear feels calmed, Schumann flashes out four measures, marked to be played much faster, which end abruptly in a dark inverted E minor chord, and which, as the title of the scene promises, are frightening eruptions of something fearful under the surface. The melody reappears working toward its reassuring G major, is destroyed, tries once more to reappear, is pierced again by the dark, fast passage. When finally the melody makes its last appearance, the theme sounds hollow.

In the original version of *Scenes from Childhood*, Schumann decided to end this disturbance by putting the child to sleep. "Child Falling Asleep" is not an ordinary lullaby, it has no sweetness. A simple figure is passed back and forth between the two hands, rocking the mind hypnotically, nothing breaking the passage of the figure between the hands until the phrase works itself deep into the bass. Then it is taken up again between the hands, now more dissonant, but also more distant, until at last the music dies away in a long minor chord. The child has drifted into sleep after nervous exhaustion.

Had they been alone, Alexander could have said to her, "You don't understand that in these two last pieces the harmony controls the melody, that is why your playing lacks depth, it sounds pretty." He could have showed her on the piano just how the disturbance of the nightmare followed by the restless sleep could be created by weighting the left-hand voices. Sometime Susan would have to admit that "Iowa," "Mother and Father," the snotty, jealous children who called her stuck up were all wounds waiting to sound. Alexander knew this much, but he was still also young. He believed they could have prepared together for the test. Sorokin's face barely lifted. "Very beautiful. We'll have to talk sometime, Miss Fields. Alex, call me tomorrow at the end of the day. I'll talk to the Met by then." When Sorokin left Alexander gave her a soft kiss. Free together; how could she avoid trying?

Most of the guests said it was a glorious wedding. Late one September morning, Alexander and Susan went to a judge's chambers in lower Manhattan, Enrico and Flavia Grisi serving as resident witnesses. The legal setting relieved them of a number of problems. Abraham Zilker would not have to enter a church. They would not have to involve the parents. Indeed, none of the parents were there.

A month before they knew there would be no mothers. It was simpler with Susan's mother; she refused to come. First she gave as a reason that she didn't want her daughter marrying a Jew; she said it once to Susan and then found she couldn't say it to anyone else. Next she said she couldn't stand being in the same room with that woman, meaning the second Mrs. Fields; she said this so nastily that Susan, who had not met her father's new wife, found herself slamming down the telephone and there was no more need to offer reasons.

Alexander did invite Gerda and Gerda did accept, even though the second Mrs. Hoffmann would be there, but a month before the wedding she fell down a flight of stairs and broke her hip and shoulder. Susan suggested that they move the wedding to Chicago, but Alexander produced various objections. That left the fathers. Abraham Zilker was barely speaking to his ex-son-in-law—it was the fight about the trust fund. Abraham thought Samuel had no right to interfere with this money. He said this frequently to Alexander aloud and to Samuel silently, a silence which Samuel matched with one of his own because the second Mrs. Hoffmann had pushed Samuel into it. The two men were pointedly ignoring each other in Alexander's studio the night before the wedding when the telephone rang. There were tornadoes sweeping the Midwest, Mr. Fields was not sure when they could fly out. Susan said, "Of course we'll wait for you." Mr. Fields said, "Don't do that, I can't guarantee anything." She put the phone down and Abraham Zilker began speaking to his ex-son-in-law about their days in the scrap trade. Both of them became wrought up. The children couldn't stop them; they were settling accounts.

Finally that moment came to Alexander which comes to every person who is the object of these nuptial festivities and he had had enough. He announced that tomorrow the marital document would be signed in the presence of the Grisis, who had originally been invited as the only spectators, and Abraham Zilker. The reception would in any event be the real celebration, by which time he hoped tempers would cool and the Fields would arrive. Everybody agreed because he sounded firm and their minds were on other things.

The Grisis were phoned and given an abbreviated version of the latest events. They agreed to stand in for Susan's side.

There were no readings of scripture, no ritual promises; the young couple had asked the judge to join them without "rhetoric," and he had obliged with the legal minimum. As the judge concluded the two-minute proceedings, each of them answered the judge's only question with "I do." They had behaved rationally in the presence of an official who had never spent an evening with them, witnessed on Susan's side by two older people who had not spent twenty years nursing her, spanking her, hoping for her, taking her to the zoo, waiting up at night anxiously while she was on her first date, making small talk with other parents at her graduation, forgiving and being forgiven once, a hundred times.

The wedding party left the judge's chambers on Wall Street and arrived at Alexander's apartment to find it crowded with people, lunch, flowers, and buckets filled with champagne. The celebration had involved a lengthy tussle with Abraham Zilker; he would pay for everything in the ballroom of a New York hotel. "Only once in your life are you married, it must be a day you and your friends never forget." The ballroom fell through with the cunning argument that, in Alexander's apartment, the celebration would feel more like home. Their cunning cost Abraham Zilker some pain: his own house had dustcovers over the furniture; his daughter spent all her time out, at the hospital or in restaurants; his ex-son-in-law lived in a community it was more dangerous for an old white man to visit, were he so minded, than it would be to return to Russia. The celebration would be at his grandson's home, the only one left in the family.

About the money, Abraham Zilker was immovable. If he could not use money for happiness, what use was it? Let her father give them some furniture, an automobile, if he could afford it—but her family was also broken, her father probably could not pay out of his own pocket and would have to borrow. "Life is like the sea, Sasha, like the sea; the tides pull in many directions. You must understand this father is swept now here, now there, and he may not admit it to you." Susan's father proved understanding; they told him it was going to be a simple affair which they would arrange themselves. Abraham Zilker was instructed to keep it simple.

When Kenzo, serving as doorman, opened the studio to the wedding party, Abraham Zilker walked in to inspect the piano, on which zakuski, caviar canapés, and steak tartare sandwiches were piled; there were bottles of champagne everywhere. Samuel Hoffmann looked at the grandfather who was beaming and proprietary, the son who was taken aback at this forbidden display. He could have told Alexander something about Abraham Zilker and pianos. The second Mrs. Hoffmann, her hair molded into an Afro but already graying, so that it surrounded her face like a halo, was talking to Akira. He wore a suit, she wore an African dress. Samuel Hoffmann, in his usual turtle-neck sweater, chino pants, and sandals, had been speaking to a young woman whom Susan had first met in the Jefferson Market; he was now reminiscing about people from the Village he had known in the old days. Susan's father and his new wife were not yet there, although they had called to say their plane was just taking off. The many young people were wolfing down food and so increasing Abraham Zilker's joy; for fifty guests he had ordered from the Russian Tea Room lunch for one hundred, "just to be safe."

Like all good weddings, the party grew hot and noisy. The second Mrs. Hoffmann, at first very much on guard, soon felt at ease in the presence of so many foreigners. Patrick, Nicola Grisi's husband, was in town on business and when Susan heard this, she insisted that they invite him. Patrick soon fell into deep conversation with Abraham Zilker about business, taxes, and politics, the old man remarking later in the afternoon to Signor Grisi that "Your boy is sound, sound all through." After an hour, Susan's father and stepmother arrived. The father was greeted rapturously by his daughter, who forgave him. Of course he would come in time.

It was going well, Alexander could see that. There had been an awkward ten minutes with a family group consisting of Abraham Zilker, Samuel Hoffmann, Alexander, and the new Mrs. Hoffmann; Alexander filled it nimbly by complaining about traveling with the cello on airplanes, which he knew was of absolutely no interest to the other three. There was a dis-astrous confrontation of Signor Grisi with one of Alexander's friends from "Musicians for Peace," in which Alexander's friend was explaining how American imperialism was no better than Italian fascism in the 1930s. Signor Grisi's face was flushed. Alexander parted them and introduced his friend to his father, who always appreciated signs of revolutionary fervor in the young. A waiter stepped on one of the cats, who showed great courage in scratching the waiter's ankle, drawing blood. All in all, it was going well.

About four, someone said to Susan, "Play something!" "Yes, yes," Abraham Zilker said, "play something, and we can sing, old songs, all the songs the maestro—" looking at Signor Grisi who looked alarmed—"all the songs we know from the old days."

"I've drunk too much," Susan replied. She was seated next to the second Mrs. Hoffmann, who had not resisted the temptation to give various bits of advice to the inexperienced bride. "You play, Sasha."

"On the cello? There's not enough room with so many people."

"Play the piano, then."

He sat down at the piano, covered with fresh infusions of food from the Russian Tea Room's seemingly inexhaustible store. He began to play a Chopin mazurka, an old piece he had learned before studying the cello, but the dishes and glasses on the piano lid rattled too much. He stopped after a few measures and motioned away Kenzo, who was starting to clear food and debris from the piano. "No, I'll play just a little something from this," Susan's score which was on the music tray. He turned to the closing scene.

It opens with simple four-part chords; as Alexander stroked each one, the plates and glasses responded in a rattling chorus. In these chords, after the child's searching, nightmares, and troubled sleep, the adult poet, according to the title, speaks reassuringly. There is nothing ugly beneath the surface. In the twelfth measure there is a sustained pause before the upper voice speaks alone in a simple melody. The pause was filled in Alexander's studio with the continued chattering of guests, friends, and relatives for whom the rattling of the piano was only one more ingredient of the celebration. Alexander played the fragile melody softly, hearing it somewhere else. At measure fourteen, when the chords begin again, they repeat the opening, calm and in repose; time is slowing down. By the last chord it seems to have stopped, on a profound, rich G major chord. Perhaps the most they could hope for together was this moment, contained in itself, when memory no longer compels.

Chapter 7

LONGING

"... *a* great honor to hear him tonight." Signor Grisi sat down.

"Thank you. Let me first say that the honor is mine. Every occasion I have had over the years to address the Musical Society of New York has been an opportunity for me to learn, as well as to meet old friends in this very congenial setting." The speaker, a man in his fifties graying at the temples, his face lined, waved vaguely at the walls of the club which allowed the Musical Society one evening a month in its library. "The good cheer of the occasion will, I hope, sustain us through the presentation I have planned for this evening. I wish to speak to you about a depressing subject.

"In the past, when you honored me with your invitations, you asked me to speak about rather technical matters, such as the physical workings of the ear or of the vocal cords. Tonight I want to take more of a risk; I want to speak about how a great composer's art is related to his medical history. Although I am an unashamed amateur clarinettist, I have no desire to play amateur psychiatrist. I merely want to present the facts as they would appear to any internist like myself.

"Throughout his life Robert Schumann had good cause to worry about the problems which finally drove him mad in 1854. His worries are reflected in the dramatic scenarios he contrived for his music: the wars of Florestan and Eusebius, the *Davidsbund*. These dramatic stories are no mere embellishment in words for pieces like the *Davidsbündlertänze*. The 'League of David'—Clara Schumann, himself, and Mendelssohn —led the forces of light against the forces of darkness, true sentiment against philistinism; honesty and openness were Schumann's ideals. I want you to understand that he advocated these virtues not naively, but because he had good cause, from the time he was a young man, to think of himself as in shadow.

"This may already sound abstract. So let me begin with a concrete question: how did Schumann ruin his right hand, and so his piano career, as a young man? In answering this question, we will begin to see what were those forces of darkness he redeemed through his art.

"I shall open by making a surprising assertion. I do not believe Schumann ever injured his hand in an accident, as is commonly thought. You all know the story. Schumann is supposed to have invented a sling, tied from his right wrist to the third and fourth fingers of the hand, to raise these fingers off the keyboard. He was supposed to have spent hours practicing in this way, so that the weak little finger and the strong index finger, forced to play as a pair, gradually became equal in strength. According to the story, one day he tied the sling too tight, attacked the piano too hard, and suddenly the third and fourth fingers snapped back, permanently crippled. In theory, I imagine, a pianist might be able to destroy his hand by such a mechanical device, but not in this case."

The doctor smiled and put his hands in his pockets.

"Consider the evidence. Schumann was in the early 1830s an open and exuberant young man, yet he was curiously indirect and elusive in writing to his friends about the cause of his hand problem. The person who put the story of a mechanical accident about was Friedrich Wieck, who loathed his son-in-law. And even Wieck does not come right out with it. He only says in *Klavier und Gesang* that the sling was invented 'by a famous pupil of mine, contrary to my wish and used behind my back to the righteous outrage of his third and fourth fingers.' Daughter Clara tells a different story. She claims Schumann wrecked his right index finger from too much practice on a dummy keyboard. The accident in either version is supposed to have occurred in 1832. Two years before, Schumann is writing of 'weakness in my right hand.' And finally when Schumann is exempted from military service in 1841, his doctor's letter states that both index and middle fingers don't function.

"Now why should Schumann have kept silent, why did his father-in-law tell one story, Clara insist on another mechanical injury altogether, Schumann admit to trouble two years earlier, and his doctors find paralysis in both hands?"

Alexander glanced at Susan, who stared, riveted, at the doctor.

"Let me be blunt. Slater and Meyer demonstrated in 1959 that the only medical explanation which fully accounts for Schumann's last illness is syphilis. Before their work, the psychiatrists were as usual concocting explanations about a man without a body. My own investigation, building on Slater and Meyer, connects this mysterious hand affliction to the syphilis.

"We know that Schumann was a gay dog in his youth, but later that he was a perfect husband to Clara. He probably contracted syphilis in the late 1820s, when he was about the age of most of you," and here the doctor smiled at the group of young people near Signor Grisi. The light in the room came from troughs set into the paneled walls. There were large bookcases with glass fronts, containing beautifully bound, un-read books. The hundred-odd members and guests of the Musical Society lounged in leather armchairs; Susan and Alexander were sunk in a deep, upholstered sofa.

"In Schumann's day, syphilis was treated by mercury, ingested orally. Now in the wrong dosages, or the wrong forms, mercury treatment could be instantly fatal. By the 1830s, there was sufficient knowledge about mercury that such accidents didn't happen; I won't bore you with the details. But, this is the important thing, the treatment even in its relatively advanced form still had disastrous side effects. One of the things the treatment could do was cause a weakening of the muscles in the hands or the feet. Schumann's symptoms at the time of the supposed hand injury fit perfectly the diagnostic profile for this mercury side effect.

"Medically, there is no question in my mind about the mercury-induced muscle destruction—I can go into the particu-lars later if any of you would like me to. The important thing is that by the 1830s a fair number of doctors knew that this side effect was likely to occur. And on this basis I would like to offer a hypothesis: they told Schumann what was truly wrong with his hand. I infer it from his uncharacteristic evasiveness in discussing the causes for this cataclysm in his life. I believe he was treated in 1830, shortly before he first complained of weakness in the hand. Furthermore, I believe he kept the nature of his illness from his wife, who knew that her father's explana-tion of the facts made no sense and was aimed only at showing Schumann's foolishness; Clara had to make up a story for herself.

"You may well ask, 'Even if he did know, why should he keep silent?' My answer, one which supports the basic hypoth-esis, is to ask you to try to imagine the shame of syphilis in the nineteenth century. It was a disease conceived by that sex-obsessed age in religious terms; it was the judgment of God on sinners. Doctors sometimes refused to treat women with syphilis, claiming that women had to be left to their just punishment. A man who had an episode of syphilis was considered unfit to be the husband of any decent woman, and in the early 1830s Schumann was the suitor of Clara, whom he idolized. It may therefore appear that he was a monster not to tell Clara, and so put their children at risk. But you must consider that some doctors in the 1830s believed they cured syphilis by treating it with mercury, cured the root infection rather than erased its first symptoms. So if Schumann kept silent, it was because he believed his secret was safe and the sin past.

"In this, the composer, like his doctors, was mistaken. Mercury does not cure. Syphilis, however, is one of those diseases which can work underground. The symptoms can fade, and then break out years later. Doctors of Schumann's time did not often connect these later occurrences to the earlier episode, and indeed, as I shall explain in a moment, the later symptoms were often quite different from the initial signs. So the doctors looked for other causes—diet, cancer, 'purely' mental affliction —and the patient was doomed. This was what happened to Schumann. From the early 1830s to 1854 Schumann experienced only occasional moments of dizziness, delusion, and headache. In 1854 the disease burst out in its final, lethal form, and the treatment he received consisted mostly of being locked up in a padded cell so that he wouldn't injure himself as he hurled around the room in his agony."

What sense could one make of this? A simple act of pleasure, probably just a chance encounter with a woman late at night after too much drinking, leading to a lifetime of punishment. Surely this was the difference.

"You see how, by working back from the last illness to its first origins, we can find out why in those early years the symbol of light, connoting honesty, openness, and truth, was so important to the young Schumann. I said I would not psychoanalyze his music, but I cannot refrain from telling a story involving the great English music critic Donald Tovey. Schumann's violin concerto, a late work, was suppressed because the family, and then the heirs, thought its weaknesses were due to Schumann's derangement. When the work was finally premiered in 1937, Tovey wrote a letter to the *Times* of London about it. Far from this late work's showing signs of madness, Tovey said, 'On the contrary, if we look for morbid elements we shall find them where we least wish to avail, in the best-loved early works.' Tovey is referring, for example, to the end of *Carnaval*, where the 'League of David' puts its enemies to flight in what must surely be one of the most tortured pieces of triumphal music ever written.

"The figure who came to epitomize the man of truth and light for Schumann was his young protégé, Johannes Brahms. As a middle-aged man, Schumann writes in 1853 about the twenty-year-old Brahms. 'Seated at the piano, he began to disclose most wondrous regions. It was also most wondrous playing, which made of the piano an orchestra of mourning or jubilant voices. . . . [H]e himself, a surging stream incarnate, swept them all together into a *single* waterfall, sending aloft a peaceful rainbow above the turbulent waves. . . .'

"In reading Schumann's music criticism as well as his letters, we have the feeling that here was a voice for directness in an age of cant. The point I am making to you might be put this way: people who are conscious of purity are seldom pure. In the tragic illness which was to destroy Schumann we find a reason for his passionate concerns. Schumann's genius, not the illness, gave him insight into what sincere, direct music sounded like. To that genius we owe the fact that there was a standard of how to edit the scores of precious masters, which called his generation back to their senses when confronted with the antics of a Paganini, a Liszt, or other flamboyant virtuosi. But no human being cares passionately in a vacuum.

"The loss of his hand was a catastrophe which Schumann bore with calm and dignity. We find him writing from Leipzig to his mother on November 6, 1832, 'I am for my part completely resigned . . . in Zwickau I will take up the violoncello again (for which only the left hand is needed), which besides is very useful for symphonic compositions. . . .' "

Six months after Susan and Alexander were married, she said to him one morning, "My left forearm is killing me."

"What have you been playing?"

"Bach, but nothing hard."

"Killing you how?"

"It started when I was making a long trill. Feel my forearm; the muscles are tight all the way down to the wrist."

Alexander ran his forefinger underneath her arm; the muscles were indeed knotted up and the veins running into the palm stood out. After three days the arm still was tight. There are doctors in New York who specialize in musicians, and Susan decided to see one of them. She had to wait two days for an appointment. On the fourth day after the attack the tightness disappeared.

"Go see her anyhow," Alexander counseled. "If it happens once it can happen again." The doctor was soothing; probably just overwork, an old-fashioned liniment wasn't a bad idea, take it easy.

A month later the forearm knotted up again, three days before a concert. This time it began on a mordant. "Help me, Sasha."

He went to a sporting goods store and bought some tennis balls. "Dr. Claude Simon's special," he said as Susan looked at them dubiously. But the tension in the forearm was not a vibrato tension; when Susan squeezed on the tennis ball, it only made her cramp worse.

Opera singers of a certain distinction can cancel concerts and the public will accept the lost evening, perhaps grumbling but understanding voice strain. Instrumentalists in general and young pianists of minor reputation in particular do not cancel;

there are no second chances. The day before Susan's concert, Alexander urged this upon her: she could not cancel, he had got through a concert having nearly destroyed himself vomiting, and she would make it. The night before the concert, the cramp spread from her forearm to her wrist.

"There's no way, Sasha, no way I'm going to play tomorrow." They had called the musicians' doctor who told Susan to soak in a hot bath and come to the office in the morning. In the morning the cramp was just as bad, the doctor clucked sympathetically, and Susan telephoned from the doctor's office to the college where she was supposed to perform. In the late afternoon, the cramp disappeared. It was too late; the college had already put signs up around the school, and if Susan showed up, there would be hardly anyone in the audience. The school's concert office was not sympathetic.

The musicians' doctor was consulted a third time. Susan gave a detailed medical history, the doctor poked with sharp tools and gave Susan various instruments to squeeze. At the end of the examination came a little chat.

"Any problems at home?"

"No, I'm just married."

"Have you been trying to become pregnant?"

"We're going to wait; both of us are busy with our careers."

"What does your husband do again?"

"He's a cellist."

"Of course, Alexander Hoffmann. Now tell me, Susan, you've never had this problem in the past. Most people do have concert-nerves, as you know."

"I don't. I like to perform. Look, the cramp went away before the concert."

"Yes, it did." A doctor specializing in musicians knows how common are deformed, stretched, or enlarged muscles. Still, "psychosomatic" glimmered on the horizon of both doctor's and patient's mind.

When Susan came home from the doctor, Alexander said to her, "I know we are very different people. All I can tell you is what tension meant to me. Your body sometimes had to go through a crisis in order for you to make deeper contact with the music. I felt more, I know that, I felt more as a result of the struggle to relax. Maybe now you are engaging the music at a deeper level, and your body is giving you signals that this growth is about to occur."

These were the most loving words he ever spoke to her. Still, her left forearm remained tense. For the first time, Alexander saw the Poussin in the living room as a whole composition, the snake in the foreground, the figures fleeing in terror no longer picturesque flourishes in the landscape but somehow its reason.

The cramp resolved into a routine. Although it came from ornaments at any time, it always vanished before she performed, sometimes only a few minutes before she was to walk onstage. There were no more thoughts of cancellation, just days of discomfort, and she was bearing up.

The prophecy Alexander made, however, proved wide of the mark. Cramp was not Susan's teacher. For a while she avoided the music in which she was the master, and tried to play the Mozart A minor or the *Scenes from Childhood* through the pain, which told her nothing about these works. Alexander's loving words were boy-kind. Nor is there a logic about when a wound opens up. They had been happy in the first months of their marriage, and Alexander had been relatively inactive, waiting for Sorokin's promised miracles to occur. All the boy-kind husband had done was pour an extra reserve of love into his playing; he had subtracted nothing from her. The cramp, they both said, was a freak of nature. The natural musician's body works no matter what its environment; put this body in a college gym for a concert hall, send it on the road for a month to play fifteen concerts, feed it fried shrimp and "my special sauce," and still it plays. When this body begins to malfunction, the environment to which it has been indifferent cannot easily help it, nor does the natural body reach out, enriched by trial, any more than a sick plant sends out new roots.

The musicians' doctor, working on other natural principles, said, "Very well, let's make a list. One, you never had this before you were married; two, your new husband is becoming famous; three, you aren't. Sorry to be so blunt."

"Alexander thinks it actually might have something to do with feeling the music more deeply."

"Um. I don't think you have a purely physical problem."

The obvious is a tyranny. Susan had got this far beyond the obvious: cramp started not when the hand began to embellish but when it finished its free work and returned to the printed line. There was no danger in an endless trill. In cramping, first the wrist tightened as though a bracelet were cutting off the blood, then the pain shot at right angles into the hand and up the arm. But she refused to stop, she kept playing; not once in her life had she ever given up. Next obvious step: Mother wants you to give up. But she hadn't had the least tremor at home. Indeed, in all ways her mother was beaten. On the telephone now, she spoke to Susan as a supplicant. And Alexander was not performing. Never in her life had Susan felt more independent. The musicians' doctor was rejected as too crude.

Alexander called Claude Simon. They were now "Claude" and "Sasha" to each other, the unfortunate review having been buried by the biographical announcement on each of Alexander's concert programs that he had been trained "by the distinguished cellist Claude Simon." Signor Grisi had never been able to bring himself to say "What about me?" and Alexander had forgotten that he and Enrico once had been something other than friends.

"Perhaps you could work with her, Claude. The problems are really like what we struggled with." Claude Simon was flattered; for a childless man there was also gratification. Life goes on as you've known it. He came to the studio just after a cramp had gone.

"Sorry," Susan said to him as he took off his coat, "but I've nothing to show you."

"I'm heart-broken. I see you still haven't fattened him up much," Claude Simon nodded at Alexander. "You can't be more of a mess than that one. Sasha, you remember the stock market?" They both began laughing as Susan stood, rather bewildered.

"Look, sweetheart, what do I know about pianists?"

"What?"

"I don't know a damn thing. Play something."

Susan played the Mozart A minor.

Alexander's agent, Sorokin, hadn't wanted to offend a new client when he listened to Susan play. The economics of offense never entered Claude Simon's mind; moreover, he took any music he heard seriously.

"It's pretty. You want to be pretty, you've got nowhere more to go. I don't hear any tension. It's absolutely beautiful, that's what you make me think, but I want to hear Mozart. For Sasha, I could do something." Alexander began to interrupt, but Claude Simon talked over him; pretty young girls with problems—you could drown in them. "Like I said, I know from nothing about pianists, and this has nothing to do with cramp. What you should do is find a tough teacher, someone who will take you back to the beginning so that you re-feel all that fluent finger work. I'll find you someone, even though you want to push me out the window. But that's what I think: you need to start all over."

Once the growth is deformed, lop it off, regenerate from the roots—if possible. He seemed to be proposing she cancel herself, she should forget and leave the city. Nobody was giving her practical advice; neither husband, doctor, nor this so-called tension expert. Claude Simon's prescription was given the week before Alexander and Susan attended the meeting of the Musical Society.

"To explain Schumann's last days, I should tell you that syphilis affects the central nervous system in three forms, meningovascular syndrome, locomotor ataxia and general paresis. In layman's language, the first affects the blood vessels in the nervous system, the second and third affect the nerve cells in the spinal cord and the cortex of the brain. The last two syndromes can come on from ten to twenty-five years after infection. Schumann was cured for symptoms of the first syndrome, which can show itself immediately, and then in 1853 began to be afflicted by a combination of the last two syndromes called tabo-paresis. This incorporates stabbing head pains, a product of syndrome two, with persecutory psychosis, delirium, and a confusion of hearing stimuli, products of syndrome three.

"It will not surprise you, from what I said earlier this evening, that Schumann came to be fascinated by mediums, table-turning seances, and other manifestations of secret voices. He believed that the dead masters could speak to him in these ways. There is the amusing story, for instance, about communing with Beethoven at a seance about the famous opening of Beethoven's fifth symphony. On April 25th, 1853, Schumann wrote to his friend Hiller, 'A wonderful force! Just think I asked it [the table] how the first two measures of Beethoven's C minor Symphony went. It hesitated longer than usual before answering. At last it began ♪ ♫ | ♩ but at first rather slow. When I told it, "But dear table, the tempo is faster," it hastened to tap in the right tempo.' With the onset of the final phase in 1854, however, the secret voices of the great composers came to haunt him in less pleasurable ways. A visit from Mozart at night would fill him with the sounds of the most beautiful choral work ever known. The next morning, the moment he sat down to write, the sounds had turned into the most terrible

dissonances—or he could remember nothing. The worst mani-
festation of sudden change from bliss to hell was an A tone
which in wonderful purity began to ring in his mind, all the
A overtones humming perfectly, and then the tone would
continue for hours, steadily, driving Schumann into a frenzy
and producing throbbing headaches.

"Mood shifts are common in the double syndrome of tabo-
paresis. The patient imagines when the attack starts that the
disorienting of his senses promises a transcendence, a move
into a higher state of relief and pleasure; as the neurological
disturbance continues, he falls deeper, farther, because he first
climbed up so high. This is particularly true of the paranoid
aspect of the general paresis.

"The figures who make Schumann's degeneration apparent
to him are the angels he imagines. They are beautiful creatures
who come to him in secret, then turn into devils. An angel sent
the A, an angel led Mozart by the hand into Schumann's
dreams. Then the A did its dreaded work of headache as
Schumann sought in vain to write down the music revealed to
him.

"Like all those in a paranoid state, Schumann was afraid of
the power of darkness in what to other men seems harmless.
Think back on his early ideals, then reflect that someone in
paranoia is not afraid of open enemies. The genius of this
madness, if I may so put it, is to scent threat when the innocent
feel only pleasure. The past crowds the details of everyday life
now like a nightmare.

"Prepared for in his youth, the conviction of such secrets is
the gate through which Schumann's physical deterioration in
the last years passes into his consciousness. February 10th, 1854,
was the fatal night when Schumann was so tortured by angelic
devils that he begged Clara to shut him up in an asylum. A few
days before he wrote to Joachim, 'We have been away a whole
week without sending you or your companions a sign . . . but
I have often written to you in spirit, and there is an invisible

writing, to be revealed later, underlying this letter. . . . I will close now. It is growing dark.' What the invisible writing revealed made it impossible for Schumann to go on.

"I do not wish to claim that the meaning of these delusions lies simply in what they tell us about the neurological condition of a patient. But you must understand that my generation in medicine wants to take some of the physical mystery out of madness without subtracting from its human meaning. So I would like to tell you something about the autopsy on Schumann's brain. Richarz, the medical superintendent at the Endinach asylum, wrote that the autopsy revealed—"

Alexander glanced at Susan. A mystery to others whose explanation one has harbored for almost twenty-five years, or a new mystery, everyone with an explanation except oneself. Was it the same disease? It seemed so long ago that Alexander had heard her glide over the surfaces of the *Scenes from Childhood*, memories of childhood that Schumann wrote when he already knew. A disease of longing? Perhaps now Susan was obeying the unspoken command to remember and regret. Yet a cramp need not drive you crazy, especially if it passes, and hers always passed. Alexander reached out his hand to Susan while the doctor described the autopsy. She drew away from him.

Chapter 8

NATURE TRANSFORMED

Around the time that Susan was consulting doctors, that Abraham Zilker was explaining to his lawyer the exact nature of his grandson's genius, that Samuel Hoffmann was happily contemplating massive peace marches in the streets, people like Nicola's husband, Patrick, who were older than thirty but not yet paunchy, were often subject to strong fits of remorse. Patrick had spent his twenties learning, as his father-in-law had put it, how to organize races in which all the horses dropped dead before the finish line; by 1970 he was a skilled insurance investor. He and Nicola now had a starter-home in a starter-suburb of Pittsburgh; they would move regularly in step to his promotions. On his business trips to New York he saw young women walking on the streets in short dresses, obviously with no underwear beneath, men in overalls similarly unfettered; the half-naked made fun of people like him. He was mesmerized by the daring of their bodies. He found increasing reasons to make business trips to the city, called his in-laws only to say he was very busy and to send Nicola's love, while in fact he prowled and told himself it was not too late.

One day in the winter of 1970 Signor Grisi stopped on a street corner near Lincoln Center and asked himself if it could have been his son-in-law and Susan he had just seen passing in a taxi. He was uncertain that it was Patrick because this clean-cut man had on an Army jacket, and seemed to be wearing some sort of beaded necklace. Signor Grisi doubted it was Susan because she was kissing this man on the lips, whoever he was.

They had run into each other on the street the day before. She also was uncertain whether the aging hippie was Patrick. At first he had wanted to duck, but they were walking straight toward each other on an empty sidewalk, and he thought, why not?

"Susan."

"Patrick? I didn't recognize you."

"I'm just, I've been doing some business in the city and now I'm just loafing."

"Well, nice to see you."

To prevent her thinking the wrong thing Patrick asked her to have a drink. Susan was intrigued. Signor Grisi had made several ironic references to the capitalist of the family without mentioning that he was a countercultural capitalist.

At drinks it was the usual family and news chatter until Patrick asked about her concerts. Susan began to describe the arm cramp.

"I don't know anything about music, but in sports that kind of thing is often a resistance to what you're doing. You know how to use the muscles, but the muscles don't want to be used. It happens often to tennis players."

Susan hadn't played, much less mentioned, sports for years. It was one thing she did at home which made her like all the other kids; she was known as Slugger Fields. Once she had told Alexander about the baseball team for boys and girls, which he thought was adorable, although it seemed, he said, a danger to her wrists. He lived his body as strategy.

Susan and Patrick began to reminisce about the small towns and farms they had known as children. Iowa and Ohio had many interesting differences, they discovered, in how people worked the land and how the towns ran. It was dinner time; he asked her if she was free. Alexander was working that night at the recording studio, starting his second record, so she was, and Patrick took her to a surprising spot. It was one of the old flaming-crepes and red-plush-walls restaurants she used to go to with her publishers and advertising men writing novels, only now the decor had been changed; there were bare wooden tables, the walls were stripped back to the brick, and there were plants hanging from the ceiling. None of the patrons had on a suit or an expensive dress. She was just about to explain to Patrick as they walked in when one of the waiters said, "Nice to see you again," to her. He had been here in the old days but now he had no French accent.

They had pink shrimp, brown rice, "organically grown vegetables from New Dawn Farm," and fun. Patrick made the obligatory disparaging remarks about insurance, and Susan was reassuring. Of course she was against capitalism, but she understood you had to make a living. Patrick had often said this to himself; since he was thirty-two and she was twenty-three, it counted more coming from her. They talked about their spouses. Susan remembered listening to a lot of wife-talk in this restaurant, but now it was different; they both had a family. Nicola, it turned out, missed her parents and New York; Patrick wasn't high enough up in the company to be transferred to the elite New York office. Susan began to describe Alexander's recent successes. It was still just a friendly dinner.

"How about for you?"

"It hasn't happened," Susan said.

"You don't say 'yet.' "

That was nice. He didn't coo and he sounded confident about the "yet."

"What's Alexander like?"

It was so hard to describe him. On the one hand his story was unusual, on the other he came out of it almost invisible: sweet, upright, most of him missing. The story passed directly into his hands.

"He likes to cook, buy antiques, read; we have cats." Most of him missing. "He's a great cellist; more than that, a great musician. I mean that. At his concerts people feel they've heard the music for the first time, just, like just them alone in a room with the music."

Patrick appreciated the loyalty. "Funny Nicola and Alexander didn't get together as a couple. Because of their background. We have cats."

In Patrick's hotel room that night, after more Iowa, Ohio, and wine, Susan was scared. For nearly three years she'd been faithful to Alexander while he became more of what she could never be and her forearm tensed. She was scared because she felt so good now. Patrick's V-shaped back seemed sheathed in a cape of muscles. He reminded her of farm laborers she had seen as a little girl, their shirts off as they worked in the fields, stretching, bending, lifting. These back muscles were now moving over her. She pushed her palm out flat to feel them give and contract as he worked himself into her.

After three years, Alexander had still not succeeded in exciting her when they were in bed. Of course she knew that after a while, sex diminishes in marriage; it wasn't that. Their love-making had always been more like friendly cuddling; so much of him was missing.

Susan and Patrick left the hotel room about midnight to have a last drink downstairs. She wanted to ask him if he was also scared, although he didn't look it. They were careful not to touch in the hotel elevator.

He was indeed feeling a little guilty in the bar so he changed the subject. "Tell me some more about this problem in your arm."

She described the strangeness of the cramp's coming and going. No, never during a concert. No, they couldn't link it to any one thing.

"I saw Alexander's old teacher and this guy said the trouble was I'm superficial."

"What a shit!"

"I wanted to kill myself. I can play almost anything and he's telling me to start over. It was particularly bad because he's a leading musician."

"Maybe that has something to do with it. People with power often like to throw it around."

"You think so?"

Patrick knew so. He described the insurance company pecking order.

No one worked for Claude Simon, but Susan appreciated Patrick's explanation. "You're right. It's a reaction." She was learning fast: a little distortion of what Claude Simon said, a little simplification of what she knew herself, and she wasn't defeated. "Something in me is resisting."

"Well, that's good." Cramp was a badge of honor.

It was curious. Alexander had spent his whole life hearing revolutionary talk; when he got together with people from other families like his, they were almost snobs about their politics: only we understand. Yet this man knew about the other side from the inside; he didn't have any of the patter— she would have to explain to him, as Alexander had explained to her, why Trotskyites were less than human—but Patrick was living what they took for granted. So she was more inclined to trust his simplicities: the pain you can't solve may come from resistance—to the Sorokins, Simons, and even Alexanders, the ones who might have a good line of talk about the system but were getting rich off it. Also, Patrick had just made her body come to life. She wasn't "into" politics, but his power to open her up seemed a kind of proof.

"When are you leaving for Pittsburgh, Patrick?"

"Tomorrow afternoon."

"Could we have lunch?"

"Sure. At the hotel."

The next afternoon, "lunch" was not quite so wonderful. Patrick was already thinking about what he was risking—home, cats, he jumped ahead and was divorced, which the company frowned on—risks so much greater than being recognized in another city looking free. Muscles, however, do not shrink overnight.

Signor Grisi saw them in the taxi after this "lunch," Susan going to the airport with Patrick.

Early that evening, Alexander asked her where she had been in the afternoon. He had accepted her explanation that she was out with friends last night; now he accepted her explanation that she was working in the music library of Lincoln Center all afternoon. His trust abashed her; it also was her first intimation that she could control him. Claude Simon, well versed in these matters, called it the "one-night-stand syndrome." You feel guilty for doing it, and you feel a little contempt for wife or hubby in getting away with it.

Susan wanted more—more sex and more relief with the handsome man, the man who shared a past with her. She became reckless. She called Patrick at the office in Pittsburgh, once even at his house, pretending to be a secretary making a business call to him from New York. She called for a week; he was coming again soon, then he had to change his plans, he was coming in a month, don't call me, it's too dangerous, I'll call, which he did once or twice to keep this crazy girl from wrecking things by telephoning the house, Nicola taking those careful messages from the unnamed secretary who gave only a telephone number, no company name. Nicola was sure to catch on.

Patrick stalled and pushed Susan away with something of a good conscience. She was rebelling, she was mixed-up, but she had to do it her own way, nobody could tell her how. Everyone has to discover himself or herself by cutting free, it's tough, you have to do it all alone. What a crazy kid. She had to learn to "hang loose," and he had had "an experience" with her.

The one-night-stand syndrome, as Claude Simon understood it from long experience, goes in one of two directions. Either you rediscover how wonderful the person you deceived is, or your little flutter didn't work out and it's the innocent one's fault. The second option is especially likely if the deceived husband or wife goes on without betraying the least suspicion or even curiosity about your absent hours of passion, noticing nothing that's happened to you. After Susan stopped calling Patrick, after Patrick stopped calling Susan, after it was clear there would be no more business trips to New York that she knew about, Susan began bitching at Alexander about the cats and criticizing his cooking in front of their friends.

Apart from the various omens people had divined from her forearm, Susan woke up each morning, as she had for the last fifteen years, facing practical decisions. If she hadn't memorized a piece for concert she had to follow memory drill, taking the printed music away from the piano—she often put it in another room—and then forcing herself through the piece. If she was uncertain about a technical matter in a piece she knew, she played the passage over and over until she had dissected in detail the finger problem, and then usually tried to work on other music with the same difficulty. This way the music she wanted to master did not go stale.

To these routines in the last few months she had added something new. She gave herself at least a half-hour a day to sight-read new music. Fauré, Russian music, anything out of the standard repertoire. The forearm cramp governed these explorations somewhat; when it was bad, she had to play miniatures rather than big pieces, yet still she kept going.

Sight-reading is a peculiar pleasure. The rule is, don't stop to correct a mistake. The excitement of discovery lasts as long as the musician is willing to surrender to sounds he or she could make better. Often, in the course of sight-reading, one will be forced to extract and invent: an enormously convoluted roll for the left hand will be replaced, spontaneously, by shaking octaves or a sketched scale. Susan's love of making up her own ornaments for early music served her well in sight-reading Debussy or Rachmaninoff; she was accustomed to inventing on the spot.

Gradually this pleasure of sight-reading extended from a half-hour to an hour, then it bit significantly into her rehearsal schedule. If she had the choice of memorizing or sight-reading, she opted for the momentary pleasures. The memory of a musician, however, is not a warehouse; unless the memory is used it erodes, though not entirely—key passages can be stored for twenty years and return intact; rather, the environment surrounding these climaxes, great effects, or difficulties is effaced if the piece is not constantly played. By the time of her experience or one-night stand with Patrick Hearn, when Susan performed in public she had begun using the printed music on stage.

Alexander thought it was another good omen, even if the performances were a little ungainly. In sight-reading, she was opening up. He offered to turn pages for her the first time she said she wanted the music onstage, which she agreed to only because she had decided at the last moment. The thin arms reached across her horizon, the square hands flipped page after page precisely, just at the last moment, then he sank back into his chair beside her and listened. After this one performance, she arranged for another woman at the Conservatory to help her.

The tumor of sight-reading continued to grow. She discovered wonderful music by Couperin and Rameau she had never known before; indeed, it must have been a secret to most people, since the library volumes were covered with dust. She almost performed this music as she played through it. Then she went on a Scriabin binge, much too hard to count as a performance, she had a Prokofiev month, even harder, then she swerved into piano transcriptions of symphonies from all periods.

Alexander, practicing two stories up in the studio the limited repertoire a cellist plays in public, asked her when she entered the transcription phase, "Why are you wasting your time on this?"

"It's none of your business."

"Of course it is," he retorted. "Hours and hours of hacking through this stuff you will never play in public. It's a waste of time."

"Sasha, we made a deal. Never to interfere when the other practices. Remember?" Free together, no self-consciousness about someone else working in the house. Yes, he remembered.

Alexander said he would make them both some tea. The detective-husband had once again discovered something about her she didn't know. She sat on the piano bench while he withdrew into the tea and most-of-him-missing and said to herself, you'd rather sight-read for yourself than perform. Until she came to New York, performing for an audience was when she enjoyed the music most. Here, people preferred hearing other people play. So you give to yourself the pleasure you don't seem to give to them. It was simple.

"I'm sorry, Sasha, I didn't mean to shout. It's just that I want to explore a lot of music that isn't, well, tied to the music business, like these transcriptions. There are a lot of things possible for the piano that have nothing to do with performing."

As he nodded gently over the tea strainer, he had, he thought, the message: whereas you, with your recording contract, your agent, and your tour. . . .

The times now refined the discovery. The word got around that Susan Fields sat in a tower studio in Carnegie Hall and played wild music for herself, and sometimes for selected friends. It was, in fact, in 1970 the best thing she could have done for her career. Along the musical grapevine, from coffee shop to coffee shop, from upper West Side apartment to apartment, the message got around that she was withdrawing into authenticity; among those drinking coffee or nestling in the apartments without an agent, a recording contract, or a tour, the message was reinforced by comparing her to her husband. You could see her do it even at the rare concerts she did give; she refused to memorize, she played from scores, it was more natural. Word along the grapevine even reached Sorokin, Alexander's agent, who thought maybe he should hear her again; people seemed interested in her.

But Susan was not adept at capitalizing on withdrawal. Whenever in the studio she took a break from sight-reading, she could hear floating down from two floors above the sound of the cello. Alexander went over and over certain passages which at first sounded like filling between big moments; the more the cello played them, the less neutral these passages sounded. She had lost faith that she could do this work. Patrick's explanation of her forearm cramp had now become part of the grapevine mythology; alone in her tower, the young pianist suffered bodily, which made whatever she was playing there even more real. Drinking her tea on the ground floor of the studio, listening to the cello obsess the little moments into life, feeling the forearm muscles pull as though they were trying to wrap around themselves, the pain seemed her admission: I can't do that work.

In the spring of 1970, Alexander was called up for the draft. The war in Vietnam was at its height, he was twenty-four, and he no longer had exemption as a student. As long as you stayed in school, even if you were studying for a degree in revolutionary dialectics, which you could in those days, you were safe. Alexander was desperate; he had no shield.

Abraham Zilker wondered if there were someone he could bribe. Many, many politicians had taken his money in Chicago over the years; graft was so normal it had ceased to be called crime and was called grease, apt for a dealer in scrap automobiles; you "greased a palm to oil the city's wheels," as Abraham often joked with the minor industrialists, who laughed discreetly. But this draft board was in New York, and Abraham's sources told him bribing draft-board officials, unlike bribing mayors or councilmen, was considered illegal. All Abraham could think to say to his grandson was, "It is a war against communism." Abraham was willing to believe this if Alexander was; the old man had worked hard for his adopted country in the last world war. But Alexander did not go along.

"It's not any such thing. We're spraying napalm on peasants to keep some crooks in power."

"Perhaps, Sasha, perhaps." It was as well he had not mentioned to Sasha his inquiries about the New York draft board. "Even so, these are the leaders of our country. I do know, from the old days, what communism does to a country. Perhaps you should trust what people in Washington say. In any event, they will never send you to the front, they will put you in Intelligence, make you an officer." He was choking on these words, but it was beyond manipulating.

Enrico Grisi, who had never bribed anyone, also found it was beyond manipulating. The week after Alexander received his notice of induction, three weeks before he was due to report, Signor Grisi made several calls to Washington. He had gathered statements from several musicians famous throughout the world, stating that Alexander Hoffmann, whom some in fact had even heard play, was a national resource too precious to be risked in warfare. Armed with these letters Signor Grisi called quiet, civilized diplomats, public officials, even a general, all patrons of music. These quiet civilized people were distressed, they were sympathetic, they had a word with this person, a word with that person, and they were sorry, they could do nothing. The general gave Signor Grisi one piece of advice.

"The only way out, right now, is if a doctor finds he has some grave medical problem. You understand me, Enrico? You find a doctor who can discover it."

Signor Grisi knew of no doctors with this talent.

Alexander almost resigned himself. Why should he be any better than the other people who were called up? On the street in those weeks he often passed peace marches filled with college students as angry and appalled by it all as he was. The boys, however, were exempt. Passing the groups waving signs, his resignation evaporated. He must find a way out.

Samuel Hoffmann learned almost too late. Father and son spoke irregularly. Alexander had been upset at the wrangling over his trust fund, disgusted at the scene in his apartment the night before the wedding. He liked Samuel and supposed he loved his father as a father, but no halo of father-power would ever surround Samuel Hoffmann's bald, worry-creased head.

"I'm going to my army induction in a few days," Alexander told his father on the telephone.

"That's terrible. Can't you do something?"

"Nothing. People," Alexander avoided mentioning Abraham by name to his father, "can't think of anything. Except that Enrico spoke to someone who said a letter from a doctor about a disease might help, but I'm healthy, there's nothing wrong with my body, yet."

"I'll call you back," Samuel said.

"What?"

"I said I'll call you back. Don't leave the house for the next hour."

Alexander thought it was an odd reaction to his predicament, but Samuel sounded emphatic, which was also unusual.

The telephone rang in just under an hour. Alexander could hear sounds of honking and trucks backfiring in the background.

"Call Dr. Adolph Green, here's the number."

"Who is Dr. Adolph Green?"

"He's the person you are looking for. I've known him since the old days."

Coming from Samuel, it seemed unbelievable. Alexander called the number he was given. A man's voice answered, "Doctor's office."

"My name is Alexander Hoffmann. I'm calling, um, about . . ."

"Yes, I have your referral. Could you come to my office in an hour and a half? These things should be seen to immediately."

"Dr. Green, you understand that . . ."

"I understand perfectly," the voice cut him short, "but I can't make an evaluation, you must understand, on the telephone."

The address the voice furnished was of a Dr. Adolph Gruen, on Park Avenue. The doctor's waiting room was beautifully decorated—leather chairs, an oriental rug, copies of *Art News*, *Connoisseur* on the tables instead of dog-eared news magazines. It was after office hours and Dr. Green or Gruen opened the door himself.

"Come in, Alexander. I've heard so much about you over the years. Sorry about the games over the phone. We had to learn to be careful." The doctor, fat, clean, and well dressed, gave a short laugh.

"I need to ask you a favor . . ."

"I know you do. When's the physical at the draft board?"

"A few days."

"Why did you wait so long? You and Sammy are just alike. Always hoping something will come up at the last minute. Let's go through your medical history."

Alexander gave him everything he could think of, including the stomach cramps. The doctor gave him a thorough going-over, Alexander thought.

"It's cursory; perhaps we could have actually discovered something through blood or urine tests. Sammy once thought he could put together a strike in a day, too. You drink?"

"Not much."

"Now you do. It's the best I can think of. I'm not a psychiatrist . . ."

"Excuse me, but what kind of doctor are you?"

"Urology. I can barely get away with this, as your family doctor. Look, the story is you came to me, you started drinking when you arrived in New York, you did it to relieve your tension but it got to be too much, you came to me through your father, your father's old friend, I've been seeing you regularly, once a week, for talks. I control your diet, talk to you, you're making progress. I give you tranquilizers but no other drugs, you've got lots of problems but I'm like a father to you, and over the last three years it's getting a little better. You're an artist; the nerves part might go over. If you're anything like Sammy you don't know how to lie. So keep it simple, that's your story, for God's sake don't embellish it. I'll give you a letter that puts it all in medical mumbo-jumbo. Keep it simple, O.K., and remember, if they start to browbeat you, if they are suspicious—and they will be—don't explain. Keep referring to the letter. You don't know anything, you just drink and you need me." Dr. Green or Gruen then repeated the essentials.

Alexander didn't like it. In the last two weeks he had begun to imagine just what it would mean to pull the trigger on a

peasant, and he was also afraid for himself, but he didn't like it.
These lies were already complicity.

The doctor seemed to sense this. "Not pretty, is it? I imagine
Sammy brought you up the way I raised my girls, you knew
but we never tried really to make you understand. Look at it
this way, Alexander. I owe your father a favor, the biggest
favor of my life. One of the people he protected was me. So
I'm doing this for him. This nice office, my girls in good schools,
I owe it to Sammy who kept quiet. I'm taking as much of a
risk as you are, I want you to understand that. So I want you to
keep control of yourself, to lie well, to help me repay this debt
to Sammy. You understand a little?"

It was a noble lie and all it led to was farce. Alexander
presented himself a week later at the army induction center,
after a sleepless night rehearsing in his mind when he too
should fall silent, when he should mumble, "You have to talk
to my doctor," his eyes rimmed red as though he had indeed
spent the night drinking; he wasn't going to embellish, he was
going to follow orders. Alexander was armed with the letter
and a copy of *Middlemarch*, which he had been reading for a
month, hard going but the novel took his mind off things. He
sat on a bench reading in a room where a hundred other young
men made nervous jokes, picked absentmindedly at the flakes
of paint coming off the walls or, in a few cases, primped in
front of a mirror. Every hour, twenty of the young men were
called into another room; through the door the command was
clearly audible to "Strip and stand at the red line on the floor!"
Alexander's was the fourth batch; he stripped and stood with
his book tucked under his arm, his letter tucked in it as a
place mark.

"Kid, what's that book?"

"*Middlemarch*, by George Eliot."

"In the army you call me 'sir,' and why are you carrying a
book? You don't need it to have your medical checkup."

"I've got my documents for exemption in it."

"I said call me 'sir' and we'll see about that."

After inspection of his orifices and then of his intelligence, Alexander was sent to the private office of a doctor.

"What's the book?"

"I'm only carrying my exemption papers in it, doctor."

"No, I mean, what are you reading?"

"*Middlemarch*, by . . ."

"I know who wrote it. Have you got to the part where Rosamond writes Lydgate's uncle?"

"Not yet."

"You know it's quite an interesting, and, I think, accurate novel about medicine in those days. You a med student?"

"No, a musician."

"Really." The doctor did not unfold the papers he had taken from Alexander. "What do you play?"

"The cello, but I'm also interested in conducting."

"Really. Who is your favorite cellist? Casals?"

"No, I don't like that way of playing. About my papers. I have a letter and a notarized prescription; that's what I was told to bring."

The doctor looked reluctantly at the documents.

"There is something irregular here. I should have been given a copy of this letter before, from your local board. Why are you producing it only now? It says you've been treated for three years."

"I didn't know I was supposed to mail it to the board."

The doctor read the letter again. "When was Dvořák's cello concerto first performed?"

"What? Let me think . . . 1896, in London."

"Who wrote *Les Nuits d'Eté*?"

"Berlioz."

"Whom do you think Mary Garth will finally marry, Fred Vincy or Mr. Fairbrother?"

"Mr. Fairbrother."

"Really. You're wrong about that." The doctor stared at the letter again. "That bad, huh?"

"I haven't touched any alcohol for seven months."

"So, you are making progress."

Alexander was suddenly terrified at the thought that he was draftable because progressing. However, the doctor continued, "We see so many phony letters here. I am supposed to tell you that, if your condition improves, you may be eligible to serve in the armed forces in the future." He smiled; he was too young to have known Samuel Hoffmann in the old days. "Enjoy the book."

Susan had been jubilant when Alexander called her at school from the draft-board center: they would have a party, a big celebration, she would meet him in an hour. He arrived at the studio before her, sat down in a chair, and began shaking. She flew into the room and gave him a big hug; the Japanese boys came in behind her, Susan having called them as soon as she was off the telephone with Alexander. Akira shook Alexander's hand, but Kenzo took Alexander by the shoulders and gently kissed him. The room was bathed in their warmth, Susan ebullient, Akira smiling, Kenzo now holding his friend, the kiss like a soft compress still on Alexander's lips.

He stopped shaking and told them the story of his interview with the doctor. Susan exclaimed, "Sasha, what a good guy!"

"Good? I could have been killed. What if I forgot my dates, what if he didn't like *Middlemarch?*"

Susan's smile died. The Japanese laughed, just like the Grisis and his grandfather laughing at the careful man with the selfish advice who was shot during the Revolution. Alexander excused himself to call Dr. Green or Gruen and then his father.

He said to Dr. Green or Gruen, "It was a farce . . ."

"All laboratories are inefficient. The tests were completed satisfactorily?"

Alexander felt they were being slightly ridiculous but he went along.

"Completely. I'm perfectly all right."

Dr. Green or Gruen then broke training.

"To tell you the truth, I wasn't thinking of you. I spent the afternoon sitting in the office, thinking of my girls." There was a pause. "They also suffer from this disability. We will meet at the regular time; please give my best wishes to your father."

"I'm tied up at the moment," Samuel said, "I'll call you right back." In a minute he was on the telephone with the honking and backfiring accompaniment. "Thank God, Sasha."

For some reason, perhaps because during the last week Samuel had worn the father-halo in Alexander's mind, he went on to describe the little scene in his apartment.

"Susan decided he's a good guy."

"Adolph? Adolph is the best. I know him from the old days."

"I know you do. I don't mean Adolph. I mean the doctor at the draft board. She thinks he's a good guy."

There was another pause on the line, punctuated in the background by "Hey, baby, what's happening?" Samuel turned to someone at his end, it sounded like a tenant from Washington Homes, and said hello Mr. Whiteside, hello Mrs. Whiteside, hello Janine, I'm talking to a man out of town, see you later. To Alexander he said, "You sound angry."

"It was a close call."

"A nice kid from Iowa," Samuel said, "she should expect the worst?" What do you want, she should be like us? "Anyhow, I'm glad it's over; I also have been unwell."

The hooting and honking continued in the background, they discussed Samuel's sinuses, Samuel said call me soon, and Alexander put the receiver down. The show business with the telephones was new to Alexander, he had been too young to understand the flood of calls which came when his father had testified; on the other hand, about this other matter his father seemed unconcerned, or perhaps you don't discuss personal matters in a telephone booth on the street.

Abraham Zilker had to be called and lied to. Alexander knew his grandfather would be upset at learning that his father had arranged for his freedom, and besides Alexander didn't think the story should be spread around, for the sake of Samuel's friend.

"You have a disease? What kind of disease?"

"Back, my spine, they just discovered it."

"Come back here immediately. We'll get you the best doctors, everything."

Alexander hated going on. "No, I'm under excellent care here, don't worry, it's nothing serious, it just means I can't be a soldier."

"Who is this doctor? What do you know about him?"

Alexander finally managed to get his grandfather off the telephone, the old man unsatisfied and aroused. Alexander called his mother and repeated the same lie, for the same reasons. When she asked, "Who is your doctor?" he was worn down and slipped.

"Adolph Gruen."

"Adolph. I see."

Finally he was through with the telephone. He came downstairs and the Japanese announced they were taking everybody out to dinner. "Let's call Enrico and Flavia," Kenzo said.

"Great, great." Alexander was delighted. Susan smiled weakly.

The dinner had an outward resemblance to the dinner at the Russian Tea Room with Abraham Zilker and the Grisis. Menus were dismissed, incomprehensible orders given, Kenzo bounced up from the table at one point for a conference in the kitchen. These are her parents. The Grisis were intrigued by the raw fish, the unspecified animal or vegetable matter floating in the black ceramic bowls. Susan mindlessly spread a large dollop of

Japanese mustard on a piece of the rubbery fish. It burned down her throat.

"Such unusual food, isn't it?" Flavia said to her genially.

They didn't like Patrick—no, that wasn't right, he said they didn't respect him. In the hotel room she'd stroked his hair when he told her this.

"Alexander, my dear, you see that military prophecy is the only reliable guide." Signor Grisi sipped the hot sake in the little cup. "You needed a disease. God provided you with a bad back. It's probably why you had so much trouble as a boy. No, Kenzo, for an Italian, hot wine, delicious as this is, hovers on the edge of the disgusting. I'm sure that's where your tension came from. Perhaps I should call this genie for my sinuses."

They weren't having much fun, the married couple. He was quite solicitous toward her, perhaps too solicitous, and she sat there glumly, not enjoying his good fortune. Signor Grisi had excised from his mind the glimpse of the young woman kissing the man in the army jacket and beads; a girl like Susan could have no interest in a rising insurance investor.

Kenzo and Akira were privy to confessions from Susan that she and Alexander had grown somewhat apart. Emotions come and go, but their friend had been rescued from the brink of something quite terrible. Quite terrible. The Japanese had a poster of Nagasaki up in their living room. Surely she should be glad that her husband had been saved from becoming an accomplice.

Alexander tried to talk to Akira about his back. Deeper and deeper into the lie, but this must be the end. No one ever sees back pain. If not noble, this back ailment among the friends he was lying to, who were giving him a dinner to celebrate the good fortune brought by the lie, was at least innocuous.

These are her parents who stood in at the wedding. Susan felt a wild desire to reveal everything to the Grisis and the Japanese about Dr. Green or Gruen. But she had given Alexander her word. Now he had changed the subject to Italy, where she had once been with her father. They could make it on Italy through the rest of the raw fish, the steaming vegetables, the green mustard, and the sticky hot wine.

After dinner, the Japanese, who were still hoping it might become a celebration, invited everyone to a party they knew of down in the Village. The Grisis tactfully declined; let the young people have a night on the town. Susan felt better the moment they disappeared into a taxi. The four young people popped into the subway.

Drugs now had a geography in the city. The white addict whom nobody would become lived in a hovel on the lower East Side; to give hard drugs a try you went to Tompkins Square. The more respectable drugs, marijuana and LSD, were sold to the west, mainly in Washington Square, where the middle-class young bought and smoked in leafy comfort. The square was now flooded with teenagers from the suburbs looking for action; New York youth tended snobbishly to avoid them by keeping to the sedate benches on the east side. Kids from the suburbs bought their drugs at the fountain in the center and then drifted into nearby Washington Mews, a charming cobbled street paved late at night with stoned bodies.

When Susan went back to the Village to see old friends, they told her the neighborhood was under siege. Their idea of Bohemian life was artists drinking and arguing at the Cedar Tavern, good bookstores, French cuts of beef, a favorite Italian restaurant where the owner would sit down for a chat. The chants of the drug hawkers in Washington Square—"Bags, loose joints, acid"—were too raw.

The party was at a loft below Washington Square, a large room with bare wooden floors and bare brick walls. People milled around drinking wine from plastic cups, there were two record players going, one with Bach, the other with a rock band; the noise of the crowd was so great that the sounds melted into the human babble. It was nearly midnight when the four young people arrived, others streaming in behind them.

They knew a lot of people here. A friend came up to Alexander and said, "I just heard. Congratulations on your back. Have some wine; get drunk!"

"No thanks, I don't want to drink." He wanted to say, I can't drink, to stop this lie at least with the other real lie, but it would never end if he kept going.

From the time he was a little boy he had gone to parties, which in some ways all ran true to form, at least the parties the Hoffmann family was invited to. There was always a mix of arty businessmen in turtlenecks, real artists in open-necked shirts, the women always wore jewelry made by sculptors, none of the women had artificially curled hair, and for twenty years it had been "Merce said to me that her lifts were superb. . . ." "It's a dubious proposition. . . ." "I'm working in mixed media in this new piece which. . . ."

The advent of drugs had somewhat disoriented these evenings. Drugs meant that something happened, there was experience right there instead of "Merce said to me." The older people did not themselves take drugs; at most, they reported on drug trips made in the company of no one at any given party. However, they were careful to be understanding of the experience the younger people were having right in front of them.

Alexander always refused drugs, hated the hype about them, and feared them. Perhaps the drugs brought you pleasure, but they could equally release the virulent ghosts who would simply take over. Smoke was no substitute for the more strategic dealings which put these terrors to work. Susan knew how much he hated drugs; all his friends did. The little whips were never flicked against his missionary hatred of drugs; only those who, like Patrick, worried that they were missing out on life felt the sting of drug hype at parties.

At about one in the morning Susan said, "I'm going to try it." Cubes of sugar had been impregnated with DMT. A young man, surprisingly wearing a tweed jacket and tie, offered her a saucer on which a sugar cube lay in the center.

"Don't," Alexander said sharply.

"Look," the neat young man assured him, "it's a short trip and Susan says she knows a lot of people here, so she won't be scared."

Alexander turned aside to ask Susan, "Who is he?"

"I don't know. I just met him. But Kenzo's taken one, Sasha, and he's fine." There were indeed so many of her friends here. She was elated, so many of them.

"I don't want you to do it, Susan."

The neat young man hovered, holding the saucer like a butler.

"Why?" I can do it but you don't dare; it might be dangerous.

"Could you go away? Please?" Alexander said to the young man, who did not seem offended.

"I'll be over in the corner."

"Susan, I want to leave here and go home." But they'd come here to escape home, just for one night.

"Nobody is asking you to take the DMT. I mean, look at the people here; they're having a good time. Tell me why you don't think I should take it." She had never taunted him before; it felt good. "I don't have to, but just tell me why not, it only lasts a few hours."

Alexander turned and walked away. Five steps from her someone handed him another red wine in a plastic cup, which he accepted mechanically and then handed to somebody else. She found the man, who was still holding the saucer, talking to another pretty girl about tripping; she reached over the girl's shoulder and popped the sugar cube into her mouth.

Guests were still arriving at the party, nobody was leaving; despite the open windows and wafts of cold autumn air, everyone was sweating. The magic cube didn't seem to work. She understood people perfectly, her head was clear, she didn't see grotesque shapes or blinding colors. She sat and chatted with Kenzo, comparing Tokyo and Iowa. Alexander came up to them. He had handed hundreds of cups of red wine to people, no conversation lasted more than two minutes, his head ached with Bach-rock-babble. Suddenly it hit her.

"Sasha! You should try some. It's great!"

Enough. It was the end of a day of successful lies to almost everyone he cared about, his life saved by farce, hours of her sulking over a minor remark, even at dinner when she was surrounded by people who loved her. And back of this day was six months of her wasting time which he wasn't allowed to comment on, a year of real pain which only made her cross with him, and which she didn't put to work—the little sugar cube instead—sniping about his cooking, about the cats, inexplicable pouting, and behind all this three years of resenting more and more his success, which came out of work and attention, resenting it as though they were competing in a race. Alexander grabbed her, spilled someone's wine across her dress, and dragged her out of the party.

In the taxi-cab Susan rubbed her hands in the sopping mess on her dress, lolled against him, and went half asleep. He shook her by the shoulders, but all she did was flop back and forth like a doll. Finally they were home, the night porter helped him get her into the elevator and upstairs. He was not going to put her to bed, she was going to come out of this and listen.

"Wake up! I'm sick of you!" He slapped her hard across the face. Susan staggered against the piano, but kept herself upright by clutching it. That was something.

"You've got to let me alone. I didn't wreck your career, I didn't paralyze your arm. I want you to stop blaming me."

She was staring directly at him, but he couldn't tell if she was hearing.

"Lots of people have your problem. You think popping these little cubes is any good? Do something, I did, you do it too. Go back to Tenth Street, find someone else, anything, just don't keep sitting in this apartment seething and feeling sorry for yourself."

Still nothing, the drugs must have sound-proofed her. Her deafness pushed him over the edge. He said to her what from the first day he had circled around.

"You don't feel anything. Do you understand me? You don't feel a damn thing when you play. What are you going to do about it? Say it's someone else's fault? You can give up, or you should get better. Can you hear me?"

"I can hear you perfectly well. You don't need to shout." It had been a short trip, just as the young man promised. Susan picked up her bag, opened the door, and rang for the elevator. It came, the doorman looked surprised—she had been on the floor ten minutes ago—the elevator door closed, and that was the last Alexander saw of her, whole.

When the police telephoned the next morning to say there had been an accident, not the driver's fault, she'd run out between cars in the middle of the street, Alexander obeyed mechanically. He notified all the parents, the friends, the Grisis last of all. In the wake of this sudden reversal of fortune, Signor Grisi was more than ever certain it was another couple he had spied that day. Alexander went through all the motions proper for a young husband. But Susan had been wrong about him. None of him was missing now. He grieved for her, he hoped for her recovery as the prospects of it grew dim, but he was also in a rage against her, not really believing she would die, sure that when she recovered they, like everyone in his family, would settle accounts. This was the Hoffmann way.

Part Four

THE FRIENDSHIP
OF MEMORIES

Chapter 9

AN EVENING
OF BRAHMS

Abraham Zilker was often asked by the industrialists at his club if he missed Russia. The correct answer is, no, I love it here. The exile, however, has a duty to himself; even if he assures others he never really existed before, he must merge in his own mind the memories of the old country with life in the new one, neither forgetting nor endlessly regretting. A person in mourning must do the same. Well-meaning friends will counsel the mourner to go into temporary exile: take a cruise, sell the old house, forget for a time and let the wound heal. Later, however, the mourner faces the exile's obligation to learn how to remember.

Various chances for withdrawal arose soon after Susan's funeral. A cellist on tour with a chamber-music group fell in her hotel room in San Francisco and broke her wrist. The manager of the group called Alexander to find out if he wanted to fill in—just one concert, but it would be a change of scene.

Alexander said no, although he had canceled his own concerts indefinitely, then he called back and said yes. In two days he was on the plane. The one concert became two, then three, then Alexander was on tour for several weeks with the group. In the air at ten, off in an airport that looked exactly like the one they had left, a carbon-copy hotel room, an hour to practice in a drafty hall, the nap before the concert, the performance for a sea of eager faces—by the end of the tour Alexander knew what he was playing only when he looked at the music on the stands—sleep and another plane.

Wearing out his body did not, however, prevent the unbidden memory of her sweating in the hospital bed.

After he returned from the tour her friends began to invite him to dinner. The geniuses in New York knew they should do something for Sasha but they were so busy. Her friends were people who had shared her past; the dinners were mostly small talk about places he did not know or experiences foreign to his own. These evenings evoked the escape he had first enjoyed with her. In a few months the friends invited him to dinner with other women, nothing forward, just a writer or a dancer who happened to be free and who happened to be at the same party.

Nothing is served by acting as though you will never desire again. He asked one of the women, a weaver, to spend the night with him. Like Susan, she made no fuss of seduction. Holding the weaver's long, supple body in bed made him, however, remember Susan's smile the first day they played together, the evening they spent guarding the cassoulet from the cats. He could not go through the steps of love-making with the weaver. He could not retrace his steps.

Susan so often had accused him of being self-absorbed, of being missing. Perhaps that was true, but now in the chaos of memory she seemed more sharply defined to him. The weaver, who became his friend, one day asked him, "I don't mean to sound cold, but why does it matter to you, whether or not you are in some way responsible for what happened to Susan? What do you get by finding an answer about that night?" It was a reasonable question, put charitably. He had a reasonable answer. "Saying I don't care how she died is like saying I don't care that she died. And I do. Sometimes I think she's more alive than ever." This answer contained the fact that he would occasionally wake up in the middle of the night, having dreamed what he should have said to Susan about the green room, the recording contract, the draft board.

The hardest moments, the softest, were solitary. The tower had now become a shrine, its *Larousse Gastronomique* and horse-hair sofa promises that if only they had managed differently, they could have been happy. The dinner-party friends thought it unhealthy that Alexander spent so much time alone in the apartment, but in this solitude, surrounded by the evidences of their shopping, he felt they were forgiving each other. The piano he kept spotless because she liked to play on clean keys. The cats Susan hated Alexander now brushed with even more gentleness, as if he were brushing her hair. And yet it was here, high above the street, where Susan had gradually destroyed her music and where she had carped at him.

After six months Alexander began to doubt that there was a way to come to terms with death substituting for divorce. The memories were implacable, they did not fade, only the evidence of happiness was disappearing under newspapers, plates of cigarette butts, and dirty dishes. The apartment was reverting to the filth in which Susan had first found it. Alexander had failed to heed the advice his grandfather was given by the man in St. Petersburg; he was trying to run forward, rather than survey the ground on which they had stood. The ballet of re-crimination between them was set to music. To begin the voyage of mourning, to launch himself upon that exile from which there might be a return, memory transformed, the dead speaking to the living, something had to happen to this music. Signor Grisi, in ignorance, made it possible.

Signor Grisi had recently turned sixty-two and retired from the opera orchestra. He spent long afternoons at the Cafe Mauro; he needed something to fill the time on his hands, and preferably something which would fill the empty chairs around him. So he offered to set up some master classes at the Conservatory; he would find master musicians to work with advanced younger ones. His first idea was a conducting class: the student orchestra could be employed and young musicians who wanted to learn something about conducting could train with this orchestra under the guidance of his friend Valleau, an ancient conductor who had often worked at the opera. It was a complicated idea which fortunately required much discussion.

Signor Grisi thought naturally of Alexander as one of these apprentices. Many cellists became conductors; Toscanini, who was a cellist, remarked once that bass instruments give a musician a good feel for the floor of orchestral sound. Alexander was intrigued when Signor Grisi made his proposal. He, also, thought it would fill up time.

Alexander imagined that in conducting he would start where he had begun with the cello, his body tense, but he did not go back. The aged French conducting master said to him: "The whole world within a box, Monsieur Hoffmann, think that there is a whole world you can conjure with your hands moving as inside a box in front of you; if you break the box, the players will not understand the wild gesture, they will cease to pay attention, and the world will vanish." The conducting master had polished this advice through long use; Alexander needed it only as confirmation; he moved economically on the podium.

The conducting master said to him, "When I can use my eyes rather than my hands, I use my eyes." This also was a confirmation. Looking at the strings when they made an entrance came more naturally than cueing with the hand. It was also better; the eyes of the string players rose to meet his eyes, the world was in a box. The hardest physical problem was learning to cue French horns, the uncertain instrument in the hands of its neurotic shepherd sometimes responding on time, sometimes not. This too he solved with his eyes; he would look down in their direction for just a moment before a horn entrance, preparing with the eyelids just as the horn players prepared with an intake of breath; he would open his eyes to signal the expelling of breath.

The conducting master said to him at the conclusion of the course, "If you want to go on with this, practice with a mirror; buy crayons and shade in the orchestra sections on the mirror in different colors. Memorize, memorize, then go to the mirror to play what is now in your head." Alexander passed an antique store a few days later, saw a Victorian mirror, and remembered the master's advice. It was a hideous mirror, framed in heavy, peeling gilt, but it was wide, wide enough to contain an orchestra in crayons. For three or four months he worked in front of the mirror an hour or so each day, soundlessly conducting various Mozart symphonies. The cats watched their owner gesture to the crayons on the glass and found nothing amiss.

Alexander mentioned casually to a friend who led a chamber orchestra in the Village that he was working at home conducting a little, and because he was off-hand the friend did not feel threatened and offered to let Alexander lead the chamber orchestra at a few rehearsals. The few rehearsals became three hours every week when the friend suddenly departed for a job in Germany. During the next few months, when Alexander was not away touring, he concentrated on the orchestra, fifty amateur musicians who played feelingly out of tune and not in time. Soon they played together and more in tune. He told them they weren't enough in tune yet, simply stating a fact rather than accusing; they asked him if he would take over permanently, the truant conductor still mining his Germany connection, and Alexander agreed if they would agree to rehearse two sessions a week, thirty weeks a year. Sorokin the agent was not pleased; important opportunities began to pass Alexander by.

A stage personality is often dangerous for an actor. He or she gets typecast, and even at rehearsals a director may force the actor to play his or her public image rather than the specific role. A conductor is always aided by a stage personality. No matter how great his musicianship, no matter how much he eschews the flamboyant gesture, the players will not give him everything until they feel a vivid human being in front of them.

When Alexander started conducting the chamber orchestra, he hadn't yet contrived this vivid person. "Mr. My-Way" a few of the players called him. Everything had to be minutely perfect; the moment the players did something Alexander felt was wrong, he stopped them and drilled them. His body was free but he was devotional and grim. The players resisted. When he drilled them in his church-of-art way, they had little tricks of obeying sarcastically. At his second rehearsal with the chamber orchestra, he drove the horn player crazy about an entrance; the horn player finally did it to Alexander's satisfaction and then kept repeating the entrance over and over while Alexander wanted to take in the whole orchestra. "I can't stop, I can't stop, for once in my life I've done it right!"

Alexander made a small discovery. At the next rehearsal, he opened with the comment: "I have found out something about this Mozart symphony which no one, absolutely no one, has ever understood in the last two hundred years." He said this rather awkwardly, just to warm them up a bit, but found it cleared the air. If he kidded himself, they stopped responding sarcastically. So he did more of it; he developed a slightly professorial air, he would say things like "highly incorrect" and smile, or let himself go on talking more than he needed to.

At first his mannerisms were simply to make the other players never laugh again with the French horn. Soon, the character he was developing began to be more important. It permitted him to say serious things freely. One night when they were to rehearse *Eine Kleine Nachtmusik*, he told them about *The Sorrows of Young Werther* and then finished, "Now look, remember when you play the music that there is another Mozart behind it, a Mozart who could understand Goethe's tale but didn't want to force his sufferings on others. They just show through the surface even of pieces like the *Nachtmusik*." The orchestra understood. He was odd, his head was stuffed with a million things, sessions always lasted longer than they should; but they had misjudged him, he had something.

Alexander sat in Sim's Bar one night and thought how little he had admitted what he wanted most: to be loved. The severe, thin young man who drilled the horn to distraction could not arouse love; it was as though a carpenter hoped that by making a perfect joint, this edge would pass into the perception of someone else in stages—how neat it is, how good a carpenter he is, how good he is, I accept him, I love him. Ridiculous. Tonight when there had been a problem with the horn players, he said, "Norman, have you ever been in Gstaad, in Switzerland? Well, neither have I. There is a famous poem about the bells of Gstaad which might apply here. . . ." Sometimes, someone would call out to him, "Enough, Sasha, let's play . . ." and it was much better, they played better, and also, thanks to this person who was an exaggeration of himself, there was something approaching love. Perhaps this was the answer to Sorokin's question, why are you wasting your time? It was more than a year now since Susan's death.

Talk about music makes most musicians uneasy. Of course they gossip about each other all the time, and like painters and architects have lots of opinions about their nonverbal art. For players, however, the relation between words and sounds is more ambiguous. Musicians stop playing in rehearsals when something goes wrong; the need to talk is the signal that the music needs to be changed. But often words are inherently incapable of furnishing the cure. A player will lean to another and go "Like this," playing a phrase, and he cannot say what "this" is. The Italian vocabulary of musical directions is no great help, more indications on a road map of which route to take than names of destinations. "Play it marcato" can be executed twenty different ways, each with its own sound. So musicians can become very suspicious of talk; too much is lost in translation.

Yet even the morose player cannot help himself. In a game of cards backstage during intermission, he will suddenly turn to another musician and say, "Didn't you think at bar fifty we should have . . . ?" The morose one is not inclined to be philosophic, to ask why this art requires something outside its own medium, what relation there is between rehearsal and the boundaries of music. It would be a waste of time, and he wants to finish the hand of poker before going back onstage.

The ambiguity of music and talk means that only a very special musician will have the words which do not make other musicians uncomfortable. This special musician uses words which make others hear themselves better. But it is the character of the speaker which determines the effect. If a man says flatly, "More mysterious, gentlemen, at bar fifty," nothing happens. The eyebrows of the speaker need to rise or his voice trails off, ". . . it's mysterious . . ." and the person who is acting well in this way has a certain distance from the words, as the words have a necessary distance from the music.

When Susan wanted Alexander to speak, to tell her about her playing, she wanted a report from one center to another. Husband and wife: he couldn't act with her, and so his reports were damaging, like direct bomb hits. But even had he acted a bit, become vivid, these reactions to her playing would have done her no good, they would have aroused nothing. "In this poem about Gstaad. . . ." Come off it, just tell me what you think.

Twice a week Alexander made the journey away from the overpopulated territory of his marriage. After a conducting rehearsal, sleep could still be disturbed by sudden bouts of anger; even when he was flushed with sex he could not give much, and people had lost the sense of adventure at dinner parties of introducing him to new possibilities. Within his orbit were a few friends, too much work, reading, a telephone call once a week to Chicago. Still he was grateful for those sessions on the podium.

When Alexander was sixteen, he had an illusion of freedom when he mastered the ghost-nerves in his body. He was nearly ten years older now, old enough to know that freedom is never permanent. And yet this facility with words, this freedom from bodily struggle in conducting, also cast him under the spell of an illusion, the illusion of relief. The miser from St. Petersburg could still bark at him, "You do not understand me, you are running forward, you are not paying attention." The words which weigh nothing drag a musician into the web of the past as surely as any vibrato fear, they entangle him more. A nerve is a report from the past, a word lives a larger life. A musician hearing through words is in danger of hearing everything. Chance made this abstract truth plain to Alexander; chance furnished him an evening of Brahms.

"Brahms started the *German Requiem* fourteen years before he completed it in 1868, when he was thirty-five. The second movement, which you will rehearse in three weeks, began as a sketch for a two-piano sonata, around the time Brahms met the Schumanns. Very little of his music from that troubled time, you know, survives in its original form. People say Brahms composed the *Requiem* to commemorate his mother's death in 1865. This is true, but the fifth movement, in which the soprano sings the mother's comfort to the bereaved, was added last to the *Requiem*, after it was premiered in 1868.

"Could the basses move their chairs a little to my right? Thank you. I couldn't quite see you all. Now, although the *Requiem* goes back in Brahms's life, it is a very tight, unified piece. Think of it shaped like a spire: the first and the last movements—tonight we do the first—are like the base of the spire; in fact, themes from the first movement reappear in the last. These are the only movements in the tonic key of F major, and they open with the same words. The second and sixth movements are also balanced, beginning with dark marches and ending with strong, affirming fugues. The baritone solo in the third movement connects with the soprano solo in the fifth movement—and then at the top of the spire is the fourth movement, soaring, very transparent scoring, harmonically far away from F major; it's in E-flat major.

"Now, in one way the words fit into this musical plan, in another way they don't. The words differ from the usual Latin text for a mass for the dead; Brahms chose from the Lutheran Bible, both the Old and New Testaments, to fit a design of his own. The words spire like this: in the first movement, those who mourn are blessed and comforted; in the last movement those who are dead are blessed and comforted, because they can rest from their labors, and their labors will follow them into eternity." Alexander looked up from the notes he was reading. "Sorry to be so flatfooted, but just try and get the sense. The second movement begins with stark images of the inevitable withering of human life, then an affirmation of our only happiness, faith in God whose word lasts forever. In the corresponding sixth movement, there is a turbulent glimpse of the raising of the dead, but then this too becomes a celebration of God's eternal power and a triumph over death. The solo movements show a man talking to men, a woman talking to her children, about loss and sorrow. And at the summit of the spire, in the fourth movement, the 'courts of the Lord' are evoked, the place where we will find heavenly rest.

"The other way the words work maybe is why Brahms chose

to avoid the Latin mass for the sake of something in his own language. If you go out and buy the Klemperer version of the *Requiem*, you'll see on the cover a picture by van der Weyden of the Last Judgment in which the Archangel Michael is weighing the souls of the dead on a scale. Some good souls are light on one side of the scale and rise toward Michael in prayer; the bad souls on the other side who are heavy sink and look down at hell beneath them. The idiots who produced this record managed exactly to miss the point of Brahms's text. All are to be comforted, the living and the dead, the good and the bad. God is greater than a judge. Movement after movement, the words end by reassuring us, they offer us solace, so that the *Requiem* teaches us in many ways, from many angles, one truth: by the last page, we who remain trust in consolation."

Alexander opened the score and put down his notes.

"Now, this repetition in the words is going to pose a musical problem, the tempo. Every movement starts slow. This repetition of time supports the wave after wave of comfort in the words. But an endless andante can quickly tire the ear; a listener might become bored by consolation. So tonight, I want to work on small variations in tempi in the first and last movements. If you would open your music to the beginning. . . ."

It had been so simple. You have an orchestra. We, St. Stephen's Church, have a choir. Let's put them together for three concerts a year, at Thanksgiving, Christmas, and Easter. The choirmaster made an offer Alexander could not refuse for the orchestra. He hesitated about himself, having no experience of singers; moreover, the works the choirmaster wanted to perform were demanding, the requiems of Brahms and Fauré, and the Rossini *Stabat Mater*. Alexander suggested that the choirmaster take over the orchestra for these combined events; the choirmaster countered by suggesting that Alexander learn through holding opening rehearsals. The older man would come in for final rehearsals and performances, at least during the first year.

For a good conductor, a rehearsal is much like a medical examination. The musical body hurts in one way or another, and the conductor, by locating just where and how it hurts, begins to discover how the composition is made. Alexander discovered that the Brahms *Requiem* can fall ill as early as the third measure of the opening movement. The upper cellos swell on the third beat of that measure; this little swell on one note appears throughout the movement and binds it together, as an expressive signature. From the cellos the swell passes next to the violas, and later to singers, horns, and flutes. All musicians tend to imitate what they hear first, so the cellos had to get it right, a round rather than a sharp increase and decrease of sound.

In coping with this problem, Alexander discovered a different tempo than the one he heard working by himself, a tempo as slow as possible. This gave the players time to make the swell without feeling pressured. But the tempo was also a risk; it verged on the static, barely moving forward. In the rehearsal Alexander began to look for ways of creating momentum without speed; for instance, he had to make sure certain long notes were sung or played at steady volume, thus forming a contrast to the swell and keeping the ear alert.

Once he found the tempo the mood came to him; the opening movement introduces the listener to a realm whose time is not man's time. The singers had trouble; they complained it dragged. "It is not Verdi's *Requiem*, not opera by other means," he replied. "You are out of the world. When the chorus enters in unison at measure fifteen, it must sound far away, as the softest pianissimo. Imagine you are monks slowly filing into church; it takes you from bars fifteen to twenty-nine to walk up to the altar and join the orchestra." This was good enough to illustrate how long it takes to develop their presence but the truth is more extreme. The singers are bearers of strange tidings: "Blessed are they that mourn; for they shall be comforted." Brahms chose as his text the only promise in the fifth chapter of Matthew which is offered to all mankind, whether they are believers or not, and it is a promise to be redeemed now, rather than in heaven or later in life. The very act of mourning, of feeling pain, contains within itself the seeds of comfort. Brahms thus chose for the rest of the movement a passage from the Psalms which speaks of him "that goeth forth and weepeth, bearing precious seed." The spacious, unearthly time of the movement is what makes this promise of comfort seem real; a divine voice tells us what in our sorrow we cannot imagine ourselves.

Even at this first rehearsal he was drawn into the word net. Solving the problem of a little swell suggested a new tempo, which revealed the mood. A thousand times he had made discoveries like this on the cello; now this familiar work led to something less comfortable. Those who mourn are comforted in their pain by God, in whom or which he did not of course believe. For the purposes of the rehearsals, he might have to pretend this faith was real, or at least playable, but he would have to pretend well. Without taking the words seriously he was going to have trouble conveying the peculiar texture Brahms created for this *Requiem*, one in which key words are set off by disturbing sounds. Tonight he had told them about the thirty-fourth measure of the first movement. "Horns and winds, you underline the word '*Leid*,' which means 'sorrow,' at the moment the singers complete a blessing on this word. Their phrase is gentle, your timbre is somber; play out." He had made a great deal of this fracture. In the apartment after the rehearsal, remembering the tussle with Susan over the break in the *Scenes from Childhood*, he glanced at the Poussin, their painting of a world divided between peace and fear. He was good at sensing fractures; tonight's shaped a blessing.

Alexander made his weekly call to Abraham Zilker: "Something new has opened up with my conducting. . . ."

"Good, good, tell me."

"I'm conducting the *German Requiem* of Brahms at St. Stephen's Church."

There was silence on the line. "You are going to conduct a requiem for Germans in a church?"

"Yes, no, you don't understand. It is a requiem in German; there is no mention of Jesus at all in it; I could perform it in a synagogue."

"But you are performing in a church. This requiem, it is with no Jesus for Germans."

"I told you, Grandfather, not for Germans, in German."

"But there are many religious works in that language which do not call themselves 'German.' "

"This is stupid. I thought you would understand. Forget it, let's talk about something else."

"Yes, anything you like. Let me only say, this concert of yours I will not attend. I wish the best for you, I always will, you know that is so, but what I am not understanding here . . . it is a simple thing, but a man, no matter how great his suffering and how undeserved, as yours has been, a man should not abandon his people. That is no answer."

Abraham Zilker's mind was entering its final darkness. Alexander hoped he could make his grandfather understand just one thing.

"I'm not performing it, Grandfather. You misunderstand, I'm just rehearsing it."

"What? Yes. Well, go on, my dear, tell me other news."

Two days later they were obliged, because of the singers' schedules, to jump to the fifth movement, the dedicatory movement to Brahms's mother added in 1868. Frau Brahms was forty-one when she married a young musician of twenty-four who was genial, unsteady, and had poor prospects. It was her last chance for a family of her own; lame in one foot, she limped badly, and expressed herself best sitting down. She was by all accounts an excellent embroiderer, with an eye for unusual

designs; she also loved poetry, and early in her courtship read it
to her young suitor, who was not interested in a good-humored
way. He was markedly handsome, with a high forehead, intense
eyes set wide apart, a straight, aristocratic nose, and strong jaw.
He looked eminently prepared to play a heroic part in life,
which his weakness and self-indulgence kept him from. They
became miserably poor.

Brahms's father did everything to seduce the young man to
his own ways. The family lived in the red-light district of Hamburg, known as "Adulterers' Walk"; the boy was constantly in
the company of prostitutes, who treated him like a pet. He once
described to a friend playing the piano for some prostitutes
singing obscene songs; the half-naked women took him on their
laps and began fondling him, trying to arouse the nine-year-old
boy. Brahms's father was amused by all this, but the child was
not seduced. His mother was his refuge from the street filled
with dirty old men, bars, and whores; a lame protectress.
Brahms's friend Herr Ernest said of mother and son, "His letters
to her breathe such a gratitude and reverence as if she had made
his childhood a paradise."

It was cramped. The elder Brahms, who played the double
bass, constantly banged the instrument going up the narrow
stairs to the room where they lived. The apartment was not
neat; Frau Brahms's infirmity made it difficult for her to clean,
and the squalor seeped in. Even had she moved freely, there
could have been no protection from the cooking smells and
stench of garbage Brahms remembered so vividly from his
childhood; the walls of their apartment seemed porous. Whatever protection she offered him contained no promise of putting
this world in order.

"To you, Janet, I want to say only not to worry about breath
breaks. The legato you seem to feel instinctively, so you needn't
be self-conscious about following the rules." Although the
soloist's tone was not beautiful by ordinary standards, thin and
at times even faint, it suited the music she had to sing, an

invalid's voice which managed to project. And her legato was indeed mysterious. Alexander tried to understand how she achieved such flowing phrases and couldn't; he suspected she didn't know either, for when he complimented her, Janet, a demure woman made up to look older than her years, blushed with pleasure but seemed surprised. On stage, she would hardly give the appearance of an enfolding matron, and that, too, was all to the good.

After speaking to Janet, Alexander turned to the chorus. "Unlike what happens in the third movement, here you do not answer the soprano's words, nor even, and this is more difficult musically, will you imitate Janet's phrasing. You will follow my breathing directions exactly, so that she can soar. Above all, sing quietly; the mystery belongs to her. By measure thirty-two, she will have built a large sound; when you come in at thirty-four, forget it, that sound doesn't apply to you." Then Alexander stopped speaking. He could think of nothing more to say, but he didn't raise his baton.

"O.K., Sasha?" Akira, who was at the first desk of the violins, said softly to him.

"What? Yes, O.K."

There had been something of a coming together between Gerda Hoffmann and her son after Susan's funeral. Whereas Samuel Hoffmann was bewildered, Gerda had been efficient; she bought food for Alexander, she helped him answer the letters of condolence. "It's hospital training," Gerda had said. "I hope you don't mind." Someone also had to look after Mrs. Fields for a few days; the loss of her daughter had driven her close to the edge. As the divorced Hoffmanns sat in their son's apartment, Gerda keeping Alexander busy while Samuel stared out the window, Gerda had turned to Samuel and said to him, "Here's the telephone number of Mrs. Fields's hotel. Please call her; perhaps you could take her out to lunch today?"

Samuel looked at his now competent ex-wife moving around the apartment.

"I wouldn't know what to talk to her about."

"Does it matter?" Alexander said.

Samuel walked slowly to the telephone and sighed; he held out his hand for the slip of paper with Mrs. Fields's hotel number on it. He stared at it for a moment, and then slowly began to dial. He reached Mrs. Fields; everything he said was correct —he didn't want to intrude but would she perhaps like to join him for lunch? In that case, would she like his telephone number if later she would like to speak to someone? She had his greatest sympathy. Goodbye. Samuel replaced the telephone on its cradle and still without looking at son or ex-wife returned to his post by the window. Alexander's eyes met Gerda's for a moment. The incidents of courage or resource in Samuel's life were surrounded by such a vast tundra of quiet, visible suffering. Gerda watched her son understand why she had left Samuel.

Writing the letters, taking walks for the few days she remained in New York, they came closer. She was frightened she might say something which might put Alexander off, offend him. Alexander didn't know why, but he also saw now that what he had taken for coldness as a boy was this fear of being rebuffed. The path of past grievances was too tangled, however, to walk back long for comfort. The best they could say was that they really hadn't known each other before.

He was so close to performing the love they could not recover.

"Alexander," the choirmaster said from the front row of pews in the church, "time is passing."

The rehearsal was not inspiring; they worked mostly on details, no more on shape. On the weekend after Janet had sung, Alexander thought more about what had led Brahms to dedicate the movement to his mother. He and Gerda really had suffered nothing, nothing in comparison.

Everyone told Alexander that the last rehearsal allotted to him would be the hardest because of the soloist, the baritone who sings in the third and sixth movements.

Mr. Grotoff was their star attraction, a singer of medium-sized parts in various operas, who always behaved as though he was doing his friend the choirmaster a favor. He disliked Alexander the moment he set eyes on him. A smart-aleck runt; probably thought he was God's gift to the world. When they began to rehearse the third movement, Grotoff groaned as Alexander, instead of picking up his baton, looked at him and said, "What's this movement about?"

"You're asking me? We can discuss it after the rehearsal."

"We can't play it blind."

"What's it about? I start, the chorus and I trade back the opening theme. Then, let's see, at measure 105 I start a new theme, they pick it up again, and they finish the piece with a fugue."

"Sure, Mr. Grotoff, that's just it, but when you trade back and forth with them, are they repeating you or answering you?"

"Huh?" Grotoff thought the runt was setting a trap. "The sopranos, yes, the sopranos follow my melody exactly."

"That's true. Now, why do you stop singing in the middle of the piece?"

Enough of this. "Because I'm tired."

"Sasha," Akira interposed diplomatically, "I'd like to know what you're getting at."

"It's just this. Mr. Grotoff doesn't give himself enough credit for the importance of his part." Akira smiled. Grotoff could be seen to inflate slightly. "True enough, he leads the singers at the opening 'Lord, make me to know mine end'—and by the way, singers, I want you to follow Mr. Grotoff's pronunciation of the German syllables exactly, they are tricky in the opening line —and the singers are his echo. They follow him in the 'all is vanity' section, and then he builds up to the dramatic question 'And now, Lord, what wait I for?' This question in Martin Luther's German, '*Was soll ich mich trösten?*', can mean 'What am I waiting for?' or 'In what can I place my trust?' Now look, at this point suddenly you singers stop echoing him and give

him an answer, '*Ich hoffe an Dich*,' or 'My hope is in Thee.'
This is why Mr. Grotoff stops singing. In his doubt, in his
recognition of human emptiness, in his evocation of the point-
lessness of striving, Mr. Grotoff has been brought to the brink
of despair, he cannot go on, and you, at that magical section at
measure 164 when the key shifts from F to D, you give him
the answer, 'My hope is in Thee.' Now how can we build up
to this?"

These were good conductor's words. The singers warmed up,
Grotoff was seduced into giving a little more than he intended.
Alexander had played the words well. But, as in the first movement, these words were more than instruments. They describe
the hopelessness of going on, and then they provide a reason for
doing so. Once at the Laboratory School in Chicago the science
teacher had said, "Religion is for people who can't solve life's
problems." The twelve- and thirteen-year-olds had all nodded
wisely over this. The baritone rehearsal was better than the
soprano rehearsal, if only because the contrast between despair
and faith is so clearly set off in the music, but he wasn't getting
any farther; he was still treating the voices of the choir like
orchestral parts.

If Alexander had been asked at the end of the rehearsal of
the third movement what he thought of his opening remarks
to the singers he would have said, "The image of a church spire
was facile, it's much darker than I thought." Leading up to the
fourth movement hope and doubt were set against one another
in sound and in word; coming away from the fourth movement
was a soprano melody which soared out of the world in resignation. The darkness he understood, but he couldn't perform it
whole.

The choirmaster could. In the sixth, "Resurrection" movement, Alexander was astonished to see the choirmaster break
all the French maestro's rules. The hands waved so wildly, it
would be impossible to follow the beat, except that the singers
followed precisely. He got more out of Alexander's orchestra

than Alexander did by cupping, slapping, and caressing the air, talking to Alexander's players almost not at all.

In the text from Corinthians Brahms made a change by cutting one sentence from the middle of the original: "For this corruptible must put on incorruption, and this mortal must put on immortality." The victory over death does not demand a victory over oneself. And the composer stopped short in Corinthians before the sentence, "The sting of death is sin; and the strength of sin is the law." Nowhere in the *Requiem* does death appear as a punishment for sin. The music makes these words happen in a stunning scene of triumph over death, beginning at the moment when the chorus declares, "Death is swallowed up in victory, O death, where is thy sting?"

The choirmaster cupped, slapped, and flailed and still the singers in this momentous fugue kept exactly to the beat. Alexander moved to the side to see better what he was doing. It was the eyes; no matter how contorted the body, the eyes were an alert general anticipating each movement on the field. When the music ended, the choirmaster walked over to Alexander, smiled, and said, "That piece always makes me sweat like a pig."

There had been a cremation; he knew now this was a horrible error. She should have been laid beneath the ground, and then, when he wanted to know what had happened to Susan, he could go to a place and stand on the ground and give himself the answer, "She is here, beneath me." He could have stood over her and done her the honor of saying, "This is no victory. We were given so much time, not by any plan more or less. I loved you, not the best I could but as I could." The answer to the question of the resurrection movement, "Death, where is thy sting?" is, "In me."

The choirmaster called the next evening to ask if Alexander could take tomorrow's rehearsal. He had to shake a cold. Alexander said he wasn't prepared.

"Not to worry. Just take them through the fourth and last

movements, so that they get used to hearing the volume with an orchestra. I've already drilled them on their own parts."

The phone rang again; this time it was Alexander's agent. They needed to set up next year's schedule; possibilities had opened up in France, they had to talk about another record. Fine, after the rehearsal.

The rehearsal was low-key, everyone marking time until the choirmaster returned. Alexander made them hear what the choirmaster wanted. At the end, he thanked everybody. He would be in Boston giving a concert when they had the dress rehearsal, but he would be back to hear the performance. He had learned so much from them, he really meant his thanks, and he looked forward to next Thursday night. They in turn politely applauded him, but not long. Sorokin was waiting in the back of the hall.

"Three percent on the first two thousand records and then a rise to six percent on anything over. Or, you could not take the gamble and ask for a flat four percent. I suggest taking the chance, why not? O.K., now on the subsidiary rights we stand firm. They sell United Kingdom, we sell Japan. Forget about the rest, O.K.? They pirate no matter what's on paper.

"About your tour. That's your bread and butter. I've lined up seven months next year, three on the road, a month off, then another four. So what about your orchestra? Come on, Alexander, it's good experience, but it's not your work. You are in town in January, back in June, you've got two or three months when people are still around, and you're making next to nothing for this conducting. O.K.? Good, now I want you to understand what this French problem is all about. Basically. . . ."

The choirmaster's cold was becoming steadily worse. He began to run a high fever. "Don't be absurd," he told his doctor, "I've conducted in poorer shape than this before. Yes, there is an understudy, but he's green; just give me something." The fever refused to go down. The doctor made one of his rare, expensive house calls to lay down the law to his patient. No concert.

The choirmaster telephoned Signor Grisi, who was an old friend. "Come on, Enrico, you said you conducted it in Rome. I can't cancel; the people at the church won't take a second chance if we waste all this money."

"But I haven't conducted in years, anything. What about Alexander?"

"He's not ready. Look, he's out of town for the dress rehearsal."

"Well, my no is final. I want Alexander to conduct this. You haven't any choice; just let me talk to him, it will work."

Gerda found Alexander in Boston to tell him that Abraham Zilker had become very ill. Alexander said he would fly to Chicago immediately.

"It isn't like that, Sasha. He could live another month. I really wanted to call because, well, I don't want it to come as a sudden shock. Don't worry, I'll let you know the moment I think you should fly out."

Alexander returned to New York to find an urgent telephone call from Signor Grisi. His grandfather must have died while he was on the plane. But it was about the choirmaster's cold.

"I can't be bothered with that, Enrico." Signor Grisi understood, but still, if the danger was not imminent. . . . "Let's talk about it." Alexander distractedly agreed.

"This cafe seems to be our office," Signor Grisi remarked as they seated themselves at Mauro's. "I have spoken to our friend several times now. He has influenza, I think. Alexander, you can sit in New York, waiting for this terrible event, or you can do something in the meantime which will give many people great pleasure. One does not mount a performance of the Brahms *Requiem* casually."

"I can't take it on. Apart from anything else, it would be crazy for a conductor without a lot of experience with singers to perform this."

"I wonder, Alexander. I listened to your rehearsal with Grotoff and it seemed to me promising."

"I'm not getting them to do what I hear."

"That, yes. Could one ever?" Signor Grisi took a sip from the cup in front of him. "It's really good coffee here. To quit would be damaging for your career, but not disastrous. But if I were you I would go on; you could. Sugar?"

"Enrico, you aren't understanding. My grandfather is dying."

"I think I am understanding very well. Your grandfather is dying, your wife is dead. On the other side is a choirmaster in bed with flu; he will recover. There are singers who have practiced for a few months; they will forget and sing something else. There is a weak soprano who perhaps should not be singing, and an excellent baritone for whom this is another night's work. This, as you know, is the spoiled mixture of life. You say you will not go on with conducting as a serious occupation. But I think the truth . . . I think the truth of this matter is that you are afraid of their side. Shall I tell you how I know this? I know because you explain too much to this forgetful chorus, this dubious soprano, this baritone, and your orchestra. You tell them so much about the words because you do not want to be consoled. More coffee? We are a little alike that way, you and me. We know how to talk things to death. As a friend, I say you should not run away from this performance."

Signor Grisi seemed drained by his burst of eloquence. He lapsed into silence. They stayed on together at the Cafe Mauro, drinking coffee and considering.

That evening Alexander called Chicago. "How is Grandfather? The same? I want you to do something for me. I want you to leave him for a few hours and come to New York tomorrow. Yes, I'm giving the concert. No, nothing at all. I want you. . . ."

He was surprised when he met her at the hotel. Her chin was baggy now, there were pouches under her eyes. Her fingers were stained by nicotine and she had grown wider. During the last two years, when he had been writing and telephoning her, he had imagined her as the younger woman he once had known. The plane ride had been rough, and under her make-up, he could see, she was pale.

St. Stephen's Church was just large enough for the musicians. The chorus was seated on risers at the back of the church; they wore black gowns with white collars. The orchestra—the men in black evening attire, the women in black dresses—spilled over the altar steps. Two rows of pews had been removed to accommodate them. Alexander sat in the third row; he planned simply to stand when it was time to begin.

The lights dimmed over the pews, and were turned up brighter over the musicians. Alexander rose calmly to his feet. He walked to the podium, put his right foot down carefully and raised himself up. He was surprised by the applause, it seemed out of place in a church. Alexander did not turn around, instead watching his musicians; the trials of the ailing choirmaster had made the rounds, the dress rehearsal had been led by Grotoff, and the singers did not look confidently at Alexander. He wanted to say, "It's going to be all right," but now he was not allowed to talk to them. So he looked at Akira. The violins do not play in the opening movement; Akira, like his colleagues, had his violin perched on his legs. Akira was also staring at the singers, slightly annoyed that they rustled their clothes and bobbed their music up and down. Since the day Alexander had first met him, Akira had been an immobile Buddha when making music. The moment a conductor waits for came to the audience; now they were still. Alexander raised his baton.

He couldn't tell if he had the opening tempo right; when the cellos entered, they sounded faster than the beat he had laid down. He knew he had it right in his head, his hand was steady, yet they seemed to be racing. The singers entered, just as they had prepared it, firm in volume, far away. There were always these little adjustments settling into a performance. He was sure the tempo worked when the singers overcame the first danger point, at measure twenty-nine; the chorus swelled roundly and precisely. Alexander imitated one of the choir-master's gestures to remind them; just before they sang he cupped his hands together as if holding a globe.

Perhaps he and Enrico had made too much of the text; he felt tonight as he had when conducting in public before with his orchestra—relaxed, released. It was an art which suited him naturally. The second danger point defeated the choir, however, as it had in rehearsals. When the chorus heard the abrasive sound of the horns as they sang the word "*Leid*" at measure thirty-four, they sang too loudly, to match the horns, and so covered over the fracture. They went on unperturbed. There was no way they could recover this mistake; the choir had permanently subtracted something from the music just to relax their nerves by singing out. Once the French master had said to Alexander, "There are two kinds of experiences conduct-ing, one the magic way in which almost everything you asked for occurs, the other, more usual way, in which you add up the gains and losses, and hope you come out ahead by the end of the evening." He hoped tonight would be the first way.

At measure fifty-five the words from the Psalms promise that those who have cried in mourning "shall reap in joy." The harp is now prominent, the words quicken on eighth notes; in rehearsal he had asked them to imagine these measures as though there were more light in the church. The little explana-tions may be facile, but as the music appears whole and there is no going back, these little aids are tested in the conductor's mind: now there is light, if the harp does its job well; I was talking nonsense, if the harpist smears the notes.

At the point marked "D" in the score, there is a one-beat rest before the strings come in on an underlying phrase. It is an important rest and Alexander knew how to do it, palm flat pushed toward the strings so that they give the rest full value. But now, by accident, he looked at their instruments, not them, and there was an impatient, too-brief pause rather than a silence.

The conductor's problem at such a moment is confidence. These subtractions which are his own fault hardly ever unnerve him in the literal way, the body suddenly freezing. Instead a lapse can break his sense of control, a feeling which often translates physically into the hand beating the time synchronizing exactly with the musical sound. The confident conductor's beat is usually a little ahead, preparing for the sound which will come. Now Alexander began to struggle against the slow tempo he had discovered, although it had seemed to fit the words so naturally. He wanted to be a little ahead of his players, in control, and so he beat a little faster. By measure eighty-eight he was forcing the eighth notes to go audibly faster than they had all remembered from rehearsal.

The singers responded too much. They were still uncertain, they wanted to run forward, they were all poised to break the mood of his ecstatic andante and race, but he was able to keep them just within bounds; he could feel the baton holding them on a leash. He had counseled Susan, "You make it too easy"; Claude Simon had forthrightly declared that her ease was superficial. From the opening of this movement, his baton arm had been sending the same message—go a little faster than comfortable.

As you tighten a bow, the fingers turning the nut can feel exactly when the pressure is right, enough pressure so that the bow wood will transmit energy from the first finger to the bow hair, but not too much pressure, so that the bow still flexes. Eyes and a whole arm are not as pressure sensitive. By the time each part in the chorus descended down the F major line, closing the movement, the singers were off the leash. The tempo was now much faster than the opening. This echoing, falling line should summarize the mood of the movement and indeed the whole *Requiem*: they shall be comforted. The words say it, the sighing down F major evokes it, but how fast can you announce "they shall be comforted" and still be believed? Like a man who rushes out the door declaring, "I will always remember you"? Evidently the comfortable tempo he had chosen had kept him from exploring the real tempo which was more than easy and less than fast.

As he struggled for control, time kept pushing forward. In the last four measures, the horns and winds were unprepared for the new walking tempo. They watched the conductor's eyes, but the eyes only looked at them, and the horns and winds did not quite conclude together. The music by this final stutter should have accomplished what the biblical text promises, grief and comfort sounding in the same notes. In rehearsal he had said, "By the end of the first movement, Brahms will have established his argument, that grief is never an isolated dead-end"; the horns and winds argued the contrary.

Akira had sat immobile through the movement, the violin propped on his thigh, hearing the flicker of things happen as they had been rehearsed, things not happen. When Alexander had sat tuning his cello in his room, the day the Hoffmanns had first moved to Washington Homes, there was a sound of grief and comfort, at least as Alexander remembered it. Now, had Alexander spoken of this sound, it would be of purely personal interest to Akira. Alexander fortunately had his back to Signor Grisi, who fidgeted when he heard mistakes, and had squirmed throughout the movement, disturbing his neighbors. Still, Signor Grisi thought he had a good idea—that playing this requiem would purge Alexander of Susan.

A few months after three of the movements from the *Requiem* had been hissed at a preview in Vienna, Brahms wrote to Clara Schumann from Hamburg on February 1, 1868, about the full production: "I am resigning myself to the thought that this

time, as in Vienna, it will go fast, too fast and too sketchily."
He was the engineer of these dangers. When the musical line
is sinuous, seamless, as in the first movement, players rush
ahead for fear of dragging. When great blocks of contrasted
music are put next to each other, players rush forward because
they know too much. This is the danger in the second movement.

The dirge with which it opens must sound as if nothing
could happen after. Life is over: "For all flesh is grass . . . the
grass withereth." Unexpectedly, the music moves into a major
key, the tempo quickens, and the chorus counsels, "Be patient
therefore, brethren, unto the coming of the Lord." Hope is then
extinguished, the death dirge returns unchanged, no development of melody or harmony. The static music exactly mirrors
the words proclaiming the withering of the flesh. Then, Brahms
shoves a new block into place; on the line "But the word of
the Lord endureth forever" the music bursts into great energy
consummated by a long and noble fugue.

To make the drama work requires discipline. The tempo
must be pulled back exactly to the beginning when the dirge
returns, there can be no fussing with new little inflections or
emphases. But the real labor is resisting the temptation to build
the drama up steadily. The interpreter has memorized his score,
he knows what's coming. The audience, however, must be
taken by surprise, rather than warned by sudden little bursts
of energy. The interpreter's restraint will thus convey the sense
of the words; there is no neat join between the withering of
the flesh and the eternal life of the Word.

Alexander was determined they would make this colossal
drama happen the right way. These building blocks of despair
and faith create perhaps the greatest sound of fissure in all
music. He was sure of this tempo, which had taken him weeks
to discover; he had taken trouble—too much trouble, the
choirmaster said, you're driving them crazy—to make the
singers breathe into the phrases of the first block differently
from the way they breathed into the second, comforting block.

Tonight they were doing exactly what he wanted. They breathed "For all flesh is grass" as though they could barely find enough air for the phrase; no matter how loud it became, the breathing phrases were kept short, the dead who have no air. The long breaths for the block of comfort made the words sound believable, these angels could fly forever without tiring. When the dirge returned, the chorus fell back into despair through the lungs; in fact they sank almost too far back, at moments it sounded as though they were gasping for air.

The long, energetic fugue which relieves this contrast Alexander had rehearsed as a release; let the singers go. Tonight, when they were finally past the contrasts between despair and hope, when they finally could breathe without thinking of what came next, the chorus, perhaps also relieved that they were going to make it through the performance without the choirmaster, that Alexander had finally got things under control, began to sing loud. They were giving everything to this fugue. Whenever a chorus playing with a full orchestra sings full volume, it courts a danger: there is so much noise that it is hard for singers to hear when they should come in. Louder and louder. He tried with his left hand, flapping down, down, to get them within a range where they could hear themselves.

At measure 219 the slips started: the sopranos came in on, rather than off, the beat, which threw the altos off the next measure. The basses became confused at the end of 283. Still the singers recovered and the audience loved it; they were leaning forward in their seats, the rafters in the church shook. Signor Grisi was disturbed: you cannot be purged through mess. The conductor buried by the fugue was also disturbed. The lessons of the music were entirely different from what he had heard in the patchwork of rehearsals.

The dead miser in St. Petersburg had been emphatic about looking to the sides and behind because it is more profitable, Claude Simon had made suggestions ranging from tennis balls to tailoring, Susan had ideas about his cooking which she put to him sharply because he was keeping his ideas about her music to himself. They all said, "Pay attention to yourself, your work, to me." But if one could not make others pay attention, one could begin to hear the world of sound stripped of authority. Alexander had lost control for no more than two minutes, a small loss if one counted all the measures in this movement. Out of control only that long, a person can hear what happens naturally. Music naturally moves to extremes. At his debut, of course, his body out of control had taken extreme measures, but this was different. The music also goes to extremes if somebody doesn't police it, an art in need of police—except that they weren't rehearsing now, this little *bon mot* was just for him.

There was a flutter of applause from the audience when the rafters stopped shaking and the movement ended. There had been a time a few years ago when it was fashionable to condone these outbursts of enthusiasm; people said, "If your audience is spontaneously moved, let them clap." Now he was beginning to understand her; when you surrender, you let mood take over. Of course for a piano player the natural mood might be un-relieved prettiness while for a full chorus and orchestra it would be extreme drama. But you let the mood take over, and the music plays itself after a fashion. The worriers want everything; they worry about good and bad because they are greedy for good and fear that bad is worse than it naturally is: if one thing goes wrong, they fear the whole performance is ruined. All the audience wants is stimulation. Tonight he would do it her way, whenever he couldn't help himself or the players in front of him, outside the circle of worry. Alexander wiped his forehead as the program pages turned. He couldn't do anything about the hot lights either. Grotoff rose and thrust his chest out. It might serve as a purge, this reliving as another person has lived.

As the third movement began, Grotoff surprised Alexander. He sang deep down in his diaphragm; the sound was colored much more harshly than when he had sung from the upper chest in rehearsals. Tonight of course Grotoff's back was to the singers, and for them to hear him as they had at rehearsals, he had to increase his volume. Moreover, a singer constantly giving concerts has to protect his voice when practicing. So next to Alexander was someone neither the audience nor the musicians could measure, a man who seemed loudly this evening to demand from God an explanation of human frailty.

Alexander took defensive action to rebalance the sound. When the basses and tenors first come in to repeat the soloist's plea for guidance, he signaled them to come in strong. The moment he had them in, he turned to the cellos and double basses and, shaking his hand back and forth in the give-me, give-me signal, increased the volume of their plucked-string accompaniment. The effect of both these moves was to strengthen Grotoff's plea.

Grotoff, hearing this sound behind him fuller than he remembered, launched into his second phrase even more emphatically. At measure thirty-nine, the strings reinforce his last word with a sudden burst of sound; although it was not marked in the score, Grotoff made his word also start with the burst. He was indeed a fine musician. Having adjusted to the unforeseen volume, he tried not to be imprisoned by it. At forty-one, on a new phrase, he brought his voice down, although the line grows ever more intense: *"Und mein Leben ist wie nichts vor Dir."* He sounded terrified by his words—my life is nothing before Thee—as though he had just made the discovery. By accident the drama started earlier than they had practiced.

Grotoff now sang the words from the Thirty-ninth Psalm, "Verily, every man at his best state is altogether vanity." They were approaching the question. Grotoff clutched the score to his midriff. Grotoff asked, bursts of breath on each syllable, "Now, Lord, what wait I for?" He went on squeezing the score after he finished singing. Alexander looked at his hands while making a gesture to the violins and saw that Grotoff's knuckles were white.

"And now, Lord, what wait I for? And now, Lord, in what shall I place my trust?" The chorus repeated Grotoff's plea over and over, following his lead in emphasizing the two notes which form the word for trust, "*Trö-sten.*" Horns and winds play in syncopation over the singers, slower and slower, ending on a weak diminished chord, a hollow sound, echoing into a void when the singers stop asking. Grotoff chose this moment to drop his hands to his sides, as though exhausted. Due to a misunderstanding, Grotoff had succeeded in making the question so powerful as to seem unanswerable.

Silence. The chorus announces quietly, "My hope is in Thee." The music swells up light and clear on flowing triplets, faith without an answer.

Measures and measure soon flow peacefully over the word "*Qual,*" the word for torment, taken from the Wisdom of Solomon, "But the souls of the righteous are in the hand of God, and there shall no torment touch them." For two years there had been no comfort in trying to weigh up the rights and wrongs of their life together, no comfort in judgment. "Brahms's deity," he told the choir once during rehearsals, avoiding the forbidden word, "is all-embracing, greater than a judge. When this deity speaks through the chorus, the sound is always serene, never harsh." These words were turning out to be true. No matter how impassioned a man was asking for answers, the response this deity makes will never consist of the weighing of souls, as it appears in the van der Weyden picture on the record cover. By accident Grotoff had pushed the demand to its limits, or rather from accident Grotoff's art had forged "Tell me, I want an answer, what am I waiting for?" into a great challenge which these singers, most of them amateurs, gliding over the flow of notes on "*Qual,*" simply avoided, faith in itself, a relaxed sound. He had lacked faith so long as he had sat in judgment, which he had done, first upon himself, then upon her—twenty-five years of greed and fear. This was the secret he had kept from her. You want to be the best, you push yourself, you pushed her, because if you don't do it right, you are nothing. The best or nothing. Without faith, nothing. He had to let go. At the final chord, he flapped his hand, give-give, and the pedal point came in strong.

In this mood he conducted the fourth movement, "How amiable are Thy tabernacles, O Lord of Hosts," according to the memory of an hour of reconciliation. One afternoon, when Susan seemed better, they talked about where they would go after she recovered. They knew exactly where: it was a small village outside of Cortona, in Tuscany. Susan had visited this village one summer with her father, and Alexander made her describe it to him in the hospital as carefully as she could remember. You take the road out of Cortona to the northeast; the road winds up a mountain even higher than Cortona itself, which is a medieval city on a steep mountain looking over a vast plain. Almost at the top of this mountain, the village appears. There are perhaps twenty houses, all in stone from a quarry off the road, probably for protection in the days when brigands lived in the wilderness. The largest house is the post office, general store, telephone exchange, and garage; in front of it is a terrace, with three tables under an arbor of grapevines. From the terrace you look down at the towers of Cortona, you talk to your neighbors, and you drink very bad wine. At the end of the row of houses along the road is a church, kept in excellent repair by the village but containing not one work of art worthy of a tourist's detour, and beyond the church, set in a garden of its own, its roof half caved in, a few windows missing, oval vaulting on the ground floor supporting a huge, open room above, was the barn which would be their house. It was for sale the summer Susan and her father visited the village. It was sure still to be.

For an hour they played house again. Susan drew the building, front view and ground plan, on a pad of paper she propped on the hospital table which swung over her bed. They would start with the roof; they would have to start with the roof, and they probably could find someone in the village who would mend it. They decided not to be fussy; their house didn't have to look as though it had remained miraculously intact from the past, they were going to let it show honest signs of habitation and change, so if it were cheaper to put asbestos tiles or even tin on the roof, that's how they would do it. Nesting, somewhere very far away.

Then they would put in the electricity. Alexander pointed out sensibly that there must be a well or at least water near the house, since it was a barn; all they needed to do was get the electricity in and they could rig up a pump or whatever for plumbing. The kitchen would be a problem, since, Susan informed Alexander, animals were never heated by fireplaces in barns. Very good, they would have a modern kitchen, white enamel appliances would be the most practical; they would buy an old china dresser for the dishes, but they would get good metal cabinets for the food, to keep out mice. The cats could spend the summer with them and also help out with the mice, Alexander suggested. Susan was pleased; it was rather stylish, she would allow the cats occasionally to spend the summer abroad. She rested for a few minutes, there was still a little time before visiting hours were over.

Tell me about Cortona.

It's half-spoiled. There are already English and American writers and artists living there, lots of tourists in the summer, some Germans in very grand houses near the Roman gate. Once you climb up above the center, it's very quiet. There is a beautiful church at the top with famous paintings by someone or other, and up where it is quiet you look for miles and miles in all directions, and there is peace.

Alexander told his forces that this movement with the lilting melodies and simple form was at the top of the spire. That meant, had he taken his own words seriously, that there must be a way down. The Brahms *Requiem* does not end with a happy consummation.

Janet had been sitting too long by the time she got up to perform. Grotoff had noticed how nervous she was before the concert, and encouraged her to sing in the fourth movement along with the sopranos to loosen up her voice. She remained silent and now rose, arching her shoulders. Alexander turned to her and whispered, "Take your time, we can wait." That only made her more nervous. She faced the audience, and Alexander started the strings, the mutes making a warm support for her. She tried to take her first two measures all in one breath and nearly lost the last note, she remembered what Alexander had suggested and recovered in the next two measures, breathing when she needed. Still she trembled and her voice shook.

They all helped her as much as they could. Akira leaned slightly to the side, turning his violin out toward her, so she could hear the support. Alexander gave the hold-back signal to the singers when they entered at eighteen, his left palm pushed out at them. There was the danger they would try to help by engulfing her, covering the voice which quavered; this would only make her force herself. For the five measures when soloist and chorus sang together, Alexander kept his left palm pushed out rigid, letting it fall only when the singers continued on without Janet.

At her next solo, she gathered some strength; Akira continued to lean toward her. She made the big sound at thirty-two, but the other players continued to hear her fear. The doctor-lecturer had referred rather ironically that night to the "hot-house passions" of the Romantic era. An inflamed passion produced the quartet, but a decent musician could play the music which resulted, Susan had played it well enough, up to a point. Whereas there was nothing hothouse about this movement Brahms dedicated to his mother, yet only an exceptional soprano could pull it off.

Grotoff sat immobile, frowning at her. By the time the chorus had named her as like a mother, the danger had passed.

Janet sang over them without wobbling; the legato she didn't understand kept her going, but no one was yielding in the movement, they were very carefully listening to make sure she didn't succumb.

As often happens when an exposed player is in trouble, the conductor's body gestures contract. His waving arms, his torso turning may distract or frighten the endangered player. He shields the gestures he has to make to others, often pressing his elbows to his sides, crouching down a bit, intruding upon the troubled player only with his eyes. When a conductor shrinks into himself this way, it is nothing like surrendering to the music; he never listens so intently as when, with a soloist on the verge of breaking down, he tries to become invisible. The mood of giving that he had enjoyed in the last two movements was gone. The natural thing to happen now was for Janet to stop singing and announce to the audience, "I can't do it." If only she could feel behind her a steady pulsing support, she might not have to make that announcement.

When Janet had finally sung her last note, slightly off pitch because her throat was squeezing with tension, Alexander took out the silk handkerchief Abraham Zilker had had monogrammed for him, wiped his forehead, and thought, "You can't blame her, it isn't Janet's fault." This music dedicated to Brahms's mother demands everything from an exceptional artist. "You can't blame her." This again was the design he had not heard before: free of blame but still unfulfilled.

At the end, the *Requiem* returns to its opening themes. The sixth movement exorcises the terrors of death, the seventh movement evokes the peace of the dead. Now the problem of the playable has come down to pacing; nearly ninety minutes of music has passed, so that the voice or hand would like an intermission. The audience has been lulled by two quiet movements. The dramatist in Brahms deals decisively with these flagging energies. The baritone soloist reveals his vision of the rising of the dead; he sees not the Day of Judgment but an apocalypse in which all those who have ever lived are set free. The chorus takes courage from him; they begin to taunt, "O death where is thy sting, O grave, where is thy victory?", a taunt which climaxes for chorus and orchestra joined together in massive chords, filling all the space in a hall, flowing into a fugue to the glory of God more sustained, more jubilant, than any which has come before. After this vision and affirmation, the peace of the last movement also is charged; knowing the ultimate fate of the departed, we who remain in life can take comfort. The melodies and words which appeared in the beginning of the *Requiem* are now transformed when they return in these last movements. Finally we have an answer—not about the purpose of life, but about the history of the dead. A death is not an ending.

Grotoff rose from his chair; he knew how to stand according to the character of what he sang. In the third movement, he had leaned slightly toward the audience as though hoping to find an answer to his question from somewhere out in the darkness. Now in the sixth he stood slightly back into the orchestra, close to Akira, and held himself straight; he was going to reveal a mystery.

The chorus set the scene. The text from Hebrews is, "For here have we no continuing city, but we seek one to come." Even in these opening notes, the ear hears something new; the singers sound as if they are plucking their notes, as are the lower strings accompanying them; a few measures later they suddenly sing in broad, liquid tones. Throughout the movement these shifts in the texture rouse the ear and contribute to the drama; no one texture establishes a routine. Alexander led them in firmly; the chorus sounded like a crowd, huddled together, waiting.

Grotoff entered: "Behold, I show you a mystery." Grotoff acted the entrance simply by turning his head up toward one of the windows at the back of the church, behind the audience, in awe of what had just been revealed to him. "We shall not all sleep." The chorus repeated after him: "but we shall all be changed," the chorus repeated in unison; "in a moment, in the twinkling of an eye, at the last trumpet." The chorus as it echoed his prophecy was rock firm. Alexander leaned toward the violins who now had a furious sixteenth-note swell; Akira was hard at work, his eyes glued on Alexander. The time shifted from four to three, the chorus reentered, the words of the prophecy were now more urgent as they sang on one beat less.

Suddenly the swell vanished into a hush, Grotoff announced that "There shall be brought to pass the saying that is written," but he didn't tell them, he too vanished from the *Requiem*, the sixteenth-note swells reared up again, the winds and horns blared, the tympani rolled, and the chorus triumphantly announced, "Death is swallowed up in victory!"

The chorus taunted, "Death, where is thy sting?" He was barely ahead of them. "O grave, where is thy victory?" The singers were no older than he, taunting a finality so far off, so singable. The chorus hit the great chords. "Where, where, where?" He raised his left hand higher each time they sang "*Wo?*" but they didn't need him, they were rapt with victory and let loose on the penultimate "Where is thy sting?" Once again, as in the second movement, the church shook.

Just as he had carefully explained in rehearsal, this time was different. Now the voices of the deity confronted death itself and these voices had to be clear. Even under the arc lights many of the singers looked flushed; he had to get them down for the fugue, but the excitement did not leave these believing faces who had almost finished for the evening as Alexander was just ahead of them, absolutely in control of the beat. The fugue would be a minefield if they didn't follow precisely, even if they were inspired. They were inspired. At measure 224, they were supposed to sing in a steady four against a syncopated three in the strings, and they didn't care, they were flushed with victory, they began to sing in three, a new mess added to the fact that they were missing entrances all over the place, just as they had in the second movement.

Akira rose slightly off his chair, turning his violin toward the singers. The chaos grew, measure to measure, eleven long measures of singers bawling in the wrong time. By the end Akira didn't care how it looked, he and Alexander would get them down together. "And for Thy pleasure they are and were created!" Finally the cacophony ceased, if only because the syncopation stopped. Akira sank back into his chair. The audience thought it was great, the Japanese boy was so excited by the music he had to stand. Signor Grisi was also nearly standing in his seat. He had given Alexander some very bad advice.

At measure 248, when the syncopation briefly reappears, the chorus had steadied into their four. Some of those flushed singers looked at their conductor rather shamefacedly; they would obey now that they had gotten it out of their systems. Alexander glanced at Akira, who shrugged. Was Brahms also the engineer of this player's disaster? Of course not; the fault, the responsibility, was Alexander's. "Thou art worthy, O Lord, to receive glory and honor and power!" Or rather, one could choose between the design of faith and the design of fault. The chorus rolled out the mighty affirmation over and over, loud and hoarse. Alone with each other in the world, no more, no less, living in a time-bound world of faults. The music ends with a triumphant explanation of death. But Abraham Zilker, who might be this moment have passed into the land of supreme promises, needn't have worried. His grandson had found his own limit; Alexander was unequal to this music.

With no more than a moment's break, they entered the finale. The law of excision, which governed the previous movement, has been revoked. The text announces a rest from labor; the music returns to the opening spirit of the *Requiem* in many ways—in the words, in fragments of melody, above all in the looseness of structure. To hold the ear in this mood of peace, it is necessary, as it was in the opening movement, to emphasize details. All he had to do was keep them going, paying attention to these details. They were not building toward anything.

You will never feel as much as you do now—perhaps not, that time is over. The last day he had seen Susan they had spoken very little; her eyes seemed to have grown large and bright as her body succumbed. Large brown eyes. He held her hand, looking into them, and she looked at him, although he had been told she could not now see well. This was what he remembered—not the bar later that night with Enrico pleading for him to return to the hospital, not the speech at the funeral. He remembered that their farewell happened then. The chorus was exhausted. Perhaps the singers had also learned. No dreams of consolation, somewhere or sometime; you must be the master of the house which is already yours. The lights were afflicting the singers; they bent their heads forward to shield their eyes from the arc lights. Master in your own house, if poorly furnished; when you give something, you can measure the gift. The singers all were obedient now; their eyes were on the baton rather than looking out over him into the audience or into the blank space behind it, where Grotoff had seen a mystery. Looking down at the baton kept their eyes out of the glare of the arc lights, and he could keep them to his beat; he would do that much for them. Gently, gently, the music drifted to the conclusion. The singers stopped, a harp chord sounded, the winds died away. No house in the woods.

Alexander lowered his baton and remained motionless, his head bent over the score. The audience did not applaud immediately, nor was there a rustle of closing programs. All of them remained together, immobile, for one moment. Then Alexander turned, stepped down from the podium and went to sit again in the first row of pews next to his mother. He had completed his mourning.

Chapter 10

CODA: AN OLD
PHOTOGRAPH

Signor Grisi sat in his apartment the next day, rather
alarmed at the small bundle in his lap. This bundle was
Nicola's first child, his grandchild. He'd never been much good
with babies; the moment this one was handed to him, it began
to cry.

Patrick and Nicola had flown out from the Midwest the day
before, for a visit and the presentation of the new generation.
They had arrived in the morning. Signor Grisi thought Patrick
might like to come to Alexander's concert with him. The boy—
he shouldn't think of him that way, Patrick was thirty-five and
beginning to go gray—Patrick never seemed comfortable in
New York; he didn't want to go to the concert, even though it
would give Nicola and Flavia time to catch up on things. He'd
made some excuse and stayed with the women in the house.

The baby was settling down. Now Signor Grisi remembered;
he turned it around so that the bundle wasn't facing him but

facing outward, its back nestled against his waistcoat. Together they watched Nicola pick up her violin. She hadn't played it in years. She began tuning and then stopped.

"How was Alex's concert?"

"It was unfortunate. Do play, Nicola. It's been a long time."

She began to play a Bach sonata she had learned long ago as a little girl; she made the same mistakes now she used to make, scratching and playing out of tune at just the same places. It brought back to both the Grisis so many other sounds from that time, the sounds of her shouting in English to other little boys and girls outside the windows, of garbage trucks on Sullivan Street in the early morning, the sounds of beginning.

Signor Grisi held the now-silent bundle in his arms and considered; although the concert was unfortunate, there had been moments. Even in the disastrous revelation moment. But he would not discuss it with Alexander. The young man had found his limit, now he would play the cello, and he didn't need Signor Grisi for that. So many had passed through his hands before he retired, so many, now all lost to him.

There was a photograph of Brahms on the wall behind Nicola. The sepia print showed the composer, in his last years, seated at a round table covered with a fringed cloth. On the table is a lamp, one glass bowl squatting atop another, the lamp surmounted by a painted metal shade; in front of the lamp is a wad of music paper, clean, with pencils and pens to the side. Although the lamp is lit, it may well be morning. Brahms used to wake before sunrise, go to this table, drink several cups of the strongest coffee, and begin to compose. There is a pot of coffee on the table.

Nicola's mistakes never made Signor Grisi fidget. Her daughter also listened unperturbed.

The composer sits at the table, his eyes bulging, staring beyond the lamp at the books which line the wall behind the table. What was the picture Alexander remembered of Brahms? It was one of the young composer, "girlish," Alexander had called him. In this photograph, the time of fragility had passed. Brahms is armored in fat, the beard covers all the features of the face except the eyes. From what one can read of the eyes, Brahms is not ready to work. Although there is nothing on the music paper, the eyes do not have that lost look of abstraction one has waiting for inspiration, or whatever it is, to come. The bulging eyes are looking at something. In the photograph he is not wearing glasses; he cannot be reading the titles of the books on the wall.

Perhaps he is looking at the past—not thinking of a memory, for particular memories make eyes lower or turn to the side, withdrawing from scrutiny of their present surroundings to see a scene again as it appeared long ago. It could be memory itself, the parade one after another of these images whose very movement is, finally, the sole proof we have that we are good animals.

On the morning of the funeral Alexander had asked, "What's it about, how can you call it a friendly art?" The answer is in the photograph. The parade before the eyes makes amends. All those we have hurt or who have hurt us pass in review; time has blunted our pain, also, unfortunately, our pleasure. We watch these figures of life pass before us clearly, uncolored by brute sensations, people in the parade who perhaps did not know one another, but all of whom we knew. We are doing them honor; each is worth remembering because of something he did, something he was. Although the evil are also indelibly in the mind, they are allowed no place in this particular procession, they are its disturbers; we are giving to those who have given to us a niche in the whole that is ourselves.

At a certain moment, Brahms will pick up his pen; at that moment the procession will reform itself into black notes, key signatures, and rest-signs on a page. These ink scrawls which mean everything to Brahms will mean nothing to anyone else; they are musical words describing an event which has yet to happen. Every person performs the act of homage through memory, it is human nature. This remembering-to-wholeness, as we detect it in the photograph, is about to be buried in ink.

Many times Signor Grisi had sat with composers at performances of their works; the composers usually left the hall angry, or needing a few minutes of recuperation before going backstage to lie and thank the players for taking so much trouble. Brahms would not have bothered, Signor Grisi suspected, with the proprieties last night. Yet because at some moment the pose will be broken and the pen will begin to fill the empty page, the composer has made a pact with you and me. We will exhume his scrawls; like an archaeologist, we never dig out of the earth all that is buried. We agree to speak for the figure suspended before his own time in the photograph. It is no pact of love; he has no interest in our plans, grievances, or hobbies. All he wants is hard work and fealty to the ink. If the truth be told, we in turn do not care just for him, no matter how great the sounds he creates; we want our voices, the voices of ambition, grief, and desire, to be heard through his. So it is best called a bond of friendship, a working friendship to make those without his gifts or ours hear the wholeness of time, to repair the wounds among the living.

The hood flopped over the front of the blanket bundle. Signor Grisi had given Alexander his answer and did not bother to push the hood back up. To the sound of Nicola's mistakes he was falling asleep.

A NOTE ON THE TYPE

The text of this book was set on the Linotype in Garamond No. 3, a modern rendering of the type first cut by Claude Garamond (c. 1480–1561). Garamond was a pupil of Geoffroy Tory and is believed to have based his letters on the Venetian models, although he introduced a number of important differences, and it is to him we owe the letter which we know as "old style." He gave to his letters a certain elegance and a feeling of movement that won for their creator an immediate reputation and the patronage of Francis I of France.

Composed by Maryland Linotype, Inc., Baltimore, Maryland. Printed and bound by Maple Press, York, Pennsylvania.

Designed by Judy Henry